THE BLOOD

The Stone's Blade : Book One

the BLOOD

the STONE'S BLADE : BOOK ONE

Helen, such a delight to dance with you. check out chapters 13 + 14 for the community dance! Hope you enjoy - There's more coming-

Allynn Riggs
5/21/14

ALLYNN RIGGS

TimberDark
publications

The Blood (Book One of The Stone's Blade)

Copyright © 2014 by Allynn Riggs
Cover design & art by Nathan Fisher,
www.scifibookdesigner.com
Edited by Melanie Mulhall,
www.DragonheartWritingandEditing.com
All rights reserved.

Published by TimberDark Publications, LLC
7683 E Costilla Blvd
Centennial, CO 80112
www.timberdark.com

ISBN 978-0-9910002-0-3 (paperback)
ISBN 978-0-9910002-1-0 (e-book)
Library of Congress Control Number: 2014933039

TimberDark
publications

t i m b e r d a r k . c o m

DEDICATION

To Morgan, the first to believe. This one is for you.

TABLE OF CONTENTS

ACKNOWLEDGMENTS

This has been a long time coming and there are many to thank for their constant support and encouragement. I thank Morgan Downing, a good friend, dance partner, and classmate in the college creative writing class where I shared the beginnings of *The Stone's Blade* as a possible book. Thanks for believing in the story and in my hopes that it would someday be published. Even after so many years, you have never forgotten about this dream and have kept asking about it. I did not forget my promise to you or the characters. Here is the first of many stories.

I thank my husband and partner, Bob, for understanding my need to write, even if he has no interest in the topic. He supported my change of careers, which has resulted in a decrease of income and an increase in my overall happiness.

Thanks to my daughter, Kristina, who practically grew up with the characters and their stories. When I finally finished the first draft, it was Kristina who told me I had rushed the ending and it needed to be rewritten. I can also blame her for the twist that opened up the story line, thus turning a stand-alone novel into a series. It was she who surreptitiously passed the manuscript on to a friend, Liz Beerman. This single act opened so many doors that I can only say, with all my heart, thank you for sharing. And by the way, book two is all your fault, dear daughter.

After searching almost two years for an agent and receiving either no response at all or the cryptic, "I don't work in that genre," when their website was pleading for a sci-fi/fantasy with a hint of romance, I met with Liz Beerman. To my surprise, here was someone outside my family or immediate friend network who loved the story and saw possibilities. At the time, Liz was on the Board of Directors of the Colorado Independent Publishers Association (CIPA). Thank you, Liz, for insisting I join CIPA.

After six months of listening and networking at CIPA, I connected with my award winning editor and writing coach, Melanie Mulhall, of Dragonheart. Melanie, for your patience and belief in my ability to learn, this simple thank you is not enough. Through your coaching over the past year, I am beginning to understand how to make a good story better. I look forward to working with you on upcoming books.

Also through CIPA, I was introduced to Nathan Fisher, a fabulous science fiction/fantasy book cover designer who can see inside my head! Thank you for making my imagination visible.

To the members of CIPA, thank you for sharing your knowledge, processes, and passions for all forms of the written word.

Also, a thank you is owed to each of my patient first readers: Kristina Riggs, who has been there since she was little and understands almost as much as I do about the people of Lrakira and Teramar and their guardian Stones; my nephew, Lewis Boyd, who read the first 150 pages and demanded to know when he could get the rest of it; Liz Beerman, who believes in the characters and asked who was going to compose "The Time

Song" for the movie; Chris Richards, who saw this years ago at a writer's conference and was intrigued by how the story developed a life of its own; and Nancy Koos, a friend and fellow dancer, who has meticulously read every version and not only still likes it, but is anxiously waiting for book two.

A different kind of thank you goes to a little breakfast & lunch restaurant in Auburn, California, Awful Annie's. They are the source of the cinnamon orange tea that inspired Ani's favorite cinnamon tea. You can check out their website (www.awfulannies.com) to order some so you can drink tea with the characters in the story.

And to all the others I failed to mention, my heart and my stories thank you.

Circle of Seven sing safe passage

Divide by two and send in deep sleep

The Blood and Balance shall each save one

Awakening three to rejoice with time's message

Time will soon come for reunion's leap

Six will sing joining three homes and suns

Renloret reread the first verse of the first song of the oldest manuscript he'd found on the shelves. The ancient language sang in his head. He wondered how the true melody would have sounded. It was a curious little song, and he wondered what it meant. All the early songs had meaning.

The sweet high notes of the nine bells crept into Renloret's consciousness and he looked sharply at the tower visible from the library's third floor windows. "Blades, I'm late," he muttered to himself as he slammed the heavy book shut, raising a cloud of dust particles that scattered in the midmorning light. He waved his hand briefly to scatter them further, then shoved the book back onto the shelf, not caring if it was in the correct space. The librarians could figure it out later.

"I can't afford to be late this time," he grumbled. "Don't have time for the lift. Take the stairs." He hurried to the old stairway and took two stairs at a time all the way to the main floor, vaulting the last four steps and grinning as he thought about how his demeanor clashed with the pilot's uniform he wore and the manner in which most pilots were perceived. He slowed to a respectable walk, ducked his head away from the stern shushings of the librarians scowling from behind the counter, and slipped out of the library and into the broad expanse of the university's central plaza. Once away from the building he glanced up at the bell tower, wishing it had not yet tolled the ninth hour, and broke into a run.

His headlong sprint carried him across the plaza's mosaic carpet of mosses designed to inspire peacefulness as he dodged around startled students. A few tried to slow his pace by shouting, but he continued on, finally disappearing through the crystalline doors of the administrative building that stood in cold juxtaposition to the ancient stone and wood buildings of the original university.

All the newest buildings were constructed with thin sheets of synthetic crystal to remind the citizens that they lived in the great city of Awarna at the foot of the Digoson Mountains, home of the fabled Anyala Stone. To Renloret, the citizens behaved as if they had advanced beyond the ancient, mystic mouthings, ignoring the fables and teachings of the Stones and their Singers. Raised in the Sancharos Peaks on the eastern edge of the continent, he'd been fully educated in those fables and tales. And now, though he had no right to be, he was concerned about the lack of respect for the Stones and the Singers. He disliked the pretentious synthetic structures the government used. He was more comfortable in the stone and mortar buildings of the past, though he would put up with a lot in order to fly between the stars.

Once in the lobby, he paused briefly to straighten his jacket and brush off the remnants of book dust from his sleeves. The lift in the corner opened to spew out its passengers and he nodded a greeting to several of the uniformed officers on their way out.

Once in the lift, he was grateful he would be the only passenger. As the doors slid shut, he said, "Main conference room, twelfth level," and the lift took off.

He pulled the small personal com-pad from his hip pocket, touched one of the twelve squares on its surface, and spoke. "Personal, date, Mevon 14, ninth bell. I'm late, again. I still can't figure out why I'm supposed to be at this meeting. Trimag insisted I attend, in uniform, at nine bells. So . . . I'm late. I never should have gone to the library. The Singers will never look to the old books for answers. But as my mother would say, 'Ren, a pilot cannot cure the world's ills. He can only escape them. Leave the Stones to the Singers. You have the stars.' I wish it were that simple."

The movement slowed and the door slid open. He leaned out, hand on the open pad, and sighed with relief. The hallway was empty.

Large double doors at the end of the hall glowed green. The meeting was already in session. Renloret straightened his jacket again, ran fingers through his hair, and marched rapidly to the doors. They opened without his asking.

"The fifth planet harbors a progressive populace. The two major governmental factions are frequently at odds and wars occasionally occur. However . . ."

All eyes turned from the star map on the screen to Renloret as he entered. The trio of gold-robed figures seated on the left side of the table stared at him in stony silence. Stone Singers.

Blades, what did I do to deserve this? He looked to the speaker. Trimag, High Commander of Planetary Safety and his main supporter, was apparently in charge of the meeting. Renloret groaned inwardly. He assumed he was in trouble—probably big trouble—but he had no idea what he'd done.

"Pilot, take a seat," Trimag said, pointing to the one empty seat, next to an ebony-skinned man in red scholars' robes whose eyes measured Renloret before turning back to face the screen.

Renloret nodded and slipped into the assigned place. He glanced at his com-pad. It continued to record. He placed it in front of him on the table, as the others had done with their own devices.

Trimag pointed at the now enlarged image of a small bluish planet with a single ringed moon and continued. "At this time, Teramar's northern continent appears to be concerned with its own problems and not those of the southern continent or the islands. War is not a consideration if we arrive soon. However, we do need to be cautious. Certain local factions strongly disapprove of the idea of alien life and space travel." Trimag glanced at the scholar. "This is what got our original research team in trouble and why the commander had to return before the research could be completed. The rest of the team and his family remain on the planet, possibly in hiding, but we are not sure."

Renloret wanted to ask dozens of questions. With only two sun-cycles of post-academy training, he wondered why he was even here. He cleared his throat for attention but halted as the glare from the Stone Singer directly across the table cut into his concentration. He shivered and wondered why *they* were present. They should be with the Stones, whispering prayers or at least asking them about this "plague." In his estimation, they should be in the library, studying the ancient manuscripts. Some of the prophecies of the Stones had already come true. Didn't they talk or sing with the Stones anymore? Or had the Singers slipped beyond them just as society had, letting other traditions slide into disuse?

The dark-skinned scholar spoke, his voice rumbling across the room, bringing Renloret's thoughts back to the meeting.

"We must retrieve them as soon as possible. Our entire planet depends on the research gathered there. I'm sure my hypothesis is correct. But I need my brother's corroboration on the findings." He hesitated, turning tear-filled eyes to the glaring Stone Singer on the other side of the table. "More importantly, my daughter may be the sole link to finding a cure. She, at least, must be returned. And her mother, please." He pressed shaking fingers to his temple in ill-hidden grief.

That same Stone Singer stared sullenly at the scholar. Anger and loathing radiated from her. Her fellow Singers whispered urgently, but she continued to stare.

A push began in Renloret's head, a deep throbbing, almost a sob. It was not only uncomfortable but unfamiliar. He stared back at the Stone Singers. The one with amber eyes and graying hair shifted her gaze from the scholar to him. He dropped his eyes in embarrassment and concentrated on listening, trying to ignore the throbbing at the base of his skull.

"We are readying a rescue crew as we speak, Commander," Trimag said as he shifted his gaze from the scholar to Renloret.

Renloret missed the look as he reacted to the conflicting titles. Exactly who was this military commander in scholar red? He again considered questions that his rank made impossible to ask.

The angry Stone Singer spoke. "We understand, Commander, more than you know. The Lentine provinces are reporting a rapid increase in the number of women afflicted per moon-cycle. The disease will reach global proportions within a few short years unless we find a cure. Within one generation there will be no more children and no women to bear them. Not even your daughter's blood will bring us back from possible extinction if the cure takes more than twenty years to bring to market. And we all know how long the research will take once the marketers get involved. Besides, how can you be sure your child is *the* cure?" Her tone was sarcastic.

"The research has already been done, Singer. Once my daughter is here, the results of our research can be corroborated, but I'm sure she is the key. We will need a number of blood samples to produce enough vaccine within a few moon-cycles of her return to protect every female. Distribution will be the only problem. Marketers will not be involved."

Two of the Singers acknowledged this with skeptical looks. The angry Singer continued to glare at the commander.

Renloret found his voice, finally, and spoke, unmindful of the consequences. "Sir?"

"Yes, pilot," Trimag said gruffly.

"I need a bit more explanation."

Trimag seemed to welcome the interruption. "The Stone Singers informed us of an ancient prophesy warning of a plague that would bring an end to our civilization unless a child with Singer's blood was brought home and balance was returned to the Stones. Combining this information with what we have from the commander's research, we *must* retrieve the team from Teramar."

Trimag turned to the star map, tapping the planet and its sun at the edge of the triple spiral galaxy. "Commander Chenakainet returned half a moon-cycle ago from this planet. He had to leave behind the rest of the research team, including his wife, child, and brother. What information he was able to bring with him has led us to believe the child is the cure. We don't know why yet, but it appears that the five-sun-cycles-old child and her blood may be our only hope for a future. Without a cure, we will all be gone in one generation."

"What about cloning?" Renloret asked.

"That would be a temporary solution, at best, according to studies done here in the past five sun-cycles." Trimag shrugged his shoulders. "It has something to do with absolute gender genetics. Evidence indicates that all females are hard-coded to develop the disease should they become pregnant through any technique. We need a true cure. The commander's daughter is our only hope."

A contemplative silence seemed to endorse Trimag's statement.

"Then it is settled," Trimag said. "A rescue team has been assembled. You, Renloret, will be the pilot."

Stunned, Renloret cleared his throat to speak, but Trimag held up his hand.

"I know what you're thinking, Ren. However, you and everyone else in this room should know that you are my best pilot." His eyes pinned the angry Stone Singer and she looked away. "And you have not been told why you were chosen. Commander Chenakainet, will you explain?"

The commander turned to Renloret. "You are the one in my vision. I saw you when I touched the Anyala Stone. I've never had a Stone-vision before. The Stone told me to find you. I don't know why the Stone chose you, but you must accept. I depend on you to reunite my family. Our world depends on you to bring the cure safely home."

All eyes in the room bore into Renloret, some pleading, some jealous, some awed, most eager to hear his response.

Renloret heard himself speak. "When do we go?" The words just formed themselves. The push in his head began again, not hurting, but calling to him, needing him. He had to see the Anyala Stone. He rubbed his neck and the push ebbed away.

Trimag came to attention. "In two sun-times you will leave with your team. I have informed your superiors. Consider yourself upgraded with honors, pilot. We salute you."

Suddenly, everyone stood and placed their left hands on their right shoulders. To Renloret's surprise, even the angry Stone Singer saluted him. Renloret slowly stood and returned the salute, unnerved by the suddenness of events and the heaviness of the group's expectations.

CHAPTER TWO

Renloret nodded his thanks to the Singer's assistant, watching as she backed away several steps with bowed head, then turned sharply and returned to her desk in the main hall. He studied the intricate carvings on the door and realized he had been delivered to the wrong Singer's chamber. Instead of Singer Selabec's office, he found himself at one of the guest offices. He turned to go after the assistant, but was halted by a female voice leaking through the door. Perhaps all the Singers had gathered in one room. Renloret checked the time and chuckled when he saw that he was early because he could not recall being early to anything, as far back as he could remember. He moved to knock on the door but stopped as the tone of the voices changed, then stepped closer to the crack.

"Yes, you should allow this," said Commander Chenakainet, his deep voice easily identifiable. "The Stone requested him specifically. I spent days locating this pilot because the Anyala Stone told me to. It didn't ask me to. I was *ordered* to find him and bring him here. And he has asked to see the Stone."

The answer from an unrecognized female was harsh. "How can you be sure he is the right pilot?"

"Shouldn't we allow the Stone to decide?"

This swift reply was met with momentary silence.

"Commoners are not allowed physical contact, by Singer Law, Commander," the woman retorted.

"Then why was I allowed?" Chenakainet asked softly.

"Because . . . because the Stone requested it," she replied with defiance.

"Yes," the commander said, "the Stone requested it. And it told me to find the pilot. It told me he was its hope, that only he could pilot the necessary mission. And as you yourself have researched, he is not a commoner, but directly connected to the Kita Stone."

"Only through his great-grandmother," the Singer hissed. "He wouldn't know how to connect with it. It takes years of training. Besides, he is a male."

"Am I not? The Stone spoke to me. I needed no training. New circumstances require us to respond in new ways, Singer. Or are you so deeply buried in your beliefs that you are inflexible?"

Silence was her answer. Renloret could hear footsteps crossing the chamber beyond. He pressed his ear to the door, not wanting to miss a word.

"Commander, six sun-cycles ago when you left, you took Selabec's daughter, S'Hendale."

He snapped back, "I did not *take* her. She demanded to leave with us. We didn't even know her true name until we had reached our destination. We tried to send her back, Diani. She refused, saying the Anyala Stone had told her she would provide the cure if she left Lrakira. S'Hendale had made a blade promise to the Stone. Everyone agreed we couldn't return her after that."

The woman, now identified as the Pericha Stone's Singer Diani said, "Selabec was so angry when she received the news. As far as the Stones have communicated, Selabec has not been in the presence of the Anyala Stone since. She said that without the blade in her possession, there was no reason to."

"Selabec has not connected with her Stone in almost six sun-cycles? How do the Stones feel about that?"

"They are not concerned. We are told that all has been planned for and that the Singer position will be filled on the return of your family. Because your daughter is only five, I assume the Stone's choice will be S'Hendale. For now, the Anyala Stone is content with being without a Singer."

Renloret held his breath. What were the rules to becoming an heir to one of the Stones? He always thought that the Stones chose from the female side of the families unless there were no direct descendant females. In that rare case, the choice was usually the next closest female, perhaps the wife of a male descendant. At least that was the standard thinking. What about the commander's daughter? Could she inherit the Stone at such a young age? How old did you have to be? Renloret wished for the musty confines of the library and time to delve deeper into the mystical singings of the Stones. He was positive the answers lay there.

"What use would this audience be?" Diani asked.

"But what harm?" the commander answered.

"I don't know." Defeat echoed in Diani's voice.

"Then let the pilot see the Stone. He needs the Stone, itself, to confirm my vision. We all need that confirmation, and only the Stone can give it to us. We cannot cease to hope. The Stone told me Renloret was its hope. Perhaps we should believe the Stone."

"Very well, he may have his audience. Is he here or must I send for him?"

"He should be here soon. I sent for him before our meeting."

"Ah, you are so confident, Commander. Perhaps . . . perhaps this youngster can save us all."

Footsteps approached the door. Renloret stepped back and jerked his jacket straight as the door swung open. The Singer Renloret recognized as Diani glared at him as he mumbled that he had been just about to knock, but stood back to let him in. He nodded respectfully to the commander and was then led by the two to a small chamber at the end of a twisting hallway. Once inside, Diani and the commander disappeared through a side door. Renloret drank in the ancient feel of the embroidered rugs and hangings and shivered. In the room's center, a large alabaster pedestal cradled the Anyala Stone.

Never this close to one of the stones, Renloret was uncomfortable. He decided to salute the dull green crystal and whispered a child's stone prayer.

> *Stone of crystal, Stone of light*
> *Stone of promise, Stone of sight*
> *See my heart, Hear my prayer*
> *See my soul, Hear my song*
> *Give your answer with loving care.*

The push returned to the back of his skull, bringing on a greenish undertone to his vision. He glanced from the ornate rugs at the base of the pedestal to the massive stone resting in its cool embrace.

A shimmer crossed the Anyala Stone's surface. He felt its mind touch his.

Come.

Renloret stepped close to touch the stone. It was cool, smooth, hard . . . and yet not hard. The shimmer danced under his hands. He closed his eyes as the Stone hummed a tune into him through his hands. Warmth spread through his body, the tune becoming words.

Pilot. You have come. You must return my blades to Lrakira. She will bring The Blood to save your people and he shall bring balance to our existence once again. You, Renloret, son of Yorsa, grandson of Ramer, great-grandson to Tivi, are the promised pilot. What is done was told eons ago. The beginning has begun and the pilot will return the blades. As we waited for the plague, we waited for The Blood and The Balance. They will save the people and us. S'Hendale has served us well. Return all, Renloret, and all will be well. You are our choice. You are our hope.

The voice faded back to a hum, leaving Renloret cool and calm.

He opened his eyes to see the faint green glow shimmer. He would "return all." His world would continue. He would succeed.

The Stone Chamber pulsed with tonal greetings as Stone Singer Diani placed her amber Pericha Stone on the third pedestal, completing the triangle of Stones.

"Where's Selabec? She should be here," Diani said.

Layson, the blue Kita Stone's Singer, shoved trembling hands into the long deep sleeves of her robe. Her voice quavered nervously. "I don't think she's coming. She said the Stone didn't want her here. Can we do this without her? How are we going to contact the Anyala Stone? How is this Gathering of Stones going to help the rescue mission and Lrakira?"

"I don't know, but I have faith in the Pericha Stone and you should have faith in Kita. They do talk to each other, you know. We're not really needed, Layson, especially now that they are in the same room."

Low tones began to emanate from the amber and blue stones, soothing the Singers' worries. The tonal telepathic communication brought frowns of concern to the Singers' faces.

"You want us to leave? But we just brought you together. I thought we worked as a team," Diani said, incredulous.

"Too dangerous? How is this gathering dangerous?" Layson implored, her voice slipping towards anger. "If I'd known that, I'd never have agreed to do this."

Diani stood before her humming Stone. "Explain this procedure."

The low tones rumbled through their minds as the Stones tried to ease their Singers' concerns.

"Yes, I know this plague will destroy us if the child is not returned," Diani said in response to her Stone's mind to mind communication. "I just don't understand how a single child can be that important? We have enough of her blood relatives here on Lrakira to simulate her blood. Wouldn't that be easier?"

Layson challenged her Stone. "Why is that tiny planet so important? How can you speed their return? The rescue team is almost there. It's been barely half a moon-cycle, how much faster can you expect? With some luck they will be home before the cycle is complete."

The Stones hummed as a trio.

"Time? Of course time is important," Diani said.

"The child needs time? For what? The pilot?" Layson raised her hands in exasperation. "Diani, do you understand any of this?"

"No," the older Singer sighed in resignation, "but since they are confident this gathering and song will guarantee success, we must allow it. And they will not answer any more questions. They mustn't waste more time."

The blue Kita Stone hummed to Layson. She turned to Diani

and said, "Kita says we have no choice. We must leave them because the danger is to us, not them."

"Then we should leave and return when called." Diani caressed her stone, reluctant to leave.

"What about Selabec?" Layson asked.

"What about her?" Diani looked at the green Anyala Stone resting on its pedestal. She knew Selabec had not been in true contact with her Stone since her daughter's defection almost six sun-cycles ago. Even so, Selabec had been furious about the pilot's audience, which Diani had allowed. Selabec had spoken to Diani just once since then and the accusation still stung. "She believes Commander Chenakainet kidnapped S'Hendale and then deliberately left her behind on Teramar so Selabec would have no direct heir."

"What does having a direct heir have to do with this?" Layson twisted and untwisted the long dark braid of hair that hung over her shoulder. "I inherited Kita from my uncle's mother. I'm not a direct heir. I thought 'inheriting' was the term everyone used."

"I guess I've had too little time to explain. You've only been connected with Kita for a few moon-cycles and you are so far away in those mountains of yours." Diani sighed. She went on to explain the history of Stone Singers and their respective Stones. The library records recorded how, though two of three Stones had maintained a direct line from mother to daughter or granddaughter, the Kita Stone had been erratic in its choices. There had even been mention of arguments between the stones about the length of time to stay within the same female line. The arguments had always ended with the Stones agreeing that the Kita Stone's choices were designed to remind the people that variety was good. Diani knew that Selabec had only one daughter and she assumed S'Hendale would want to inherit, though S'Hendale's abrupt departure six sun-times ago seemed to suggest otherwise.

Layson stopped twisting her braid. "Doesn't Selabec see the opportunity for her granddaughter? She is still in the same line if S'Hendale refuses to join with the Stone upon her return."

"No, I've tried to discuss it with her. I'm not sure she even realizes she has a granddaughter. She is adamant that S'Hendale will inherit. She sees nothing beyond that. The sooner S'Hendale returns, the sooner Selabec will be appeased and we can let the Stone resolve the issue of inheritance."

Kita and Pericha hummed in agreement, the sweet song indicating approval.

Layson smiled. "Best to leave it all to the Stones. If this thing they plan to do works, then fewer women will die and we, as a people, will continue. I had hoped to have children someday, but with this plague affecting only women who have recently birthed or are pregnant, Karvlet and I have put off that thought, though I'm eager for a cure." A wan smile crossed her lips as she gestured towards the chamber door.

Trusting the Stones to call when needed, the Singers exited arm in arm.

The air in the chamber began to oscillate with a humming duet. The Anyala Stone added its harmonics as soon as the door latched, and the chamber throbbed with joy as the Stones conversed freely and planned the time-song. It had been many hundreds of years since the trio had been in such close proximity. And though they were in constant contact, the power necessary for the coming song had required this "gathering." The harmonics built gradually as they readied themselves to twist the time line. So much could go wrong, but this was such a small twist compared to the Song of Saving choreographed by all seven Stones a thousand years in the past. This little twist would be the beginning of reunification. The birth had occurred. The pilot had been chosen and was nearing Teramar. He would return The Blood and The Balance, thus ensuring the survival of Lrakira's people. This one small twist would solve so many things.

The triangle of crystals glowed. Energy flashed off the walls—visual music as they danced with time. The Stones twisted the tune and changed the melody, and time gladly followed. Success was near. A few more phrases and it would be done. Only the tiny planet at the edge of the triple spiral would be affected.

The Anyala Stone slid into the last movement of the song. A few more measures would twist a few more years. Just two or three were needed now, then the ship could land and The Blood and The Balance would come home. The Stones' charges would be saved and reunification could proceed. The Stones were joyous; the song almost complete.

A shadow passed between the lights and music. The Anyala Stone faltered on its note as the amber blade entered its core, stopping short of its soul.

The shadowed figure snarled, "You'll not keep her from me any longer. She will return."

The Stones' melody screeched in discord. The twist jerked wide of its mark. On a faraway planet with a ringed moon, the other three crystalline Stones were jarred from their hibernation by the cry of pain and loss. They rushed to add their voices to repair the melody of time, to keep it contained. Five Stones joined, not in joy as had been planned, but in a fight with time. The ruined twist grabbed the ship. Time skipped forward uncontrolled. The rudely awakened Stones of Teramar struggled to ensure the pilot's survival. Scattered and hidden across the planet, they could barely protect the ship. They surrounded it in a cushion of red, yellow, and purple song. They could do no more. The rest would be up to him.

The Stones of Lrakira cried in frustration as the tune disintegrated. Despair flooded the room, pulsing angry amber and blue. The connection was lost. The fate of two planets rested in a pilot who did not know his importance or that The Blood and The Balance were now grown. Kita and Pericha sobbed.

The door burst open. Stone Singers Diani and Layson raced to the triangle of stones and stopped in their tracks, aghast. Selabec's hands were wrapped around the jeweled hilt of the amber blade, which was buried deep in the Anyala Stone.

"What have you done?" Diani and Layson gasped in one voice.

Time hiccoughed just as Renloret set the final coordinates for the landing. The blue-green image of the planet shifted on the screen.

"What was that?" asked Sharnel, the rescue team's leader, as he strapped into the seat next to Renloret.

"Don't know, Sharnel. I hope it didn't screw up the coordinates." Renloret began checking his numbers, his fingers flying over the command panel.

"Blades, Ren, we're approaching too fast," Sharnel said.

Lights began pulsing as automatic alarms sounded and Renloret said, "We're in for a bumpy entrance." He toggled the communications switch. "Kiver, leave off the language prep and harness up."

"Doing so now, Pilot." The response came from the personal quarters' section near the back of the ship.

Before Renloret could acknowledge the researcher, the planet's image shifted again and the command panel bent and slid away from Renloret's grasp. "Oh, Stones and Blades, help us." A mind-numbing pain pushed inside his head, shutting everything else out. Despair filled him and he screamed. On the screen, the two continents of Teramar rushed up to greet him through a purple, yellow, and red pulsing haze. He fought the pain in his head and the forces wrenching his ship. An explosion burst the command panel. Renloret watched a slice of metal pierce Sharnel's chest.

Sharnel grabbed at it, his eyes wide.

Renloret turned back to the screen.

Time slowed.

Steep canyon walls loomed into view and trees barreled at them.

The sleek ship twisted.

Renloret saw stars, beautiful stars, stretching across the

canyon opening. His thoughts flicked between the confidence of the Anyala Stone, the expectations of his world, and now, the certainty of his failure.

CHAPTER FOUR

*A*ni.

The telepathic call was insistent. Ani rolled over, pulled the blankets tighter, and snuggled deeper.

Ani.

A whisper echoed in her dreams. She buried herself under the covers, trying to ignore it.

Ani!

The whisper became a shout and brought her fully awake.

I'm awake now, Kela. What have you got? Even through her grogginess she felt the urgency in his tone.

Help.

Help? Explain, please.

It wasn't like Kela to do this. Where was he anyway? She sat up and perched herself on the edge of the bed to get her bearings. The coolness of the wood snapped her to alertness as her feet touched the floor.

There's been a crash in the canyon.

What are you talking about? Ani immediately got up and fumbled for her clothes

Get up here and help me.

Kela's mental voice had never sounded so imperative.

What kind of crash, Kela? Ani finished buttoning her shirt and shoved her long legs into heavy work pants.

How am I supposed to know? I'm just a canine. Now hurry up.

I'm on my way. I'll pack a few things first.

She added a sweater over the shirt in the faint glow issuing from the fireplace and managed to locate the first aid kit under the sink. She stuffed it into the backpack that always rested near the door.

I'm almost ready. What time is it anyway?

She moved to the counter, pulled a drawer open, and felt around in the semidarkness to choose a blade. After strapping on her favorite leg sheath, she pulled on knee-high boots to cover it.

You don't want to know. Just hurry. I can smell at least two bodies.

Ani reached far back into the drawer and pulled out a hand-light and three small round disks. She studied the disks briefly, not knowing if she'd need them, grimaced, and stuffed the miniature holographic projectors in the pack's front pocket. Rummaging through an overhead cabinet, she located a box of folded black bags. She never considered she'd have reason to use one of them again. On Kela's thought, she took two. Grabbing the light jacket off the wall peg, she zipped it, shouldered the backpack, and stepped outside.

The horizon had not yet tinged itself with pink and gold. She shivered in the cold. *Why are you always getting me up before dawn on a wild honker pursuit?*

Kela's reply was indignant. *I have never chased wild honkers.*

It is before dawn, though. I can't even see Starlight Ridge. Ani negotiated her way across the small clearing in front of the cabin to the trail.

After almost a year of neglect, the trail to the canyon showed signs of overgrowth. She had forgotten just how steep it was. Her lungs burned. Ani searched her mind for Kela and got no answer, though his mental presence reassured her. She made a face, sucked in more air, and continued the climb. The hike to the canyon seemed longer than she remembered. It was clear that her year at the university hadn't benefited her physical condition, but the altitude probably didn't help either. She'd have to correct that later, after she tackled whatever crisis this was. At the top of the grade, a few hundred yards from the canyon opening, she paused to listen. The forest was too quiet. It made her nervous. Branches snapped to the side of the trail.

"Kela! Is that you?" Ani yelled, hoping to scare off any large creatures. It wouldn't do to run afoul of a hunting kreline. "Kela?"

Yes, it's me. What took you so long? He emerged from the heavy timber at the canyon's opening and looked at her expectantly.

She switched back to telepathic mode because that method didn't require air. *Well, it's a long story and trail. You know that little ravine half a mile back? It's not so little anymore. Must have been some rainstorm earlier this spring to gouge it so deep.*

Quit complaining and follow me. He slipped through the trees towards a small creek.

Ani grimaced and followed, not sure of what to expect.

Did you bring them?

Kela's question caught her off guard. "Bring what?" She ducked under a branch, wrinkling her nose at the smell of burning brush.

The holo-cams. We're going to need them if we want to keep this a secret.

Ani stopped at the edge of the debris field. "Why should we keep it secret?"

The canyon floor glowed dimly in spots where remaining flames were reflected by large metal pieces. Smoke billowed from a huge engine that lay several yards behind the rest of the craft. It couldn't have crashed more than a few hours ago. She approached slowly, assessing the scene. Her first impression was that it didn't look right. It was massive compared to the planes being introduced to the skies above Teramar. Those only carried two or three people; this would have carried ten times that many. She hoped there wouldn't be any scaled, winged, or multi-limbed aliens inside. She wouldn't be able to handle that. She stepped gingerly through the plowed up ground, shoving her emotions deep so she could do the job confronting her.

"Kela, why keep it secret?" she repeated.

Because it is necessary for your safety. Kela's tail waved as a signal near a chunk of twisted metal. *A body is here.*

"My safety? I hardly think a plane crash is a threat to my safety unless it crashes on the lake house or the cabin." She lifted a panel to reveal an arm and swallowed hard. She placed two fingers on the wrist and paused her own thoughts to concentrate for several seconds. No pulse.

What about the alien rumors? Kela reached under Ani's hand to grab the material around the arm and pulled.

"Are you going to start that up again, too? You're as bad as the boys from the university." When Kela did not answer, Ani grabbed the shoulder, or what was left of it, and pulled the body clear of the wreckage. A large gash across his upper thigh proved he had bled out.

"Doesn't look too alien to me." Ani studied the battered body and put a fist to her stomach to keep from throwing up. "Very human, in fact. I hope this is the only one." Relief flooded over the sick feeling in her stomach.

It's not. I can smell at least one more.

Ani winced. With a brief blade salute and a glance at the fading stars she said, "May the blades honor and protect him." She tossed back the loose strands of hair that had escaped from the braid. "Kela, you have not answered my question. Why should we keep this hushed? I'd want to know what happened if this person was a friend of mine or a family member."

Kela jumped over some long metal pieces. *Look over here and then decide for yourself.*

Ani followed. The largest piece of wreckage loomed near the front edge of the burned area. She shivered. It didn't look like any aircraft she knew about. It was too large even in two pieces. Perhaps it was a Southern experimental craft of some sort. Hadn't Uncle Reslo mentioned something about intercontinental aircraft being designed by an upstart company down there? Kela stood by a panel with painted letter-like designs. As Ani got closer she felt a tremor course through her body. She shook her head as her vision took on a greenish overtone.

"Kela, I think I'm going to be sick. Everything looks green."

Just look at this panel. Do you recognize it at all? Kela sat next to the panel. *You won't get sick; you're too strong for that.*

Ani knelt next to Kela and leaned on the panel for support. "That's what you think." She brushed soot and dirt from the panel to get a better look at the designs. The metallic surface didn't feel right. Waves of green again threatened her mind, along with the unbearable need to find someone alive. With a deep breath, she shoved the thought of her churning stomach down with her emotions. Her fingers traced the designs. "Nope. Don't recognize them at all. Not related to any language I've studied at least. Maybe it's Southern code or something."

A deep groan caught her attention. "Was that you, Kela?"

Nope. He turned his head to the front section of the wreckage.

"Someone's alive. Let's find him." She stood shakily as waves of panic increased the nausea already straining her control. She leaned on the panel again and jerked her hand off as if it burned. "Kela, I don't feel so good."

I suppose you could be reacting to some of the fumes. But I've been here longer than you and I don't feel sick.

Another groan redirected their attention. Ani stepped inside the opening to the right of the panel. A man was still buckled in his seat, a large sliver of metal pinning him in place. Ani closed her eyes in horror at the look on his lifeless face. She whispered the death blessing, "Blades, protect your spirits," and brushed her hand over the man's staring eyes to close his lids. She could return to handle this one after she located the source of the sound. The screen in front of him glowed green.

Kela looked at Ani. *Perhaps this is why you are seeing green?*

"Perhaps." Ani rubbed her temple again as she began to study the interior. "This man couldn't have made the noise I heard. There must be someone else." She moved a seat that had been ripped from its base into the middle of the small room. A leg dropped off the armrest. Another groan sounded as the leg hit the floor. Ani retrieved the hand-light from the pack, knelt, and reached her arms along the leg, noting the blood soaked fabric. "Got to stop the bleeding on that," she muttered.

She shook his foot. "Hey! Can you hear me? I'm here to help." There was no response. The space under the console limited her ability to get a good look at potential injuries. Ani would do what she could first, then get him outside and back to the cabin before contacting the sheriff. Silently she cursed the distance between her and the village. Then she remembered she hadn't checked to see if the tel-com at the cabin was working. She knew she was on her own for at least a couple of days, and with a long sigh, she did what her mother had taught her.

Using both hands, she felt his leg bones. There were no obvious breaks, only a cut on one shin. She crawled further under the console, pushing debris away from the man's torso. The light showed no blood along the front of his abdomen, but she palpated anyway. It seemed okay and the even rise and fall indicated he was breathing. No ribs appeared to be broken. Moving upward to his shoulders and neck, she pressed her fingers to the side of the windpipe. A steady bump under her touch brought a thin smile to her lips. The hand-light showed red stickiness covering his cheek. She ran a hand to the source, a cut above one eye.

He twisted away making anguished sounds. She didn't

understand any of them, though they were definitely words. She backed out slowly, lifting the side of his body only enough so she could slide her hand along his back to check for blood. Her hand came out dry. Ani stood and stretched while studying the surroundings.

Kela crawled under the desk-like structure along the man's body. He snuffled at the man's neck. A hand came out of the darkness, slapping Kela across the head. He shut his eyes but stayed close.

I think he's fine. He just smacked me.

Did you deserve it? Ani asked, returning to the cramped space.

I was checking his pulse.

You put your cold nose on my neck and I'd swat you, too. But you're right, he must not be too bad off if he's doing that.

As carefully as possible and trying not to cause further injury, Ani slid him from under the console. Once she had more room to maneuver, she leaned over the man, gently lifting his eyelids, and used the hand-light to see if they responded evenly. She expelled a breath in relief. They did.

Kela had moved to her side. *Well?*

Equally reactive, that's good. The two gashes on his scalp and the slice on his leg are the only visible injuries, though a more thorough exam might be needed to assess possible internal damage. But he's alive, for the moment. Ani fumbled with her pack. Her vision clouded green again, this time pulsing like a heartbeat, and she pushed the heels of her hands to her temples. This was not good.

"What's wrong with me?" She managed to open the pack and blindly pulled out some of the items, scattering them on the floor. The pain increased. Her heart rate jumped as a burst of fear overcame her. What was the danger? Where was it coming from? She struggled for control as an overpowering desire to escape the craft swept through her. Glancing around the space for an intruder of some type, she realized all she could see was waves of color, purple, yellow, and blue, along with faint shades of green. She shook her head.

What do you need? Kela's tone was curiously calm, oblivious to her panic. That made her angry.

"My eyesight, damn the hells! This is not going to work. I can't do this in here. Got to get him outside." Tears ran down her cheeks as she grabbed the man under his shoulders, braced his head with her hands, and dragged him towards the opening. Her back complained at the strain, but she gritted her teeth and kept moving. He moaned once more, then his body went limp.

Once outside and off the burned area, Ani collapsed against the base of a tree, the man's head resting on her lap. She closed her eyes and breathed deeply. Each breath eased the headache and assisted in releasing adrenaline's grip around her heart. Kela's cold nose at her neck startled her, but she did not swat him away.

"Thanks." She opened her eyes.

The early morning sun peeked over the canyon edge, giving her normal light to see by. Before she moved him again, she brushed dark blood-crusted hair from his face. His mahogany skin was a bit lighter than hers and well-shaped eyebrows arched below his pain-furrowed forehead. She ran her fingers across his temples and over his scalp, feeling for any dents or lumps on his skull.

"Kela, get the stuff from my pack. I can see what I'm doing

now." The green fog obscuring her vision was subsiding and her headache began to fade.

Kela dropped rolls of bandages within reach and sat down to watch.

Ani placed a wad of gauze on the man's scalp gashes and wrapped it tight. The bleeding had eased from the ragged cut on his leg, at least for the moment. She decided to just wrap it until she could get him to the cabin where she would clean and stitch it. That complete, she paused to rub her head, trying to ease the tension. Kela came to her side and pressed close; Ani reached her arm over and hugged him tight.

She glanced at the wreckage. The strange metal reflected the first rays of sun as it topped the tallest trees. "I've never seen a craft like that before, not even drawings." Ani turned her head away from the disturbing view. The man's human face reassured her. Not alien at all.

Ship or plane?

Ani sighed. "It can't be a plane, it has no real wings." She let the thought hang suggestively.

So? Kela pressed.

Ani ignored the question, not wanting to pursue the subject further.

Burying her face into Kela's fur, she whispered, "The holo-cams are in the outside pocket of the pack. I agree we need to keep this a secret. Too many things . . . leading to a conclusion I don't think I want to know. I need more time to look at the pieces before I let Taryn or the military up here."

She paused, hugging Kela tighter. "All the hells, do you suppose

Dalkey will come back if he hears about this? If I know him, he'll want to be here to prove something to me, the military, the media, and perhaps to himself. I need to talk to this survivor."

She took off her jacket, rolled it up, and placed it under the man's head. "Hope he can give me some answers." Her fingers traced the pain lines across his forehead. "Kela, get the pack. I'll need your help in setting up the holo-cams."

She reluctantly took her fingers off the man's face, then stood and brushed off pine needles and dirt.

"After we've activated the holo-cams, we'll have to decide how to deal with the two bodies. And we'll have to take this one to the cabin."

She looked down at the man. Blood showed red through the bandages, but not in excess. He'd be okay long enough for her to set up the holo-cams and deal with the bodies, if she was quick about it. Most of the bleeding seemed to have stopped. She thought there were two possible problems: internal damage and a concussion. She'd have to get him to the cabin to do anything about those things. And to do that she'd have to make a litter of some sort first, because she was not dragging him all the way to the cabin.

She looked into the trees, searching for large dried up branches that could be used as a frame for a litter while continuing to mutter a list of things to check. Reaching into the pack, she drew out a palm-sized disk and twisted the top half until it popped up several inches and emitted a low whine. Then she tapped in a code on the underside of the device. The whine disappeared as she set it on the ground a few paces away from the unconscious man.

One third of the valley floor fuzzed in her vision as the hologram concealed part of the crash site. She stepped past the device towards the crash. It came into view again. Kela pressed another holo-cam into her hand as she walked across the debris field and found a place for it. Kela followed with the third. Together they placed the last one and Ani again backed away from it. Trees appeared undisturbed, the creek ran along an edging of bushes, and flowers slowly opened in response to the light now beginning to fill the bottom of the canyon. The one thing she couldn't hide was the smell of smoke, which would dissipate within a few days. Hopefully, that would be long enough for her to find out what type of aircraft had ripped up her property.

She stepped forward again and the wreckage fuzzed into focus. Kela moved towards the first body, and she acknowledged it with a nod. "I think we ought to bury them."

How?

"I brought a couple of stasis-bags." She shivered at the thought of enclosing someone in a bag, in stifling confinement, reasoning with herself that they were already dead and wouldn't know. It was just like a casket, and for some reason a casket was acceptable—if everyone was positive the person was truly dead. "We can cover them with enough stones to keep out scavengers and they'll be all right until I have more time or can get some help." She pointed to the edge of the canyon where rocks had naturally piled up due to an old slide. "How about over there?"

Good enough. I guess.

Ani noted that Kela didn't sound sure as she drew her knife from its calf-sheath and entered the aircraft. Once the two bodies were in the stasis bags and covered with rocks she could build a litter and get the injured man to the cabin. Then she could consider what to do next.

Poking her head out of the wreck, she said, "I wouldn't mind some help."

Kela laid his head across the chest of the wounded man. *I'll help you best by staying here.*

"Okay, but the next time something crashes, you're doing the hard stuff." Her green eyes glared at him. "You could bring me the stasis bags."

Sighing dramatically, Kela nosed through the backpack and delivered the bags, dodging her swat of irritation, then returned to the tree and placed his head on the man's chest.

Two hours passed before Ani was finished burying the pair of stasis bags and securing the wounded man to a primitive litter. Using some webbing stripped from the wreckage, she tied the handles to a loop over her shoulder and began the tedious trek down to the cabin.

A small round-eared, fuzzy-tailed hopper scooted from under the bush as Ani tossed the last of the cleaning water over the porch railing. She grinned and tucked a few stray strands of hair behind her ears as the hopper zigzagged into the trees across the clearing. Why did she think she knew the unconscious man who was now at rest in her bed, bandaged and clean?

She shrugged and drew her arm across her forehead, staining the shirtsleeve with sweat, then set the empty bowl on the top of the railing and took a deep, slow breath. As she released the breath, she opened her mind to her surroundings. The evening insects droned rhythmically. A kreline's hunting cry echoed from somewhere beyond the trees. The soft clicking of claws on the porch decking announced Kela's arrival. He licked her hand and bumped it with his muzzle, insisting she scratch behind his ears. Without thought she rubbed deep into his fur eliciting a purring rumble.

Kela's question came softly into her mind. *Do you think he'll survive?*

Not wanting to disturb the night sounds just beginning to calm her, she answered telepathically. *Yes, the major injury is the gash on his leg, though he may yet develop signs of a concussion. The cuts on his head will heal just fine. I'm surprised he has only those injuries. Mother would have said, "The Stones have a plan for him." But why here and why now? I just wanted to have some time off with no one bothering me. I shouldn't have stopped at Gelwood's. I'm sure Taryn will find out about that scuffle from his father. Perhaps I should contact him in the morning. I don't want him to come out here looking for me.*

Kela harrumphed but kept silent. Ani closed off the direct communication with him to consider the possible consequences of the incident.

She'd scuffled at Gelwood's grocery with three boys on their first year break from university. Actually, it hadn't been much of a scuffle. They had made aggressive advances on her, not knowing that she was a blade instructor. And they had brought up the whole ridiculousness about aliens. She'd dispatched them without much physical damage to them, only damage to their pride.

Ani was confident Gelwood would inform his son, the sheriff, of the incident and she did not look forward to the admonishment that might result. She shook her head. She'd only wanted to get away from the university for a few weeks, relax at home where she wasn't under constant scrutiny from the military and politicians because of her uncle's "retirement" to the southern continent. And now she had an aircraft of some sort, possibly from Southern, crash on her property. If Taryn wanted to talk with her about the incident at Gelwood's store, she would have a lot more to explain than the incident with the boys.

Ani opened her mind to Kela. *If I call Taryn and voluntarily confess to protecting myself from the unwanted attention at Gelwood's grocery, maybe Taryn won't press me and I'll have a few days to figure things out. And I'd like to understand what's going on before I fill in Taryn about the crash.*

Kela made a sound not unlike a low grumble. *It wasn't your fault and there was no harm done, right? Gelwood will explain what happened and Taryn wouldn't hold you responsible anyway. And until we know more about the man inside the cabin, why should you risk anyone finding out about the crash, including Taryn?*

She considered Kela's question as she stretched, easing the ache in her shoulders from burying two bodies and dragging the wounded man to the cabin. Though the trail from the crash to the cabin had been downhill, it had not been smooth, and she'd almost spilled the man off the litter several times. The leg gash had been messy to clean, but once it had been stitched, it didn't look too bad. The scalp wound would be hidden by hair after it grew back from where she'd trimmed it. Her examination of every cut and bruise had done nothing to answer the nagging thought that she should know him.

She wanted to discuss the decorative scars on his wrists with him. The designs and the fact they were actual cuts and not tattoos indicated he was from Southern. No one else she knew, except her parents and uncle, were from Southern. With her uncle in hiding there and her parents both dead, she felt very alone. Seeing the championship scars on his wrists reminded her of her Southern connection and that, in spite of her friends here in Star Valley, she was probably the only Southern bred person on Northern. Common sense said otherwise, but the tensions between continents had escalated in recent years and even her own blade champion status had not relieved the scrutiny she received from the military because her family had hailed from Southern.

She pushed away from the railing, gathered up the damp towels into a bundle, went back inside the cabin, and dropped the towels in a basket for a later more thorough cleaning. Then she took three blankets from the closet next to the bed and placed them on the rocking chair seat. She eyed the open rafter beams and decided to hang the blankets lengthwise to provide a makeshift wall separating the bed from the rest of the large main room of the cabin.

Kela seated himself out of the way and watched her hang the blankets. He interrupted her thoughts. *I think we ought to keep the crash a secret. Only he survived and I've not seen any signs of rescue personnel arriving, though they probably wouldn't show up until sometime tomorrow anyway.*

Ani stepped off the footstool she had used to reach the rafters and turned to look at the man before commenting. He was breathing heavily, hopefully in response to the narcotic she'd slipped between his lips before she stitched his leg wound. It would keep him asleep at least until morning.

She whispered, "I agree, but how can we keep this a secret? Surely someone saw the aircraft coming in too low and in the wrong place. If not, someone surely saw the smoke. The village is only ten miles from here and no airfields are within one hundred and fifty. Maybe Taryn already knows about it."

Then why hasn't he contacted you? Kela insisted.

"I don't think the tel-com is working, per usual. Listen, Kela, I'm tired beyond being useful. I'll check it in the morning. If he didn't leave a message, I'll call him. Okay?" Her whisper was laced with exhaustion.

Okay. Just want to cover all the tracks. Kela curled onto the rug near the bed.

Ani straightened the blanket that covered the man. He moved, agitated by unknown dreams and pain. He mumbled foreign words.

Ani pulled another blanket from the closet and wrapped herself in it as she sat down in the rocker next to the bed and began to rock. The wood runners created a soft beat against the floor and Ani began to hum a lullaby from her childhood. The man seemed to relax and his breathing eased as Ani closed her eyes to concentrate on the almost forgotten notes.

CHAPTER FIVE

The tel-com on the desk buzzed. Sheriff Taryn Avere smiled as he tapped the receive button. "Good morn, Daneeha. How was your off time?"

He turned a page of the night shift report as he waited for the secretary to respond. His father had mentioned that Ani was back and would be calling, and he wondered if Daneeha was buzzing him to say that it was her. He had no idea when she would contact him, but he didn't want to miss the call when it came.

"Just fine, sir. Sorry to interrupt so early this morn, but there's a call for you from a General Stubin Dalkey. He says he's from continental headquarters." Her squeaky voice jumped even higher when she repeated where the general was calling from.

Taryn paused in his reading and raised his eyebrows in surprise. "*General* Stubin Dalkey? Last time we talked he was only a sergeant. I wonder what he wants now." Taryn closed the report file and pulled out a clean pad for taking notes. "Okay,

Daneeha, you can put him through, voice only, please." He took a deep breath and released it.

"Good morn, General." He couldn't keep the smile out of his voice at the title.

"Glad to know someone in authority is on top of things in that little splat of a town. Now here's what you're going to do—" the general began, disrespecting both Taryn's position and the jurisdiction in one breath.

The demanding tone grated on Taryn's nerves and he interrupted. "*General* Dalkey, demands without explanations will get you nothing in this 'little splat of a town.' We may be small, but we know the laws. What is it you'd like us to do?" He considered turning on the video so he could see Dalkey. Obviously, the general didn't remember him from the previous year. Taryn had narrowly avoided a riot at the Chenak funeral when the then Sergeant Dalkey had incited the mourners.

"Our space surveillance has detected a downed plane near your valley, Sheriff." Dalkey spit the title out. "I need your permission to search for it."

Taryn straightened up and began making notes on the pad. "And what kind of plane is it? I've received no calls from the outlying areas about any type of crash."

Dalkey cleared his throat noisily. "You don't need to concern yourself with that information. I just need your permission to search for it."

"And just where do you intend on searching, General?" Taryn asked. He didn't feel any real inclination to grant permission.

"The Chenak holdings," Dalkey responded.

Taryn stopped writing. "General, do you remember the last time you were involved with the Chenak family? Your accusations nearly caused a riot at Mrs. Chenak's funeral! Do you expect me to let you near the family again on an unconfirmed downed aircraft search?" Taryn dropped his voice into a menacing range. "A restraining order is still active against you personally, if you need reminding, sir." He would protect his jurisdiction, even from continental headquarters if necessary. Taryn slapped on the video as Dalkey countered.

"I need not be reminded. I have orders to check this out." Dalkey looked up noticing that the video had been connected. A look of surprise flickered across his face as he apparently recognized Taryn. "So, you are no longer an underling."

"I was the sheriff a year ago, while you were a mere sergeant. And now you are a general? How'd you manage that promotion? Even so, *General*, I cannot let you near the Chenak holdings. I will offer any assistance necessary to search the area in your place. As I stated, no calls have been received as yet. I will let you know if I find anything." He reached to end the transmission.

"A moment, Sheriff," Dalkey said, holding up his hand. "You don't know what you will find; I do."

"I'm sure you do, General. However, it *is* my jurisdiction and you'll have to wait. If it's an alien landing force, I'll ask for reinforcements—and call you so you can come and watch. You will not embarrass this 'little splat of a town' again. I'll call you with what I've found out. Leave your com-code with my secretary."

He ended the call and went back to work. A rap at the door

brought his eyes up. "Yes, Daneeha."

The door opened a crack. "I've got General Dalkey's com-code. Should I hang on to it or toss it?" Daneeha's squeaky voice sounded hopeful to Taryn. Even if some of Star Valley's newer residents misunderstood the research the Chenak Group had been doing, they all had expressed horror and sympathy at Mrs. Chenak's funeral when representatives from continental headquarters had arrived—with Dalkey leading the way—to examine the contents of the casket just before its burial. The barbaric manner in which remaining family members had been treated had made a lasting impression on the village folk. None who had been at the funeral of the well-liked Mrs. Chenak would be too forgiving of anyone from continental headquarters, especially the man who had led the "raid" on the casket.

Taryn sighed. "Unfortunately, you'd better hold it until tomorrow. I need to check on something." He rose from his chair and put on his jacket.

Daneeha scurried to her desk. The mouse-like voice fit her precisely. Even though she only came up to his waist, Taryn knew she was less mouse-like than she looked or sounded. She'd always been staunch in her support of the Chenaks. If not for their medical research, her husband would have died long ago. Taryn remembered Daneeha at the funeral, bereft at the loss of a friend who had played such a definitive role in her husband's survival. Her face now showed disappointment as she retrieved a crumpled bit of paper from the waste can.

"Okay. Why's he calling here again, anyway? Didn't get enough last year, you suppose?" She stabbed the note on to the bulletin board with a pin.

"Guess not. I've got to talk to my father. He said Ani was back. I'd like to know a bit more before I jump to conclusions, but it appears she may be under surveillance. Dalkey would use any excuse to get close to the lake house." Taryn slipped a hover key from the wall hook. "Even a hoax."

With surprising strength, Daneeha placed a tiny hand on his arm. "Keep the tel-com open. I'll let you know if any crash news comes in."

Taryn paused, grinning. "Better take care of that eavesdropping or I'll have to write you up."

"Write me up if you want. Dalkey won't know what hit him if he tries to pull another stunt in this 'splat of a town.'" She squeezed his arm tighter and then released him. "Tell your father I'll be up to get the groceries I ordered yesterday when I'm off for noon break."

She turned back to her desk, all business as she snapped a blinking light off and spoke into the microphone of her tel-com headset. "Good morn, sheriff's office." But she waved at Taryn as he left.

Taryn waved to his father as the hover car settled quietly on the gravel drive. The driver's hatch opened with a soft swoosh of air. Taryn slipped out and greeted Gelwood with a firm hug across the older man's once broad shoulders. Taryn stayed by his side as they maneuvered around the hover car towards the house. They paused at the bottom of the steps as Gelwood shifted his crutch out of the way so he could use the metal railing for support.

"Melli!" Gelwood called through the screened door when they reached the top of the steps. "Taryn's here. Can you bring out some tea?"

A faint voice answered, "Good morn! Tea is coming. I'm adding a cup for you, Taryn." A light clatter of cups being placed on a platter followed his mother's answer.

Gelwood eased himself into one of the chairs that faced each other to the left of the door. Taryn moved the small round table from between the chairs and placed it in front of his father. His mother pushed open the screened door with her back as she carried a tray with three cups and a large pot with steam drifting from the spout. Taryn whisked a third chair into place opposite his father as Melli set the tray on the table and seated herself in the proffered chair. She reached over and patted the empty chair's cushion.

"Now, Taryn, sit and celebrate this lovely spring morn with us. I've made your favorite." She smiled as she poured the tea and offered the first cup to her son.

The cinnamon scent tickled his nose. He sipped cautiously, knowing that Melli's teas were notoriously hot. It was better for the digestion she often said. He nodded in thanks as the hot liquid spread the spice throughout his system, invigorating and calming at the same time.

"Mother, it is a fine spring morn, made better by your tea and company."

Melli winked at her husband. "So grown up he's getting, Gelwood. We've brought him up fine, we have."

Gelwood nodded as he cooled his drink by blowing across the top, wrinkling the tea's surface.

Melli turned to Taryn. "So, what do you have on your mind this morn?"

Taryn cleared his throat. "I know you'd like nothing better than to sit on the porch with father and me until morn is done, but I need some information."

His parents paused, a long look passing between them. He knew that they knew he wanted information about Ani.

Gelwood leaned forward, placing his cup on the table. "Son, didn't you get my message? I sent it right after she left the store yesterday. Why're you waiting? She's going to slip away for sure if you wait too long."

"Hush, Gelwood," Melli said, breaking in. "Let them work it out. If they're not meant to be together, we must accept it. You shouldn't push so hard to make them more than friends. We're lucky they have a friendship. She could have gone to Southern with her uncle."

Taryn waited. His father had always insisted that he could make a marriage commitment with Ani if he would but ask, while his mother had been happy enough that he'd been friends with Ani and nothing more. His mother always seemed reluctant to encourage a romance between them, but his father was all for adding Ani to the family.

"Taryn, do what your heart tells you," Melli finally added.

"Thanks, Mother." Taryn set his half empty cup on the table.

"But it's not just Ani I need information about. Have either of you seen or heard anything unusual about the Chenak property in the last few days?"

They both shook their heads. "Why?" they asked in unison.

"I got a call from a *General* Dalkey about a downed aircraft of some sort, and we all know what sort he thinks it is. Second, he says it's—"

Interrupting, Melli demanded, "Is this the same Dalkey from the funeral last year?"

"Yes. He thinks the craft is on the Chenak property." He waited for the explosion; it came from his mother.

"Are you going to let him crawl over Ani's property like he crawled over her mother's casket!" She slammed the cup down so hard Taryn feared it would break.

"No. I even reminded him of the restraining order. But I also said I would look into it."

"Look into what? His imagination?" Melli snorted in ridicule.

"Perhaps," Taryn replied, "but as the sheriff, I have the responsibility to look into the possibility of a crash no matter who reports it. Please understand that I will protect the village and its surrounding population from another fiasco." He stood. "Not to please Dalkey, but to follow the laws I pledged to uphold."

Defiance lit his mother's blue eyes as she, too, stood. "Don't lecture me, Taryn. I'll wait until I see the creature himself before I kill him for what he did. *If* he shows up."

"Mother, just do me the favor of keeping open ears for anything unusual when you're in the village over the next few days. Will both of you let me know if anything is discussed or rumored?"

Gelwood spoke quietly. "I'd best tell you now what occurred at the store. If Dalkey turns up, it could get ugly. Ani had a run-in with some of the semester break visitors. I couldn't stop them. They were a bit rude in their conversation. Mroz had tossed them out of the bar the night before for the same reason. Ani dealt them some quick blows and stayed away from the produce display as I requested. But one of them asked about the alien connection. You'd think stuff like that would've ceased after so many years, but the stories still float around."

Taryn rolled his eyes in disgust as his father continued.

"I think she managed the situation, though she did tell them that she'd be more than happy to cut them up for the aliens' meal, *if* she knew any aliens." A weak smile flickered across his face.

"Wonderful. Just what I need, people being eaten by aliens living in Star Valley. Wouldn't Dalkey love that?" Taryn sighed. "And that altercation explains why she's not at the lake house where I expected her. Do you want to file a report?"

Gelwood shook his head. "She handled them just fine and outside of a few displaced canned goods, which the youngsters reshelved at her suggestion, there was no harm."

"Good. Saves me paperwork. I left a message on the lake house's com on my way over here, so now I'll try the cabin's tel-com, though it's been known to not work for weeks. I wish she'd fix it properly. If I don't get through in the next day or so and she doesn't contact anyone in the village, I'll go up and see her."

He grimaced at the thought of her reaction to his presence at her sanctuary, though that would be better than having to tangle with her after Dalkey did something to antagonize her. Taryn was sure Dalkey would show up, and soon, if he didn't get the information he wanted.

"Taryn? You okay?"

His father's hand on his arm made him realize he'd been standing there for some time in silence. "Yes, Father. I'm fine. I need to let Ani know that she may be under surveillance by Dalkey."

"Do you think he would do something like that after last year?" Melli asked, clearly worried.

"I wouldn't put too much past him, Mother." Taryn looked at the hover car and moved toward the stairs.

"You can use our tel-com," Melli said, placing cups on the tray and nodding to Taryn to get the door. He followed her in.

CHAPTER SIX

It had been a rough night. Ani had dosed the man a second time with the narcotic to ease his sleeping and she added a liquid antibiotic hoping to prevent infection. She had also checked his eyes for possible concussion several times since he had not wakened enough to talk. She worried that she had not calculated his weight correctly and had overdosed him. During her exam she had marveled again at the finely drawn patterns on his wrists, so like her mother's, but with delightful differences. She was positive he was from Southern. And though a Southerner was unwelcome in most parts of Northern at this time, except perhaps in Star Valley, where a family from Southern had brought medical assistance so long ago, she did not think there would be any trouble. She would have to ask when he was well enough to be questioned. Until then she'd be patient and try not to assume anything before hearing his tale.

While the man slept she worked on the infrequently used telcom hidden in the cabinet near the wood burning stove. Just after breaking her fast she succeeded in sending a quietly spoken message to Taryn's office explaining the difficulty in contacting him and requesting a response. She tactfully neglected to mention the crash. It had been less than thirty hours since she'd been called to the crash scene by Kela and she had done all she could and the one survivor was alive. She expected Taryn to call sometime later in the day when news of the crash would hit the local stations. Then she could confess and he would come up and take over. She was confident Taryn would figure out a way to keep her name out of the news so she wouldn't be connected with any more alien insinuations. She shoved the tel-com screen into its narrow slot under the cabinet when Kela scratched at the cabin door.

"Coming, Kela." Her voice sounded out of place after so many hours of silent communication, but the whispered message to Taryn had distracted her into speaking aloud. She opened the door and Kela pushed his way in with the early morn chill and headed straight for the rug in front of the fireplace.

The wood box is low, Ani, Kela said as he curled up with a sigh.

"So, I've got to get it myself now?" she replied with her hands on her hips.

Guess so. How's the invalid? Kela raised an eyebrow and tilted his head toward the blanket wall.

"There's no fever and no sign of concussion, but he hasn't fully regained consciousness either. He's still drifting in an out, not really lucid enough to talk yet. I just sent Taryn a message about the tel-com not working. I'm expecting him to answer once he gets to the office, but in the meantime, you can help me bring in more wood to keep *you* warm."

She grabbed her jacket and headed out the door. Kela slipped out behind her before the door swung shut. Ani knew she'd have to split the wood logs, but she welcomed the exercise. She was annoyed at Kela's freedom the past several days while she'd been cooped up in the cabin watching over the injured man.

That night in the rocking chair convinced her to locate the cot in the attic. She hoped to have fewer muscle aches tonight. However, not all the kinks had been worked out and she needed to stretch a bit before swinging the ax. She considered warming up with the stylized moves her uncle had taught her but decided against it. It had been too long since she'd practiced, and she didn't have the time to do them correctly. A few simple stretches would ready her instead.

Soon, sharp whacks echoed in the little clearing as the ax bit into each log. The physical labor felt good, and she removed the jacket as the exertion warmed her. Ani split more than enough logs for both cooking and heating before stacking several in her arms to reenter the cabin. Kela had been watching from his perch on the top step, and she handed him one of the smaller pieces. She smiled as he grumbled in her mind.

Renloret kept his eyes shut, letting his other senses tell him about his surroundings. Soft musical sounds lilted in from an opening along the wall. They were similar to the songs of the feathered flitters of his home world. A breeze, carrying the smell of fresh leaves and damp, cool earth, brushed across his face. He wondered what had awakened him and took stock of his condition. No restraints bound him. He lay on a wide, comfortable cushion. His head ached, his left eye felt swollen, and his right leg was stiff. Air hissed through his teeth as his breath caught at the pain when he stretched his leg gingerly. It was probably broken. He considered his options.

"I'm alive," he muttered to himself as he opened his eyes. "I'm bandaged and clean. By whom? Why? By all the Blades and Stones, I should be dead." A breeze and more of the flitter-like songs came from the open window. The curtain's movement revealed glimpses of dark green and blue foliage and a brilliant blue sky. He noticed that the wall was made of logs stacked on top of each other, the spaces between them filled with some type of plaster.

He shifted position to get a better look at his surroundings and his leg muscles complained sharply. He lifted the coverings to get a look at his leg. Thankfully, it was not broken, but the long gash running the length of his lower leg was more than enough to warrant the tiny crisscross stitches that tracked a jagged line next to his shin. Tender to his touch, those stitches seemed to be doing a good job of holding the skin and muscles together. Without the advanced care from his own medics, he would carry these scars for life. He lowered the coverings, feeling the soft smoothness of the inner covering and fuzzy warmth of the outer blanket.

He reached up to feel his face and head. A bandaged cut above his left eye explained the swollen feeling. His fingers felt the five stitches beneath the thin covering. Another stitched cut above his left ear probably accounted for the headache.

There were blankets hanging from the ceiling rafters, blocking his view of the rest of the room. Whoever had rescued him and stitched his wounds had also made an effort to give him a sense of privacy. Curious. How long had he been lying here? Considering his injuries the subdural healing aid would have kept him unconscious for at least twelve bells. Was he the lone survivor?

His mind trailed back to the last things he could recall before he lost consciousness. He knew the mission's leader had not survived and considered the possibility of Kiver's survival in the back portion of the ship. Had Kiver strapped in? What about his own injuries? Would he have to carry out the mission alone? Was it even possible to return home? Was Lrakira doomed? Had he managed to land—or crash—in the right area of the planet? Would the language he and the rescue crew worked to perfect be correct? The list of questions piled up with no answers. Footsteps outside the window interrupted his contemplation.

The footsteps were followed by a loud clattering and whispered curses. The voice was female.

"All the hells, Kela, get out of the way! Put the wood in the box, not on my toe. All the noise probably woke him up." There was a short pause. "What if he's awake? How should I know? If that didn't wake him, he's worse off than I thought and we should take him to the clinic. Go check on him. I've got lunch to finish."

Renloret slowed his breathing and shut his eyes, feigning sleep.

A warm presence arrived near his hand at the edge of the cushion and he resisted the temptation to jerk his hand away. Regular warm breaths puffed gently on his wrist. Renloret turned his head towards it and opened his eyes.

Blue met blue. The animal's ears were upright and its overall expression seemed surprised. They stared. It seemed to Renloret that the animal was taking stock of him every bit as much as he was taking stock of it. Then the animal licked his arm with a rough tongue, and Renloret relaxed. The animal turned away, slipping under the heavy brown curtain. Renloret again let his senses talk to him. There was another being beyond the curtain, the one who had spoken.

As Ani reached for a can of soup in the cupboard, she noticed the flashing light that signaled a message on the tel-com. She pulled the tel-com open and inserted the listening plug in her ear. It was Taryn. At least her message had gotten through. Opening the can and dumping its contents into the pan on the stove, she listened to the message. She glanced at the blanket wall in alarm when she heard Taryn's specific request for information about any aircraft crashes near her property. Guilt swept over her until his warning tone mentioned General Dalkey. She decided to keep the crash quiet a long time—even from her best friend—if Dalkey was interested. She'd wait until eve to answer, depending on the condition of the injured man. As she put the tel-com back and returned to the soup, Kela nudged her knee.

"Did you wake him?" she asked softly.

Kela looked back at the blanket curtain. *No.*

"I'll check on him again in a minute. Ready for lunch?"

She set a large bowl of soup on the floor for Kela and tossed him a biscuit from a box on the counter. Then she served herself and took the bowl over to the table. Deliberately sitting so she could face the hanging blankets, she ate her soup while studying the curtain, thinking about the man behind it. Kela rattled his bowl wanting more soup.

"You're going to get fat if you continue to eat so much," she said as she dished up more vegetables for Kela, leaving most of the broth in the pot. Then she got a small bowl down from the cabinet and began to fill it with the hot liquid. "Maybe he'll be awake enough to eat today. I hate having to slip in a spoonful at a time. He comes so close to choking."

"I believe I could manage some liquid on my own."

The rich baritone issuing from behind the curtain startled her and she missed the bowl with a ladleful of soup, splashing the searing liquid across her other hand. "Aye, all the hells!" She scrambled to plunge her hand into the bucket of water standing near the stove.

Kela laughed in Ani's mind. She glared at the dog, realizing that he had known the man was awake and listening. She gave him a mental tongue-lashing for deceiving her.

But I didn't wake him. He was awake when I went in.

Turning her back on him, she wiped her hand across her jeans, noting the redness of the burn. It would have to wait until later because she now had a fully conscious patient to deal with.

Placing one of the biscuits on a plate next to the bowl of broth, she advanced toward the blanket curtain. The curtain had been a mistake because she couldn't see what the man was up to. She breathed deeply before stepping into the makeshift room.

He was sitting up with his head against the wall, eyes closed, the sheet and blanket pulled up under his arms. His thick sable hair hung across his forehead giving him a disarming boyish look.

Ani cleared her throat to announce her arrival before she spoke. "I've got some soup and bread for you to . . ." Her voice faded to nothing as she looked into the dark blue eyes that opened at her words. When he broke into a smile, she felt the warmth of a blush color her cheeks. She avoided a return smile by looking down at the floor.

"I'm sure I won't choke now that I'm awake. It smells delightful."

He reached out and took the plate and bowl from her hands. His smile deepened; Ani's blush deepened as well. She snatched her hands back to her side.

"Thanks to you . . . uh, how do you name yourself?" He sipped the hot broth from the spoon, eyes maintaining contact with her.

"My friends call me Ani," she replied, still avoiding direct eye contact as she scrambled telepathically, calling for Kela's help.

Help? You need help with a wounded man? Not in this lifetime.

The man took a bite of the biscuit and chased it with another sip of broth. "My name is Renloret."

"Renloret." It tasted good on her tongue. "Sounds foreign. Where do you come from?" Ani asked. Then she responded telepathically to Kela, accusing him of being no help.

Why can't you treat him as if he were Taryn? You sound flustered or something.

"Oh, shut up." Ani slapped her hand to her mouth as she realized she had responded aloud.

"What?" asked Renloret.

Ani blocked the mental connection to Kela as he began to laugh in her mind.

She recovered quickly. "How's the soup?" She pulled up the rocking chair to sit next to him.

"The soup is fine. It is the first good food I have ingested since we left on our mission." He paused, placing the plate and bowl on his lap. "Speaking of we, what has happened to my companions?"

While his words were casual enough, his look was imploring, and it took Ani's breath away. She considered the question as she worked on the proper wording of an answer. She could not reveal the existence of the stasis bags to outsiders. The bags were such a scientific and medical breakthrough that her mother and uncle were the only others who knew about them. And her mother was dead and her uncle was now hiding out on Southern. Knowledge of the bags and how they worked would have again put Star Valley under extreme scrutiny, and that was one thing Ani would not be responsible for.

"Both were dead when we reached the crash. I placed them where they would be safe and yet recoverable when needed. Their bodies will be fine until I get directions on how they are to be processed. I don't quite know how to explain other than they are suspended in time, sort of. When their families are informed,

I will release them for whatever ceremonies or procedures are proper for their beliefs. We also disguised the crash site as much as possible. Until I know whose side you're on, I'll keep quiet."

She paused, thinking of Dalkey's interest in the supposed crash. She decided on a quick test. "Should I contact General Dalkey for you?" She couldn't keep the sarcasm out of her voice at the title. She stared at the floor, trying to think of something else to say as she waited for his response.

"General?" Renloret popped the last piece of biscuit into his mouth.

Ani fidgeted in the rocker. "A General Dalkey was asking about a possible aircraft crash near the village. He wasn't clear about why or even where the crash was. I'm assuming your aircraft was experimental and he might have a reason to be interested. Though why you chose my mountain to crash on is beyond me. I've had my fill of the current military in general, and Dalkey in particular!" She stopped, surprised at her own vehemence in front of a stranger, and then continued. "I'll keep you a secret unless you want to contact him. Kela thought it would be appropriate not to tell anyone until we could talk to you."

Ani blushed again as she realized she'd been rambling, which was quite out of character for her.

"Who is Kela?" Renloret asked as he set the empty plate and bowl on the small table next to the bed.

"Kela? Oh, he's my . . ." she hesitated and looked over her shoulder. *Should I tell him you're a dog and we communicate telepathically?*

I think it would be better to leave out the telepathic part, Kela suggested through the last of his meal.

"Your what?" Renloret prompted.

"Kela is a dog, a very special dog that my uncle gifted me with a long time ago. He's more like a friend."

"Interesting name, Kela. It means leader does it not?

Ani's eyes widened in surprise. "Not many people know that."

Kela arrived whispering, *Fascinating. Aren't you and Reslo the only ones who do?*

Ani placed a hand between Kela's ears and gave him a scratch. *Mother said it was from an ancient Southern language. Perhaps he is from Southern as I suspect.* The redness of the soup burn on her hand glared against the white fur, and she winced as the fur brushed its edges.

"You should rest, Renloret," she said as she stood. "We'll talk more, later."

She stepped around the blanket, now glad of the barrier. Several calming breaths were needed to shove her girlish reactions to Renloret's good looks far enough away to ignore them.

"Hells," she whispered, "I forgot about the clothes." Raising her voice she said, "By the way, your uniform couldn't be mended to a wearable state. I can get some clothes that might fit. I believe we'd both be more comfortable if you had something to wear other than a blanket. It would take two to three hours for me to get them here. Could you handle being alone for that length of time?"

"Yes, of course. Ani, I do appreciate your vigilance in keeping the crash secret for now. It would prove embarrassing to some very important people. I will be out of your way in a short time."

Ani wondered which "very important people" would be

embarrassed by this accident. She hoped General Dalkey was one of them, though she didn't think he was all that important in the larger scope of the government, even with his promotion. She grabbed the largest backpack from its hook and sorted through the pile of items to be cleaned to find what remained of his clothing. These she dropped into the central compartment of the backpack and headed out of the cabin. *Kela?*

I know. Stay here and make sure no one but you gets close to him and he doesn't leave. Does that cover it? Kela's tail wagged as he cocked his head to the left.

I wouldn't have said it quite like that, but I guess so. See you in a couple of hours. She jumped the stairs and headed toward the trees.

Once out of sight of the cabin Ani paused. She needed a moment to think about the consequences of her actions. There would be trouble with Taryn when he discovered she had deliberately omitted information about the crash. And how was she going to get the bodies of the two who had died to their families without revealing the nature of the stasis bags? Plans for reviving the medical research center would have to wait until all of this was sorted through. She cursed the improbable combined timing of the crash and Dalkey's reappearance. But as the saying went, you could only sharpen one blade at a time, and getting some clothes for the man in the cabin was the first blade that needed sharpening. She would sharpen the others as time allowed. She headed down the trail, intent on her mission.

Renloret settled into the comfort of the mattress. The food would replenish his energy and his leg wound would be healed sufficiently in a few more days. He reviewed his portion of the rescue mission, as well as his training on how to behave under the present circumstances with a new culture. At least he had managed to land in the correct federation, and the bio-taught language had proven correct. He was confident his training would prevent any major mistakes. Her comments about what side he was on could prove problematic if violence had erupted between the continents in the short time it had taken to travel here. And he was not sure why Ani had been surprised at his knowledge of the meaning of Kela's name. He was sure it had been supplied by the bio-teacher. How else would he have known it?

He would also have to work on his accent, in order to fit in better. If he was going to rescue this rescue mission and his world, he was not going to get any help from dead team members. He wished they had included him in their planning, other than that which related to his role as the pilot. He'd have to retrieve any information remaining at the crash site. But first, he needed to be healthy. Once that was achieved, perhaps he would ask the girl's assistance in retrieving the information and searching for Commander Chenakainet's family. The fact that she was reluctant to inform the military was to his advantage. Renloret smiled as he settled further into the pillow and closed his eyes. As he drifted into sleep, his last thoughts were of the girl's brilliant green eyes—not just any green, but Anyala Stone green.

The path through the trees greeted Ani like a trusted friend. Being there calmed her, but she could not think of anything other than those haunting eyes. Never before had anyone affected her that way, not even Taryn. She had to be systematic. When she almost lost her footing as she clambered over a fallen tree, she chided herself for letting a good-looking man with the darkest blue eyes she'd ever encountered scramble her senses. Continuing her half run down the path, she refused to think too much, glad to concentrate on her footing.

At the lake house, Ani studied the surrounding area before leaving the tree cover. If Dalkey or some other unwanted presence was lurking nearby or had been there, she needed to know. Seeing nothing to rouse suspicion, she ran along the pool's edge to the large potted trees and dug into the second one until she located the key to the back door. Blowing off the dirt, she walked the rest of the way, unlocked the door, and went in.

Ani was soon standing in front of her parent's old room at the end of the hallway on the second floor. She had spent little time in the room in the past several years, but she knew there had been some of her father's clothes in the trunk at the foot of the bed when she'd closed up the room after her mother died. She raised her hand and struck the cool carved wood of the door with her fist. The knocking sounded hollow. "Blades, why should I knock? Old habits, I guess." Her voice echoed in the wake of her knock as she pushed the door open.

The room was dark except for the single shaft of light filtering through the crack between the heavy burgundy curtains covering the entire right wall. They concealed a large double-wide doorway of glass, with additional glass from floor to ceiling running to the corners. Her parents had called it their "gateway to home." When she was little, Ani had often asked why they had called it that, but they only smiled at her and told her she would understand when she was old enough. Since her mother's death, Ani had felt a disquieting sadness that the reason for the unusual name for the wall of glass seemed to be the one thing her parents had never shared with her.

The balcony, which lay beyond, overlooked the small meadow that had once been Ani's playground. The happy memories of her family made borrowing her father's clothes easier. Surely her parents would want her to help a person in need, and Renloret was in great need of clothes. Ani flung open the curtains and the light flashed off the polished oak floor, even through the layer of dust. The sun's midday trail had just begun, so she knew she had plenty of time to look for the clothes. She hoped they would fit well enough for Renloret to get by until she could make or purchase ones to fit better.

Brushing the dust from the top of the huge trunk, Ani snapped the clip locks open. The lid was heavier than she remembered and the hinges creaked in protest. She waved her hand through the cloud of dust disturbed by the trunk being opened. The cedar smell of the trunk's interior filled her lungs. Her mother's favorite soft sweaters graced the top layer and Ani fingered through them. The next layer held silken treasures that Ani had seen for the first time the previous year. Nightgowns, robes, camisoles, slips, even "merry widows" and "teddies," as her uncle had called them when she'd asked. Barely twenty-five years old, grieving and essentially untried in love or even dating, Ani had put them away without thinking that she might have use for them in the future. Now she blushed as she considered how she might look in them and how Renloret might react.

She forced herself to focus on the task at hand, placed the slippery silks next to the sweaters on the floor, and dug deeper into the trunk. The next layer held several flannel shirts and about a dozen cotton shirts her father had worn so long ago. She pulled the top one out and spread it on the floor. Dumping the remains of Renloret's uniform from the pack, she pawed through the pieces until she found the intact arm. She laid it on top of the flannel, noticing that the uniform fabric felt more like the silks and satins of her mother's personal items than what she expected from a uniform. Lengthwise, the sleeves seemed to match. Locating the back of the uniform top, Ani checked it against the width of the flannel shirt and smiled as the flannel showed extra inches beneath the flimsy uniform fabric. A few extra inches would be no problem. She could take in the seams if necessary. Ani pulled out the remaining flannel shirts, along with three cotton ones, and stuffed them into the pack.

After placing the rest of the shirts on top of the sweaters, Ani dug into the trunk's depths again. This time she pulled out two pairs of faded blue work pants. She compared the length with the one uniform leg she'd salvaged. Her laughter filled the room as the tattered uniform extended more than five inches past the end of her father's pants. She had always thought of her father as quite tall, which was evidently a childish memory, because she now realized he had been a man of ordinary height. This Renloret might be slightly taller than Taryn. Ani sat in the midst of the clothing and decided he could use a pair or two of shorts as well as two pairs of pants augmented by deep cuff-like extensions. She pulled out five pairs of pants, all in varying shades of blue, and stuffed them into the pack.

The bottom layer contained dress slacks with coordinated jackets and several small boxes. Ani opened one of the boxes to discover two belts and a buckle. She tossed the box in the pack. The others she let rest unopened. She could reminisce another time. Piling the unneeded clothes back into the trunk, she let the lid fall with a bang and puff of dust.

Before she closed the curtains and left, Ani paused to let the sun warm the room more, yearning to hear her mother's footstep and call to dinner. She knew the call would never come, but the desire to hear it would always be there. "I love you, Mother. I miss you and Father," she whispered with a sigh. "I hope you are together and happy."

The fire radiated cheery warmth, lighting the room with its orange glow. Renloret sat in the rocking chair, his stitched leg elevated on the stepstool. A flash of lightning filled the windows, followed by the sharp rumble of thunder. The cabin shook. Rain splattered the now dark windows. He was reminded of the many storms in his home mountains, so far away. The storm had arrived on the heels of Ani's return with the clothes he now wore.

She'd handed him a stack of shirts and announced that he'd have "shorts" to wear in a few moments. He'd had no idea what shorts were until she'd tossed two pairs of pants with very short legs onto the bed. The legs had been cut off above the knee so the fabric would not rub against the stitches on his shin. Her next pronouncement had made it clear he was to get dressed by himself, and when that task was complete, he was to call for assistance to the rocking chair near the fire.

Renloret had gotten the shorts on but had struggled with the closure device Ani called a zipper. Still, he'd managed it and the final results were quite satisfactory. The shirts were all a bit too broad across the shoulders, but at least the arm length was right. He wondered who she'd gotten the clothes from but had not asked. The first clap of thunder caused him to choose one of the softer, almost fuzzy, shirts in a dark blue plaid pattern. He relished the warmth now, even with the fire. Before calling for assistance he'd run his fingers through his hair, wincing as he pulled hairs near the scalp stitching. He felt awkward for the first time. He knew he should be in control, but the thought of those intense green eyes in the sculpted bronze face shook his resolve to be all business.

He couldn't shake the feeling that the girl was important, though he didn't have a clue why, except to help him heal and point him in the right direction. He also couldn't shake the feeling of attraction to her, but knew he had a mission to accomplish: locate the commander's family and find a way to return home with the one possible salvation for his world—the commander's young daughter.

The fact he was the lone survivor and needed native help to accomplish all this was overwhelming, but he had yet to back down from a challenge and wasn't about to let a crash and injury get in the way.

Renloret studied the young woman across from him. Her head was bent close to her sewing as she added what she called cuffs to a second pair of long pants. He was fascinated by her total concentration on the work. It allowed time for him to study her. Her long black hair was braided into two plaits hanging behind her ears. These Teramaran bipeds so closely resembled his own species that it was no wonder there had been little discussion of the research team's possible discovery. The commander had said the differences between the two far-flung races were negligible, similar enough to allow offspring without difficulty.

He felt a flush of desire at that thought and shifted his position. Though Ani had been caring for him for several sun-times, he had been aware of her for less than half a sun-time—or day, as she called it. He'd reacted to beautiful women before, but this "girl" brought up thoughts and feelings that confounded him.

Ani looked up at his movement and he shifted again. She smiled and laid the sewing on the table to her right.

"Does your leg hurt?"

"No, I am just stiff and thinking too hard," he replied.

"I suppose you do have a lot to think about. Would you like some cinnamon tea?" She stood and stretched her arms to the ceiling. "I'm almost finished with the second pair. In a couple of days, once the stitches are removed, you should be able to wear them. Hopefully, the weather will warm up and you won't be chilled by the wet spring we're having."

Lightning flashed and the cabin shook in response to the accompanying thunder. Renloret noticed the slight shiver that rippled across Ani's face. She seemed bothered by the ferocity of the storm. He wondered why, but refrained from asking. It was the type of question you'd ask a good friend, and though the general conversation had been light and cordial, they were not good friends.

"Cinnamon tea sounds good," he said in response to her question, not knowing what cinnamon really was. The bio-teacher provided the language, not the experience.

He watched her at the wood burning stove, wondering at the dichotomy of the relative high technology mentioned in the mission reports and the apparent lack of such in his current surroundings. He worried again that he'd crashed on the wrong planet, or at least on the wrong part of the planet. Some isolated, backward areas still existed on his home world, and they'd had space travel for many generations.

Ani returned to him with two deep cups in her hands. He reached for one of the cups and their fingers brushed as he took it. He heard a light hiss as Ani took a sharp breath through her teeth.

Kela bounced to his feet from his curled position in front of the fire, his long back hairs standing straight up, his head low and menacing. Ani's eyes flicked to the dog and back to Renloret.

"Did you burn your hand?" he asked.

A blush of color darkened her face and veiled her eyes even more as she answered, "No, not this time. However, the tea is hot, so take care until it cools off." She sat in her chair, both hands wrapped around the cup.

Kela stared at him as if what had occurred was his fault. Ani reached a foot out and nudged Kela's chest. He lay down but continued to glare at Renloret.

Renloret sipped the fragrant tea. It was very hot, but the heat enhanced the taste. It was similar to the sonte-spice tea imported from Buchres Island, the largest of the islands on Lrakira, and he wondered if cinnamon would taste the same if planted on Lrakira. He watched Ani stare at the fire through the steam from her cup. The silence was comfortable. He chuckled.

"What's so funny?" Ani asked, turning to him.

"My brother would find this a laughable situation." Thunder rumbled like a deep belly laugh.

She took a sip of tea. "How so?"

Renloret had always been nervous and clumsy around beautiful women and he couldn't believe how comfortable he felt in this one's presence, at least most of the time.

"Oh, he's always finding ways to tease me. Thayech would say the crash was deliberate just so I could get a girl to look at me." He smiled in spite of the aches in his leg and head.

Ani got up, tossing her braids. "I bet you have many girls looking at you, but perhaps you just don't see them. Even with the bandage on your head you're handsome enough for me." She slapped a hand to her mouth, smothering the exclamation that followed. "Hells! Did I say that out loud?"

Renloret raised his eyebrows in spite of the stitches on his head.

Kela rolled over and sighing heavily.

Ani muttered, "Oh, shut up, Kela," stood, and turned her back to Renloret.

He looked from the girl to the dog. Did they understand each other? He dismissed the idea, deciding that it was just coincidence, and Ani was probably embarrassed, though her comment did please him.

She turned towards him again. "Enough chitchat. You are quick to recover after being in and out of consciousness for a few days. I need information to help me decide what to do with you."

He looked her over, standing strong and defiant in the light from the fire, and grinned, considering four or five things he wouldn't mind her doing to him.

"Watch it," she warned softly. "You're in my territory and you'll have to keep your thoughts clean or to yourself." She glanced down at the dog and added, "I told you to shut up."

Kela rolled over again, placing his head and muzzle on his front paws, ears laid flat, tail thumping softly against the chair, seeming to apologize.

Renloret was struck by the conversational behavior that appeared to pass between them, but chose to ignore it for the moment. More important things had to be discussed. He cleared his throat and took another sip of the cinnamon tea.

"Your pardon, Ani. What information do you need? I will try to answer most of your questions."

"Why should I know you?"

He stopped in mid sip, caught totally off guard by her first question. "What?"

"When I pulled you out from the crash, I felt I should know who and what you are. But I have never met you before. I would remember you, believe me." Her voice was soft, almost pleading, as she repeated, "Why should I know you?"

Renloret shook his head. "I would remember you, too, if we had ever met, but that is impossible. This is my first time on . . . this continent."

The rain tapped and danced against the windows and the roof, filling the sudden awkward silence that hung between them. Ani returned to her chair and rocked back and forth several times before leaning forward.

"Okay, on to perhaps more pertinent questions. Why are you on this continent?"

He took another sip of the tea. He'd already decided how much he could tell her. "I'm on a rescue mission of sorts. Several of our people were here doing some research. A recent misunderstanding with a local government separated them and the leader had to return alone. I was to pilot the ship so my colleagues could focus on retrieving the remaining people and their research.

We'd hoped to be unnoticed, considering the circumstances."
He hoped that implied he understood the conflict between the
continents rather than his alien status.

"But something went wrong as I was preparing to land and I
crashed. I apologize for the inconvenience I have caused. I also
thank you for your efforts to rescue us and for being discreet
about our presence, though I am curious about how you are
managing that. I assure you, I will only be in your way for a brief
time—just until I figure out exactly where I am, where I should
be, and how to contact my people. Then we will return home and
all will be well."

There, he had laid it all out just as planned without revealing
anything "alien." And though her eyes darkened, Ani did begin
to nod her head. Maybe he had pulled it off.

"That's about as plausible a story as I'll get, I guess," she said
with a sigh. She shifted in the chair and swallowed some of her
tea. "Depending on your next answers, I'll decide how much
I can help you. First, do you have any contact with a General
Dalkey? If so, do you want me to inform him of your crash and/
or mission?"

He had no reason to lie. "You already asked that and my
answer is still no and definitely not."

"How many people do you need to rescue?" she asked.

"At least three, perhaps more. My colleagues were the ones
who handled the details, though I may be able to locate specific
information if I can get to the crash site. I am hopeful that not
everything was destroyed."

"What kind of research was being done?"

"All I can say is that many lives depend on the results of the research *and* those I need to rescue, assuming that they are still alive." He suddenly realized Commander Chenakainet had no way of knowing if his wife or the all-important child had survived the incident that prompted his return to Lrakira.

"Fair enough." She straightened and then settled back into the rocker, sipping tea.

Renloret eased back into his chair as well. He drank the rest of the tea, letting the spice tingle down his throat to settle, warm and soothing, in his stomach. Would she be able to help him, or even want to? Or would she be forced by politics or local laws to turn him over to the authorities? Would his presence bring harm to her?

"Renloret?"

His name was soft on her lips. A shiver ran down his back as her hand touched his shoulder. He'd been staring into the depths of the empty mug, twisting it slowly as he contemplated her decision and how it might affect his world, and now looked up at her.

"I'll help."

Those two words reduced much of his tension. He now had an ally. He wasn't alone anymore. Relief made him aware of how tired he was, and the leg throbbed in unison with his head. He wanted her hand to stay on his shoulder and tipped his head to the side, sandwiching her fingers. Her simple touch seemed to ease all his aches, except the ones in his heart. Those would not ease until he had returned everyone to Lrakira—before it was too late.

She squeezed his shoulder. "I'll help you find your people."

A pulsing noise emanated from the cabinets above the counter near the fireplace and a green light began to flash at the base of one corner. The mood shattered.

"That's probably Taryn." Ani sighed as she stepped away, unmindful of the echoing disappointed sigh Renloret let escape.

Kela stood and pushed his head onto Renloret's lap. Renloret stroked the soft fur between the dog's ears and whispered, "So, do you understand what we say?" The canine wagged his tail and moved closer. Was that a yes or did he just want a scratch between the ears? Renloret turned to watch Ani as he rubbed the base of Kela's ears.

A small flat screen slid down from the front edge of the cabinet. She tapped at the bottom of the screen and then placed a small object in one ear.

"Good eve, Taryn. What're you calling for? Yes, I got your message. No problems up here now that the tel-com is fixed."

Renloret continued to watch her. She seemed at ease.

"Yes, it's raining here, too. Yes, I'm staying dry, and yes, I have enough food for a few more days. You're as bad as my mother would be. I'll see you when I come down for provisions."

Renloret couldn't tell if there was a face on the screen and could only hear Ani's side of the conversation, but it was obvious that she was familiar with this Taryn. Would she reveal his presence to this person?

"Thanks for the warning. Keep me informed. I'll stay up here until I hear from you. Give my cares to your parents. Tell Melli the new batch of tea is best when brewed very hot, just as she insists. See you in a few days." Ani removed the object from her ear and touched the screen's edge. It slid back into the cabinet.

Renloret stretched. "So, you *do* have technological conveniences."

"Only out of necessity up here, I assure you." Ani returned to her chair and finished her tea. "I would have preferred not to have a tel-com here, but it is isolated and Taryn gets so worried about me being up here alone."

"Who is Taryn? Your boyfriend or husband?" Renloret stopped, aware of how inappropriate the second question was and aware, too, that this Taryn could quite possibly be female. How could he assume anything from a one-sided conversation?

A slight smile on her lips, Ani said, "Jealous already? I'm flattered."

Renloret shrugged, relieved in part that his first assumption had been correct. But he was also relieved that his unguarded, personal questions did not appear to be endangering his mission. Struggling to keep his voice smooth, he replied, "Not jealous, just curious. Should I be concerned for my mission if this Taryn knows about the crash and me?"

"Relax. No one will know about the crash or you until I'm ready. And I'm not ready yet."

Renloret wondered when she'd be ready and then what would happen. "Do I get a running start when you *are* ready?"

Ani flashed him a brilliant smile as she answered, "Perhaps."

The rain eventually petered out to leave the air clean and woodsy. When they decided to retire, Renloret settled into his bed wishing he was in his home province high in the Sancheros mountains, perhaps camping with his brother. The responsibility to complete his mission and "return all to Lrakira" threatened to overwhelm him, but he would do his utmost to see his world survive—or die in the effort.

He stared at the shadows dancing across the ceiling as Ani went about her preparations for sleep. He was definitely drawn to her, and he marveled again at the similarities between their species. He knew that the myths of the seeders were now considered to be true because so many species were alike. But to locate such a species so far from Lrakira, Renloret knew in his soul it had to be either unimaginable luck or planned by some great power. His thoughts were abruptly halted as the girl's shadow revealed that she was brushing out hip length hair.

On Lrakira such length was a powerful symbol. Only the Stone Singers or those in line to be a singer kept their hair so long. Renloret wondered about this little planet's perceptions and beliefs. Perhaps he would have a chance to discuss them with Ani. Logic said that the length of a person's hair had no bearing on their abilities, though his brother wore his at shoulder length to advertise certain prowess to the women—or at least that was his brother's explanation. Renloret smothered a chuckle.

Ani's shadow continued to taunt him as she pulled the shirt over her head, flipping the long tresses to her back to reveal a very feminine profile. Stifling a groan and a curse, Renloret shifted his gaze to the farthest corner of the cabin, but the sensuous shadow danced across the ceiling and deep into his being. He pulled the covers over his head, hiding, and took several breaths, concentrating on sore muscles. Then he peeked out at the ceiling.

Thankfully, both the shadow and firelight were becoming dim. Ani was softly humming a melody he thought he recognized, one sung to him when he'd been a child. He smiled at that unlikelihood, pulled the covers up again, and allowed the words to the melody to slip through his memory as he surrendered to exhaustion.

CHAPTER EIGHT

Kela stared at the sleeping pilot. Upright ears flicked with each sound of Ani making the morn's meal. If he could communicate with the pilot as he did with Ani, he'd have all the answers he needed. But Kela needed more exact information before revealing what he suspected. Renloret stirred and mumbled in his dream. Kela scooted closer and placed his muzzle near the pillow, whining softly in hopes of waking, but not startling, the pilot.

Kela was suspicious of Renloret's explanation to Ani about his mission. If this was the rescue Reslo and Shendahl had been expecting, they should have arrived within a few months after the attack on the research center. Why was it twenty years late? This crash could be mere coincidence, but the facts didn't fall in rows, especially after so many years. Another unnerving coincidence was how close to the anniversary of Shendahl's death this was occurring.

The pilot stirred again. Kela ducked as an arm flailed near his head.

Renloret jerked upright, sweating, staring wide-eyed. He whispered to the dog, "I should have died with them. I cannot possibly do this by myself. I do not know all their names or how many need rescuing. I crashed my ship. I was just the pilot. Oh, blades, why did I survive?" He buried his head in his hands.

Kela placed both front paws on the bed and shoved his head under an arm, stretching his tongue to lick an already damp cheek. He was beginning to understand the pilot's dilemma.

Kela sent a mental query as he continued his licking. *Ani?*

Breakfast will be ready shortly.

Kela heard dishes being placed on the table as he continue licking. *He's awake.*

Did you wake him?

No, a dream did. We need to help him, soon. He was just the pilot, not part of the actual rescue.

How do you know that?

He told me.

Okay, what are you proposing?

How soon do you think he'll be able to move freely enough to get to the crash site? Kela asked.

Two to three days at a minimum, depending on how bad his head hurts, but the stitches shouldn't come out for another week. She sounded thoughtful as she added, *Perhaps I could go get what he needs. Save him the trip.*

The blanket curtain moved as Ani peeked into the makeshift room. "Kela! What are you doing?"

Startled at the out loud exclamation, Kela slipped his head out from under Renloret's arm and backed off the bed. *Sympathetic licking. It works for other dogs, why not me?* He tried to sound hurt.

Renloret had raised his head, blue eyes red-rimmed. "I do not mind."

"Well, you should. He's not supposed to be on the furniture." Ani placed her hands on her hips, eyes flashing at Kela.

"Oh," Renloret replied. "I have not been here long enough to know all the rules. I apologize." He wiped tear trails off his cheeks.

Kela watched Ani soften. "It's not a problem, Renloret. Kela should know better."

Yes, I should, but the pilot needed a hug or something. Kela placed a paw on the bed, daring Ani.

"Kela, I'm warning you. Don't push me." Ani stepped closer.

Kela stood his ground for a full second then turned and dashed under the curtain. He heard Ani laugh and knew he wasn't in too much trouble, so he posed a question. *Why don't you ask him what information he needs from the crash? Perhaps you can get it for him.*

Good idea, Kela. Now be a good dog and let me handle this.

Kela watched her feet move to the rocking chair next to the bed. The chair creaked as she sat and began rocking. Kela padded back to the makeshift room to watch and listen for clues to the pilot's real purpose.

"Renloret, I want to help but I've a feeling you were just providing the transportation for the actual rescuers, and you don't have enough information to locate these people. Right?"

He nodded. "You've been talking to the dog?"

"Well, sort of. It's a bit complicated," she replied, side-stepping the question. "Perhaps I can locate the information you need and bring it from the crash to the cabin. I can also get some maps, show you where you are, and help you get to where you need to be." She directed a bold stare at Renloret, daring him to refuse her assistance.

Kela watched, amused, as the two people just stared at each other. How was anything going to get done if they stopped talking every time they looked at each other? He whined. *Ani?*

She blinked. "What?" she said aloud.

Kela barked softly.

"I'm still considering, Ani," Renloret said, clearly assuming that the "What?" had been aimed at him.

Kela issued the equivalent of a dog snort at this.

Ani stood. "I'll go up and see what I can find. You'll be able to make your own visit to the sight in another day or so. But I could look for specific things and let you know if they are there or even bring them here, today."

"If you have implements I can use to draw, I can show you certain symbols to look for and describe objects that may aid in speeding my search," Renloret replied, all in one breath.

"Hells," Ani said, "you have a way of using as many words as possible to get your idea across. Who taught you my language? I know you're not a native speaker." She smiled as she took several sheets of paper and a pen from the small table next to the bed and placed them on his lap.

"That will have to be answered later." He picked up the pen and began drawing.

Ani watched as he drew. "Those three were on a panel to the left of where I found you," she said as she pointed to a series of markings. "They were blinking green. Well, I think it was green. Most everything seemed to be green at the time."

Renloret stopped writing and looked at Ani. "Everything was green?"

"Well, I may have been bothered by the smoke or fumes. I didn't feel too well until I'd gotten you away from the crash. Then everything cleared up just fine." She kept her eyes focused on the paper and tapped the sheet. "What does it say? I don't recognize those."

He pointed at each set of symbols as he described them. "These are the labels on compartments that may contain the information I need. Inside you should find long, narrow cylinders, about a hand length long. Bring as many as you can find."

She nodded, hair slipping over her shoulder.

"I will also need at least one of the following devices." He sketched as he described what he called a portable vial reader. "They may be located near the rear of the ship, perhaps in our sleeping quarters."

As he handed the papers to Ani, it appeared to Kela that he was being careful to not touch her hands.

She folded the sketches and tucked them in a pocket on her shirt as she got up and moved towards the curtain. "Okay. I'll be back in a few hours. I'll leave something to eat on the table. If you feel like moving around, I don't think you'll have any problems. But if you get light-headed, sit down. Oh, and don't wander off from the cabin. There's a kreline in the area and you never know how they will react. You're safer staying put. If your vision doubles, tell Kela and I'll be back quickly."

He looked at her quizzically.

"Look, let's just say that Kela and I have a deep connection and understand one another. Trust me on this. If you're in trouble and tell Kela, I'll know and will be back quickly."

She disappeared through the split in the blanket wall, but her voice continued. "Kela, you stay and keep watch. Let me know if anything happens." Then she returned to pull back the curtain and look directly at Renloret. "Don't forget to eat." She tossed a muffin at him and backed away, the blanket covering her exit.

Kela sidled next to the bed, his eyes alternating between the muffin and Renloret's face. Saliva dripped from the tip of his tongue. He aimed his thoughts at the pilot, wistfully hoping to be heard. *It's good manners to share with friends.*

Though he could feel Ani's presence, he would have to concentrate on that presence to "see" what she saw. He didn't do it very often because everyone needed to be left alone and, of course, some things were meant to be private. He'd never told her just how much he could see and feel, especially when she allowed him free access. He could feel each type of mental block the two of them had devised when privacy was desired. Mostly it was direct communication that was blocked. He and Ani seemed to always feel each other.

Kela placed a paw on the edge of the bed and whined to encourage the pilot to share the muffin. If telepathic communication didn't work, then perhaps simple begging would.

Renloret's face was impassive. Kela looked at him, head cocked to the left, tongue relaxed over very sharp teeth. They stared at each other until Renloret broke the silence.

"If you are so smart, Kela, you know I am not going to give you the muffin. But if you bring me the green shirt from the stack while I put on these shorts, I will split it with you."

He slipped from the covers, reaching for the shorts hanging over the end of the bed, keeping a hand on the rocking chair to steady himself. Kela dropped the shirt in front of Renloret before the man had managed to get into the shorts completely.

"Now how did you do that?" The green shirt had been the third one down in the pile. "Should I watch what I say when you are around?"

He pulled the shorts up and zipped them.

Clearly, the man was ignoring his promise. Kela slowly closed one eye and cocked his head to the side, tongue again rolling out in a fair imitation of a laugh.

Renloret shook his head. "Must be the concussion. But I did promise."

He broke the muffin in half and offered the smaller piece. Kela shook his head.

"Oh, all right. Here." Renloret popped the offered piece into his mouth and tossed the larger one at Kela, who swallowed it before Renloret could straighten up.

Renloret slipped the shirt on and made his way to the table. More muffins and fruit were artfully arranged on two plates and mugs of cinnamon tea steamed in the brisk morning air. One, half full, sat next to a plate missing sections of fruit and muffin crumbs. He sat at the full plate and began to eat.

"I will be just fine after a meal," he said, looking down at Kela, who had settled in a patch of sunlight that was streaming in from one of the windows. "Then I will have to consider what to do next."

Kela looked up at him and gave him a slight, but perceptible, nod.

Ani approached the crash site, mindful of Taryn's warning. She stepped inside the holographic image and made her way to the remaining sections of the aircraft, ducking through the gash to where she'd found Renloret. No lights flashed after three days, though she blinked several times to clear off the faint green hue in her vision. No upset stomach or headache, no demanding feelings to do something. Relieved, she let out the breath she'd been holding.

She located the panel door with the three symbols on it, retrieved the paper from her pocket, and pushed at the panel's center symbol. It took long seconds before the panel slid to one side, revealing neatly racked cylinders with colored tops. She removed all and gently placed them in her backpack. The panel closed and Ani snatched her hand out of the way in surprise. She'd have to discuss the aircraft's automated systems and long battery life with Renloret.

Now to find one or more of the cylinder reading devices the pilot needed. She worked her way to the back of the craft, unfolding the paper to check Renloret's drawing. A mangled door stopped her progress. Turning into the space where the door once stood, she was drawn by the sudden appearance of green light peeking through the cracks behind a panel. She wedged her fingers in the crack and pulled. The panel bent; the green light intensified.

Ani squinted to see the interior. Three of the desired machines lay unharmed on the shelf, though they were too large to be pulled through the widened crack. She glanced about the room for something to use as a lever and found a strip of metal from some piece of furniture. It appeared to be the correct size. Gripping it firmly, she jammed the metal into the crack until it hit the back corner of the cabinet and used it as a wedge against the door. She pulled hard and the panel released with a screech, sending shivers down her back. As she reached for the devices, the green light faded and there was no longer enough light to see. She dug into the backpack, brought out a small handheld lamp to finish the job, and then used the lamp's light to study the interior of the cabinet for a light fixture. There was none. She shrugged. But as she turned to leave, another faint green glow in the room made her pause.

Four more cylinders lay under a strut, and as she stuffed them in with the others, the green glow faded. Flashing the hand lamp around the room, she tried to locate the source of the mysterious light, but found nothing. She tied the pack closed and made her way out of the craft, adjusted the pack, and headed back to the cabin, satisfied with this first retrieval task.

The sun was high in the sky as she arrived at the cabin. The night's rain had added moisture to the air, and insects drummed rhythmically in the first real spring warmth. Renloret sat on the top step of the porch, one hand resting on a sleeping Kela's head. No wonder she'd heard nothing from Kela. He'd obviously decided the pilot was safe enough to take a nap when he should have been on guard. She decided to teach her four-legged protector and new friend a lesson.

Silently, she maneuvered to the other side of the cabin where the trees stood closer and the underbrush was thick. She slowly pulled a broken branch from between some large rocks and examined her choice. It was not her usual weapon, though she'd been trained to use whatever she could. The branch was a little longer than her arm span, fingertip to fingertip, and slightly tapered to one jagged end. Sturdy and thick enough to wrap her fingers comfortably around, it would suit her purpose. A few practice twists of her wrists proved it to be pleasing to handle. She decided to keep it as part of her arsenal. Her blood began to pump, her breathing deepened, and her eyes glowed with remembered exhilaration of the last time she'd competed in the dome.

Two long years ago she'd been the champion—the first female champion the continent had ever had, though her mother had made inroads at the regional competitions when Ani was seven. The government had applauded and asked Ani to train combat troops. She'd declined the combat position to be closer to her mother, who had suddenly become quite ill. Instead, she satisfied the government by teaching small basic courses while at the university, a few hours away. The classes had kept her mind off her mother's constant pain and shriveling body. One year of teaching incompetent sluggards the rudiments of self-defense had convinced her she should have taken the combat position.

A year ago, she had found her mother in the last stages of an unknown disease when she'd returned home to discuss her change in plans. All plans fled as her mother wasted away.

Ani had trained one class at the university since the funeral. Even with the tensions rising between the continents and full-blown war imminent, she did not feel compelled to keep up with competitive blade fighting. This trip home was supposed to help her regenerate and find a reason to stay in the valley. Maybe she would even decide to compete in some manner again. She needed a purpose.

Perhaps this pilot was reason enough. She smiled in anticipation.

The branch was warm in her hands. Humming a snatch of song her mother used to sing to her before each competition to settle her nerves, she placed the backpack at the base of a tree and peered at the cabin. Kela was still asleep and Renloret appeared unsuspecting. This would be fun. Kela would be so surprised.

She charged out of the trees, branch held diagonally across her body.

CHAPTER NINE

*H*e's *been stretching and practicing,* Kela yelled in Ani's mind as he scrambled off the porch.

Ani ignored the warning. Renloret followed the canine smoothly, neither concussion nor stitches slowing him. She noticed the movement of his hand to his calf, where she would have hidden a defensive blade. A flicker of consternation crossed his face as his hand grasped nothing.

With a grin, she changed her tactic. Instead of startling Kela and having a bit of fun, she now faced a warrior. Excited, her heart rate jumped. Then he smiled. She chuckled, knowing she could not pass up this opportunity. She passed the staff behind her, giving him the first opening. He moved away from the cabin, trying to get the sun in her eyes. She swept the staff around, controlled and precise, just as he feinted forward then he slid to the side. Anticipating such a move, she shifted her weight and whipped the staff back across her body.

The branch smacked Renloret's ribs hard enough to knock

him off balance. He coughed as he rolled back onto his feet, smile gone but respect in his eyes.

Ani snapped the branch to her side, nodding in salute. "Sorry. I meant to catch Kela napping. He looked too relaxed on the porch. But then I couldn't resist wiping that smile off your face."

His smile returned and he sidled closer. "Where did you learn moves like that?"

When Ani reached toward his cheek to pick off some leaves, Renloret slipped his hand around her wrist, twisted, and bent over. A plume of dust danced away as her back hit the ground, pushing the air out of her lungs.

"Who's smiling now?" he asked, reaching out to help her up.

She grabbed his hand and kicked out and over, slamming him into the dirt. They both lay there, head to head, silent.

Kela approached the pair, growling at Ani. *He's at least a Level Five from what I saw of the exercises he went through an hour ago. Did you consider his concussion and leg injury?*

Ani started to giggle. *They obviously don't bother him too much. I haven't been thrown like that in quite a while. I think I like this pilot.*

Kela snorted at her and nosed over Renloret.

"I am not hurt, animal, though my head is ringing and my leg stings," Renloret said as he pushed Kela away.

Ani stopped giggling. "Kela, we're both fine. A bit dusty, but fine." She stood, brushing off twigs, leaves, and dust. Then she studied the man sitting in the dirt. "I suppose if you're well enough to go a short round and throw me within the first three moves, you can explain a bit more about your mission so I can assist you properly." Pointing, she said, "The stuff you wanted from the crash is in the pack at the base of that tree."

"You still want to help?" he asked.

"You just proved your story—at least in part. You have the training I'd expect, even if you are from Southern. And you haven't trained with anyone here in Northern or I would have known about you. But I hadn't thought you'd recover so quickly from three days of semiconsciousness. There is more to you than meets either my eye or Kela's."

Kela moved closer to Ani and she absently scratched the base of his ears. He whispered in her mind, *There's much more, Ani, but I'm confident he will not harm you. And I believe he'd be your match in the ring.* He looked up at her. *It is good to see you energized again.*

She ruffled the top of his head.

"You also surprised *me*," Renloret said as he climbed the porch steps.

"Perhaps I was unfair to you. A few years ago I was the Northern Continental Doubles Champion with Taryn."

"I underestimated your abilities," he replied, sounding confused.

Renloret braced a hand against the porch post, sat down on the bench, and rubbed his forehead.

"Something wrong?" she asked, taking a seat next to him.

"I'm beginning to think so. I don't remember a woman being announced any kind of champion. I think I would remember that, even though I am from Southern. Perhaps it's the bang on my head."

Ani placed her hands at the base of his neck, applying pressure to the muscle cords. He closed his eyes, exhaled, and seemed to relax a bit.

The tel-com buzz was annoying. Taryn slapped the switch on. "What now?"

"Sorry, sir," Daneeha replied, "but Bokswin just called. He saw a milit transport headed up Starlight Pass. He's telaxing a report right now."

Taryn shouted, "Get it in here!"

Daneeha slipped in and laid the report, still warm from the machine, in front of him.

"He stopped at your parents to send this. He recognized Dalkey and didn't like what he saw. He wanted you to know," she said.

"My thanks to him and you, Daneeha. I apologize for shouting." Taryn scanned the report, anger and suspicion building with each word. "Hells, he's after Ani again. I didn't think he was so close. I thought I had a few days to prepare. I'll warn her on my way. Maybe I'll get there before she kills him." He stalked through the office, Daneeha trailing after him. "Let my parents and Bokswin know I received the telax. Also, I don't think I'll need reinforcements, but keep a couple of the men around until I call."

The tel-com is blinking, Kela said, nudging her knee.

Ani slipped her hands off Renloret's neck. "Sorry, but Kela says the tel-com is blinking, and I should get it this time." She stood and pointed again to a large needled tree near where she'd appeared only a few minutes before. "Don't forget the pack."

"I will retrieve it." He heaved an audible sigh and without a glance at her, stepped off the porch.

Shaking her head, she entered the cabin and slapped the pulsing light. The screen slid down filled with Taryn's face. He was frowning.

"Where have you been, Ani?"

"Sorry, I was in the meadow—practicing." She glanced back to the doorway as Renloret entered with the pack. She decided to lie to her best friend. "I've got a private student up here for a couple of weeks. If he survives what I put him through he may enter the regionals at the end of the month. I'll introduce you later. Why're you calling?"

"Look, you've got bigger things to worry about, now. Dalkey's back and I received notice he was headed up the pass toward the lake house."

Her mind suddenly numb at his announcement, Ani refused to respond. She gritted her teeth against the groan that threatened. Why now? Life was just getting interesting again. She glanced at Renloret sorting the tubes just out of Taryn's line of sight from the screen. She turned a practiced bland expression back to Taryn.

"Ani, love, you've got to let me handle this," he said.

"No, Taryn, this is between Dalkey and my family. We knew he would try again after . . ." She couldn't finish the thought. "I really think he's crazy, Taryn."

"I know that look. You can't kill him, Ani." His tone was a warning.

Her face stayed immobile as she said, "I won't kill him, yet. I want to know how far he's willing to push his obsession, especially after last year. How'd he get out so soon anyway? I thought his superiors had locked him up for counseling?"

"I haven't received a response from my inquiry on that yet. We certainly weren't informed of his impending release like we were supposed to be. I can arrest him if he crosses the property line or at your word."

She sensed the hope in his voice just as she sensed her own rising anger.

Trying to keep from snapping, she said, "I won't give it unless I can't handle him. Do you think he's still alien-addled? Just look at my family's connections! How could we possibly have hidden aliens when we were constantly in contact with military and medical personnel?"

She raised her hands to her forehead, expelling a burst of air through tight lips in disgust. "I'm sorry. You've heard all this before. If I can't convince him to leave with common sense, then I'll throw him off." She paused. "You know, on second thought, you'd better be there to catch him, 'cause if he takes one step in the wrong direction I *will* kill him."

She slapped off the screen before Taryn could talk her out of confronting Dalkey.

Unaware that Renloret had stepped up behind her, she turned and smacked face first into his chest. Inexplicably, she wanted to dissolve into his arms as they closed around her. She allowed herself to lean into his shoulder for a moment, wanting to just forget the past. But before she could lapse into weakness, she pushed away and wiped the tears of frustration off her face to find Renloret calmly staring at her.

"Aliens?" he asked.

"It's a long story, Renloret. I've got to go explain to a psychopath that I've never met an alien, much less helped hide one. I'll explain later—unless I'm jailed for murder." She opened a drawer revealing a surprising array of blades and accompanying sheaths, chose one, slid it over her lower arm, and closed the drawer. "Don't think about using these unless you're in real danger. None of the sheaths would fit anyway."

Kela, keep him out of trouble. If I'm not back for the eve meal you will know I've been arrested. She jumped the stairs and disappeared into the trees. She was glad she had not stored the wheeled vehicle at the lake house. She could make a more impressive entrance driving in than if she just walked up to her home. The path branched. Taking the left hand route she hurried down the mountain to the hidden garage.

Kela stood across the doorway, barring Renloret's attempt to follow her. He was close enough to hear Renloret's whispered comment, "Never met one—until now, that is."

Kela accepted the unconscious rubbing at the base of his ears from the tall alien and decided not to interrupt Ani's angry thoughts. It would be best to discuss the identity of the pilot later, when she was more likely to be open to who and what he was and why he was here.

"I think we will have a lot to discuss when she returns. Ani will not like what I have to say. Well, Kela, it seems we have some time to ourselves and you have proved more intelligent than the bio-teacher informs me by virtue of the green shirt you chose, perhaps you are smart enough to lead me to the crash site. Will you do that?"

Kela wagged his tail and barked once. Then he backed up, leaning down on outstretched forelegs, his tongue lolling across his teeth in an attempt to laugh. He backed out onto the porch, inviting the pilot to follow him.

"I take that as an affirmative." Renloret snatched the empty backpack from the table, adjusted the shoulder straps, and joined him on the porch. "Lead on, Kela." Then he paused at the top of the stairs, staring intently in the direction Ani had gone. "She will be all right?" he asked.

Kela barked softly again, dancing on his front paws, eager to leave the clearing. Now that he had confirmation of Renloret's alien status he hoped all his suspicions would prove to be correct. Any rescue mission that was twenty years late was still a rescue mission.

Kela noted that the injured alien was well enough to keep up with him, and they made it to the crash site in good time. Once inside, Renloret looked around until he found something to use as a wedge, and a panel screeched as it opened enough for him to reach inside. A smile crossed his face as he grasped something.

"There you are, old friend. I thought you'd be lost in this heap." He pulled a leg sheath and blade from the cabinet and stuffed them into his pack with the paper maps. "Found it, Kela. Let's get these back to the cabin. I need to explain a lot to Ani."

He winced as he stood and bent to examine the bandage on his leg.

"Kela, I think I've managed to compromise some of the stitches. Ani's not going to be happy with me is she?"

Kela shook his head from side to side, waited as Renloret shouldered the bulging pack, then hopped out of the wreckage and onto the ground.

"Wait, Kela. If you can understand what I say, can you show me the device hiding all this? I know it's a type of holograph."

Kela appeared to contemplate his request and then moved off to sit near a fist-sized rock at the base of a bush. He barked once and placed a paw on the rock.

Renloret picked up the "rock" and turned it over. The switches blinked orange. "How simple. Ingenious design and . . . if I touch here . . ."

The air shivered in front of them revealing the section of the ship they'd just left. Renloret toggled the switch again and the canyon repaired itself.

"How many did it take to hide the crash?" Kela barked three times and Renloret laughed. "Again, more technology than I'd been told." He returned the "rock" to its place and shifted the pack. "Let's go."

CHAPTER TEN

Ani's knuckles were white-tight on the steering wheel as she arrived at the lake house. A large military transport sat in front of the mansion's entrance. She ground her teeth in anger and growled as she climbed out. The double doors stood open as soldiers halted their activities at her arrival.

A young man marched down the steps, his palms facing her. "Citizen, you're not allowed on this property without the written permission of the owner. Please return to your vehicle and remove yourself," he said, oblivious to her identity.

Ani suppressed a vicious chuckle. "I *am* the owner, Private, and none of you have my written permission to be on my property. Now remove yourself, your comrades, and that monstrosity. Now!" She strode up to the astonished man and demanded, inches from him, "Where is your commander?" Her blood warmed at the prospect of another exercise and she itched to release the blade strapped on her wrist. A calming breath pushed the excitement away. This youngster was not her target.

He gulped, eyes shifting sideways as his comrades moved away, showing their lack of support. "I . . . I need proof of your identity," he sputtered.

Ani pulled out a thin black folder and flipped it open to reveal her photo, residences, and university identity card. She snapped it closed again as he reached for it. "I repeat, where is your commander?"

"Ah, Miss Chenak, we weren't expecting you," he said with a glance behind him to the house.

"I bet you weren't," she said.

"The commander was hoping to get this cleared up before you arrived." He moved aside as he gestured towards the doors. "If you'll wait in the foyer, I'll announce your arrival."

"Thank you, but I've no need to be announced at my own home." She took the steps two at a time.

Once inside, she glared at the men in the foyer. They exited, glancing back fearfully. Ani noted the scrapes on the stone floor and the dirt tracked in by a multitude of boots. She followed the heaviest trail to her father's library. Impressed and a little surprised at the audacity Dalkey showed by his rapid takeover of her family's main residence, she assaulted the double door. She noted that all but one of the men stood at her entrance.

"General! You have five minutes to remove your personnel and equipment from my property." She captured the lone seated man in a cold green glare.

The general had the decency to look surprised, though he left his dirt encrusted boots on the desk. Sweeping her arm around the room she said, "At least they stand in proper respect. I'll not repeat my demand."

The general unfolded his fingers from across his belly and moved his boots to the floor. He grunted a release, letting the men scuttle out, leaving him to suffer the homeowner's wrath.

"You have not followed the laws, Dalkey." Ani saw the flicker of uncertainty that crossed his face.

"That should be *General* Dalkey," he said.

"Why are you here?" she demanded.

"I contacted the sheriff about a possible downed aircraft in the area, but he was no help, so I decided to lead the search myself to prevent any further contamination and to protect the people living in this valley." The beginning of a smile dropped in confusion at her unrelenting stare.

"Did that sheriff give you permission to seize my home? Did that sheriff have any prior information of this . . . this crash? Did that sheriff offer to look into the matter first and then notify you of the results? Did that sheriff—"

The general slammed his hands flat on the desk and shouted, "No, no, and yes!" He thumped his chest for emphasis. "I have to protect this valley from aliens. No one else knows how they look or what they can do to us."

"How do they look? Have you ever seen one?" Ani waved her hand in dismissal. "Are these *aliens* the same ones you decided had removed my mother's body from her casket to experiment on?"

"I was protecting this world," he replied, "protecting you!"

"You attacked my mother's casket with an axe at her funeral to protect me? To protect this planet?" Disbelief raged in her voice. She put her hands on the desk in front of the general's hands, brought her face within inches of his, and fought for self-control.

"Yes, Miss Chenak, I did. I believed I had good reasons for my actions, though in retrospect, the timing was unfavorable." He smoothed his shirt as he stood. "My men and I will leave as you've requested. Contact me directly if you encounter anything unusual on your property. The sheriff has not the wit or experience to deal with what you might find." He gathered a stack of papers into his arms and marched out of the room, back straight and eyes ahead. He did not look back.

Ani remained leaning across the desk, staring at the now empty chair, her mind churning. That was not the reaction she'd expected. She reviewed the scene and struck the desk with both fists in self-recrimination as she realized she had lost control and not gained anything. She walked to the window and watched the last of the men climb into the hovercraft as a smaller vehicle hummed to a stop at the staircase. Taryn stepped out. He spoke to the general, glancing at the still open doors at the top of the stairs. The general neglected the proper salute before closing the transport's hatch. Taryn watched the transport disappear down the narrow drive, then turned to the house and ran toward the stairs.

Ani turned from the window and sat down in the chair behind the desk. Her soul began to crack.

Taryn skidded to a stop just inside the door to the study. "Ani?" She seemed to stare through him. That was not a good sign. A chill quivered down his spine.

"He's gone," Taryn said.

"I know," she replied. Both hands were behind her head and her unfocused eyes were a flat, dead green. "I should have . . ." Her left hand snapped forward.

He felt the push of air against his cheek as he glimpsed a small silvery blade whip by, a finger width from his face. Her hand slapped the top of the desk a blink before the thunk of the blade hitting the door reached his ears. He remained still, watching her. She was in a very dangerous mood. Other than on the tel-com, he'd not seen her in almost a year. Her eyes brightened with tightly controlled rage and other emotions he couldn't describe. She clasped both hands in front of her. They were trembling. He wondered if this encounter was her breaking point. She continued to stare at the door and the vibrating blade.

"Ani?" he whispered, wary.

Finally she focused—on him. She took a shaky breath. "Sorry about the knife."

"You missed." He tried to smile.

Her face softened. "I meant to."

"Welcome home," he said.

"Taryn, you have such a way with words." A brief smile flicked across her face as she sat back in the chair.

He crossed the room and leaned over the desk, looking straight into her eyes.

She seemed to study him, as he remained stretched over the desk. Another, softer, smile flickered across her lips. "I've always wondered what it would be like to have a man lay across the desk for me."

He raised his eyebrows in surprise. "Me?" he asked.

"No." She stood and moved around the desk to the door. "Not anymore."

He expelled a breath in defeat. "I'll either learn or die lonely," he said as he watched her wiggle the narrow blade from the door.

Her long fingers caressed the damaged wood. "Mother wouldn't approve of this."

"She'd understand," he replied. It was like talking to someone who was hallucinating.

"At least it wasn't the crystal blade. I was smart enough to consider those consequences." She shrugged and jerked the blade out.

He watched her slip it into the wrist sheath. He should have remembered that was her favorite weapon. It had come too close a few minutes ago. He shifted into his formal role as sheriff. "Explain what happened here. I need to know so I can prepare."

Her hands returned to caress the door, ignoring him.

"Ani!"

She whispered, "I yelled at him like I was a child. I almost cried. I lost control." Her chin trembled.

Taryn shook his head in denial and said, "If you'd really lost control, Dalkey would be dead. You did it on purpose. You wanted him to provoke you so you'd be justified! You needed more than just his trespassing."

She nodded, refusing to make eye contact. "Then he said you wouldn't have the wit or experience to deal with whatever he thinks has crashed and gathered up some papers and just . . . walked . . . out."

Taryn stared at the bewildered young woman. "He just walked out?"

She stared at the desktop. "I lost it. I thought I'd dealt with all the possible pain and rage, but what he did at Mother's funeral! I still can't believe . . ." She ran shaking fingers through her hair, lifting and straightening the long strands. "The nightmares are going to come back, Taryn. I still hear the axe." Tears, for the first time, slipped over and slid down her cheeks. She whimpered. "Why didn't I kill him—then or now?"

Her yearlong control shattered as Taryn gathered her into an embrace. He shivered as he remembered she hadn't cried at the funeral. The first blow of the axe to the casket had immobilized everyone. She had screamed—just screamed for hours until exhaustion and damaged vocal chords silenced her. It had taken Taryn and other attending military personnel to haul the raving Dalkey off the casket and far away. Hadn't Dalkey been locked up for psychological observation? They were supposed to be informed when he was up for release, but since Dalkey's contact two days earlier, Taryn's inquiries had gone unanswered. Taryn couldn't believe Dalkey's audacity. The anniversary of the funeral fiasco was only days away.

Taryn kissed the top of her head as she sobbed. He had dreamed of holding her again, but not like this. Still, he would take whatever she allowed, though he was confident she would return to her carefully controlled self after the pent-up tears dried. And he would be just her friend again. He held on, letting her soak him in her grief. They remained that way for a long time.

The sun had slipped towards the mountain horizon before her

tears ceased. Tree shadows crossed the windows, darkening the room. Her breathing had calmed and she lifted her face, allowing him to brush his thumbs across her cheekbones, slipping wet strands of hair behind her ears. He kissed her forehead, held her chin in both hands, and wished he could turn back time.

She placed two fingers against his lips, shaking her head. He sighed and tightened his embrace briefly before releasing her.

"Feel better?" he asked.

"Much," she said, placing her palms against his chest over the fabric wet from her tears. "I guess I'll now have to thank a madman for helping me."

"Let's not be too hasty, Ani," he said, tucking another strand of hair behind her ear, his fingers lingering on her face.

His heart ached. He would never be able to recapture the past. So this was what being her friend felt like versus being her lover. Perhaps in time he would accept that she wasn't destined to be his. More than a year ago, Melli had tried to tell him when he had explained their breakup. He had refused to listen. He lamented the wisdom of mothers. They always said there was someone for everyone. You just had to be patient and you would know when that someone came along. Taryn thought the sentiment was offered only by parents to soul-shattered sons. Well, he'd best put forth a better front than that if he planned on remaining in contact with her. He knew he wouldn't want to live without her in his life, and if a friend was what she wanted him to be, then that was what he would be. A smile finally spread across his face and carried into his eyes. She returned it.

Taryn risked returning to the subject of Dalkey. "Dalkey's

walking away was not what you expected?"

"No," she said softly.

"Not exactly what I'd expect either. I didn't tell him you were home, so he wasn't expecting you at all, much less having you confront him face-to-face. You caught him in the act, Ani. Whatever he was up to, you just spoiled his plan. He has to regroup. That'll give us time to figure out why he's out of the hospital and in your life again."

Taryn paused. He needed to find a way to keep her safe while he checked on Dalkey. He remembered the student in the background of the tel-com screen. The young man would be a convenient diversion. "Were you planning to stay up at the cabin training that student for a while?"

She nodded. "I planned to stay at the cabin for a month or so, apart from visiting Mother's grave next week. Why?"

"Let me know when you go to the cemetery so I can be there, too. You could even bring that new student of yours. You said you'd introduce us later." He wanted her thinking of something else, anything else, and he was curious about this sudden appearance of a private male student.

"The cemetery is none of his business and who I have at the cabin is none of yours," she said, lifting her chin, daring him to question her.

Taryn narrowed his eyes at her defensive reaction—unexpected and interesting. He decided to push the subject to see how much information he could get without questioning the man in person. Ani was usually a good judge of character, but she'd been under a lot of stress the past year and he hadn't seen her often enough to know how she had changed.

"You know, Gelwood assumed you were alone when you picked up food. Where was this *student* then?" He emphasized the word student, trying to get another reaction.

She hesitated. Her eyes flicked downward and to the right, and he knew she was about to lie.

"I dropped him off earlier with Kela. I knew you'd make a fuss if I brought in someone you didn't know. I hadn't had a chance to tell you I was considering training again."

"A plausible answer, but I still want to meet him," Taryn said, trying not to let his concern show. She'd never lied to him before. What was she protecting him from? "He's not just any student, is he? You've never brought other students to the cabin. Why him and why now?"

A blush colored her face as her eyes flicked down and to the right again. "He's from Southern and he thought he could pick up something new by training with me for a few weeks. He's looking for an edge to compete in Southern's continental blade competition. What with all the uncertainty between the continents I couldn't just announce to the entire continent I was training a Southerner, could I? Now, will you stop it? You're acting jealous."

"You may have a point about training a Southerner so soon after your uncle moved there but you could have forewarned at least me." The blush surprised him but it brought up yearnings he'd try to ignore. "And perhaps I *am* jealous. You know how I feel about you."

"And you should know you are my best friend—emphasis on

friend. Anything closer doesn't feel right to me anymore." She pulled both his hands to her lips. She kissed each one lightly. "My heart is sorry you're not *the one*."

"Is *he*?"

"I can't answer that. Besides, I've only known him a few days."

Taryn squeezed her hands. "You should see your eyes, girl. They say a lot more. You'd better let me check him out, though, for your safety. For all you know, he could be a spy for Dalkey."

"He's not a spy for the *general*. In fact, he doesn't want contact with any military or government people. He just . . ." She stopped, biting her bottom lip, and averted her gaze.

Taryn gripped her hands and demanded, "Who is this person?"

She pulled at her hands. He refused to let go, knowing she could hurt him if she wanted to.

"Ani, answer me."

"He's just a student I'm considering training," she said, her voice tense.

"You're lying," Taryn replied.

"We're still negotiating the terms, so it's not a confirmed contract. Dalkey has horrible timing. My student will only be here a few weeks at most. Now, please let go."

He let her hands slip away. She was still lying, sort of. There was a taste of truth to her last words. "Ani, I'm—"

"He's asked me to help him. It's important to me. Please don't get in the way. I need to do something positive."

"All right, but you're correct about bad timing. It couldn't be worse. Are you sure he's not what Dalkey is looking for?" He studied her face for more lies.

"An alien?" she said with a laugh. "He's every inch a man, Taryn. He's no more alien than you or me."

Her easy, honest laughter relieved Taryn's concerns. Perhaps training this student would help her come to terms with her mother's death and keep her out of trouble so Taryn could do his job. Perhaps she'd even compete again. Maybe they could renew their partnership, at least in the blade ring. The beginning of a smile faded as her words sank in.

"Just how much of him have you seen?"

"Enough."

"But you said you've only known him for a few days!"

"I don't have to tell everything, even to my best friend or the sheriff." Sparks of glee glinted in her eyes.

The look was so endearing he wanted it to remain.

She patted his shoulder. "There, that's what I want to see. You didn't come all the way out here to discuss my training someone. You came to protect a citizen from a crazy maniac. Well, the maniac is gone and the student is not an alien, so this citizen is just fine, Sheriff Avere." The corners of her mouth turned up a bit.

"You do have a point, citizen. Officially, you'll promise to keep me informed if you see any aliens or any other unusual activity on your property?"

"Oh, I promise I'll scream for help, Sheriff Taryn." She straightened to wave her hand from her forehead to her heart, a blade-master's oath. "I most truly promise."

"I just want you to be careful. I'll look into why Dalkey is here and rummaging through the valley. But in the meantime . . ."

She raised her eyebrows. "Yes?" she said, drawing it out.

Taryn took a breath and continued. "Before I forget, I should tell you there's a sing and dance at the village hall. Why don't you bring this student? What did you say his name was? Where exactly is he from?"

She wagged a finger at him, shaking her head.

"Okay, no more questions. Just bring him. Melli and Gelwood will be there. They'd like to see you."

Ani nodded this time. "For your parents, we'll be there." She headed to the foyer. "Come on. The entertainment's over for today."

He followed her out. Ani stopped to examine the gouges in the wood where the locks had been pried apart by Dalkey's men.

"I'll file this as a break-in. Anything stolen?" Taryn asked using his sheriff's voice and pulling out his notepad.

"I don't think so, but I'll look around and let you know at the sing and dance."

They stepped down the stairs together. Taryn pulled her close as they approached her vehicle. "Take care, Ani." He kissed her forehead, knowing her lips were off-limits. "It's good to see you again."

She reached up, drawing her long fingers across his forehead and down his cheek. "It's good to see you, too." Her hand paused on his jaw. With a light pat of her fingers she withdrew her caress. "Give my regards to Melli and Gelwood. Thank you for the invite." She slipped into the seat of the outdated wheeled vehicle.

Taryn waited in the evening light for the sound of the engine to be swallowed by the trees before getting into his own hover-car. His heart ached. Perhaps it was time to move on, but to where or to whom he didn't know.

CHAPTER ELEVEN

The shadows lengthened as the sun's last flickers edged the clouds above the mountains. The flitters' evening songs tantalized Renloret with childhood memories of other nights on another planet, so far away and yet eerily similar. Kela lay at the edge of the porch, watchful but unconcerned. Renloret stopped what he'd been doing and marveled at the intelligence of the canine. He had been reading some of the info-vials Ani had retrieved and hoped she'd return soon so he could show her the maps. Perhaps she'd be able to help him identify his current location.

He smiled as a small furred creature hopped in and out of the brush near the clearing's edge, nibbling at the grasses. The bio-teacher identified it as a mountain hopper. Renloret's eyes took in Kela, whose ears had moved. The dog seemed content to watch, another sign of advanced intelligence.

The mountain hopper froze in mid-nibble as some horned beasts cautiously entered the opening. Renloret took the cue from Kela and remained immobile, hoping to view some of Teramar's larger wildlife. The bio-teacher catalogued them as tri-pronged sueders. Three animals entered the clearing. A fourth animal hesitated briefly then stamped a foreleg before moving into the clearing. Two tiny versions of the tri-pronged sueder scampered ahead of their mother. Their antics and obvious joy at being released into a large open space brought a chuckle from Renloret. Every creature within view froze and stared at him.

The largest tri-pronged sueder snorted and lowered his head, shaking the trio of horns that curved and branched from his brow. When Renloret remained motionless the male whistled a two-tone note and the females returned to their grazing. The twin young scrambled to their mother's belly, heads butting her udder as she alone continued to stare at the cabin, a silent challenge. Renloret watched them feed until scatterings of stars appeared across the sky, seeming to invite the pilot to join them. While he never tired of the stars, he knew he'd never see them all. He reasoned that he was still young and if he managed to complete this mission, he'd go to as many as possible. He frowned at his own "if" and changed it to "when."

Snorts and stiff-legged stamping from the tri-pronged sueders startled the pilot. The females and young faded into the trees; the male was the last to leave. The bushes rustled. Kela stood, tail waving back and forth, a low rumble vibrating his chest.

Ani walked into the narrow pool of light that stretched from the cabin's open door into the clearing. She stopped, put her hands on her hips. "Well?"

Kela bounded down the steps and placed both front paws high on her chest, tongue washing her neck. She laughed and pounded his sides with her hands then pushed him off. "Enough, I said. I've only been gone an afternoon and you act like I'm back from the dead." She looked at Renloret, still sitting on the porch.

Memorizing her smile and the sound of her laughter, Renloret could not account for the sudden ache in his heart at the thought that a successful mission meant leaving her behind. The overwhelming urge to kiss her made it impossible to breathe. He struggled to say something intelligent and blurted out, "You frightened the sueders." He stood to further cover his discomfort.

She glanced around. "Sorry, it's calving season, so they're jumpier than usual."

"Your presence means you were not arrested, so can I assume you did not commit murder?" Renloret asked.

"Don't assume too much. Just because I was not arrested doesn't mean I'm not in trouble. I should let you know the sheriff is my best friend, but . . ." She pointed to the open door. "Why are you letting all the warm out? The sun is down and it's still spring. Let's go in and I'll try to explain what happened."

She ran up the steps and grabbed Renloret's hand, trying to pull him into the cabin, twisting him off balance. He snagged Ani around the waist and pivoted to back her against the side of the cabin. He looked down into eyes that flickered, first with surprise, then with wariness. An inviting smile caressed her lips and he leaned closer.

Kela barked sharply. Ani used the distraction to duck under his arm and into the cabin. Renloret closed his eyes and struck the wall with a fist. What had he just tried to do? He'd never behaved like that before. Why did this girl affect him so? He'd only known her a few sun-times and he was out of control with desire for her. He sucked in a breath. How could he face her now? Another breath. Something bumped his thigh. Renloret looked down at Kela's forepaw pressing against him. The animal's ears were fully cocked, his tongue lolled over canines, and his eyebrows were raised in a comical look that Renloret felt obliged to answer.

"I apologize for moving in on your girl, Kela. I do not know what made me do that. I am not that type of man." He hesitated as he looked into the cabin. "But she does something to me. I have not figured it out yet, but she does something. And it is going to be a problem if I am not careful." He pushed away from the wall and entered the cabin, determined to figure this *girl* out.

Ani was standing at the counter, water running into the basin. She cupped her hands and splashed the water on her face several times, then grabbed a towel hanging above the basin and buried her face in it. Renloret reached to cup his hands under the still flowing water, elbowing Ani to the side, and splashed his own face. The cold fluid helped to resettle his thoughts to where they should have been—the mission, instead of a certain girl.

That girl handed him a towel. He buried his face in the softness, patting around the stitches above his eyebrow, then peeked over the edge. She wasn't there. He turned and saw her at the table, seemingly unbothered by his actions. She was studying the numerous maps he had spread out. She picked up one of the readers, drew a finger across the screen and down to the array of small pads, and pressed one, smiling as the screen lit up.

He moved to the other side of the table. Keeping a solid object between them might help keep him focused. How would she react to his technology? Would she figure out his alien identity?

Kela climbed onto one of the chairs at the table and seemed to peruse the scattered documents. Then he turned to scrutinize Renloret. The intelligence behind those pale blue eyes shook the pilot. This was truly an alien planet if all animal companions were as sophisticated as this creature. Renloret cleared his throat. Ani glanced up and quickly averted her gaze back to the reader in her hand.

"Well? Will you still assist me?" It was the one thing he felt comfortable saying. He had to focus and Ani was probably his only chance to recover the mission and return all to Lrakira. Was there enough time? He had the distinct feeling that time was important but didn't know how much he had. He rubbed at the pressure that began throbbing at the base of his skull.

He sat down and watched as Ani placed the reader on the table and chose one of the contour maps. She shook her head and turned it slowly, alternatingly bringing it closer to her face and at arm's length.

"Shut up." Ani whispered, waving her hand at Kela. Then a look of understanding spread across her face.

Renloret could barely hear her words.

"These are much more sophisticated than Uncle led me to believe. I didn't think the satellite had returned information yet. Hells and blades, what would the Northern government give to know about this."

Kela whined.

She slapped the map with her hand, pinning Renloret to his

chair with a glare. "Which government are you spying for? Speak the truth and fast or I'll kill you here and now." She flexed her wrist and a thin blade appeared in her left hand.

Renloret threw his hands above his head and flash-reviewed the information from the bio-teacher. There were only two large continents, one in the north and one covering most of the southern half of the planet. And a chain of islands decorated portions of the equatorial zone. The bio-teacher had not given much information about the politics of the planet other than hint at occasional rivalries and widespread skepticism about alien life forms and space travel. Since he hadn't been scheduled to interact with the general populace in order to find the stranded scientists, he'd not been given political information. He was just the pilot. He prayed to all three stones on Lrakira that his answer would be correct as he sputtered, "Southern."

Ani held her pose for a few more seconds, then slid the blade up her sleeve. Renloret now remembered her putting it on before going to meet Taryn. She sat back in the chair. "You'll live a little longer, Renloret. Spying for Southern might be disquieting, but not as disquieting as spying for Dalkey."

Judiciously, he kept his hands up. "But I'm not spying for anyone. I'm just the pilot of a rescue mission that now needs rescuing. As I said before, I need help in locating some people. When I find them we'll go home and won't bother you anymore."

She raised her eyebrows questioningly. "Home to Southern?" she asked.

"Home." He glanced at Kela. The animal actually winked at him. Perhaps the alien topic should wait until the mission had been accomplished. Holding his arms overhead was proving uncomfortable. He tested his own believability by lowering them, though he was ready to raise them again should Ani or Kela make aggressive moves. "You still haven't answered my original question."

Ani frowned, rubbing her neck and then her temples. "All right. I'll help. Show me which map has your desired location." She sounded tired. "Get off the table, Kela, please."

Kela jumped off and went to curl in front of the fireplace, maintaining eye contact with Renloret.

Renloret uncovered a specific map and spread it flat, relishing its texture. He hadn't had pulp paper in his hands for years, outside of the library's history section, but the mission had required its production due to some technological gaps in Teramar's command of science. Teramar seemed almost ready for space exploration, but they still relied on ancient methods for recordkeeping. He'd been lucky to find the maps undamaged, and he hoped they would speed his efforts in locating the missing personnel.

"I'm curious about one thing, Renloret." She pointed to several markings on the map. "I'm an expert in several languages and these make no sense."

"Code—top secret," Renloret lied. He made a mental note that on future missions, if he got home from this one, all materials would be marked in the correct language. Something so simple could make contact impossible or disastrous.

She nodded. "I'll accept that, for now. You'll have to translate then. Where were you supposed to land?"

He pointed at the map. Ani studied the area around Renloret's finger. She moved to the end of the table and leaned across, pulling the map closer.

"Oh, my," she muttered as she looked up.

His heart dropped into his stomach. "How far away am I?"

"Not as far as you might think."

"How far?"

"About twenty miles." She studied him closely. "That spot is the next valley over to the west. You would have crashed there if you had made it over this ridge at the end of the canyon." She frowned. "So just who are you looking for? Depending on how long they've been there, I may know them. Your stay could be shorter than you thought it might be."

Renloret found himself trying to hide his disappointment. He grabbed one of the readers and fingered it on. "Well, the info vial that had the roster was damaged and unreadable. I believe eight were on the original mission. Names may also be on one or more of the other vials, but I have not looked through them all."

She reached for one of the vials from the stack. "Show me how to use this reader of yours." At his hesitation she added, "All in code, aren't they?"

He nodded.

She passed the vial to him, careful to make no physical contact. "I'll fix dinner while you check the rest of the vials. We can take the list to the village dance. Almost everyone in Star Valley will be there. Someone may know someone on the list."

Renloret stopped the reader's scrolling. "Village dance?"

"Yes, Taryn invited us. Evidently, he wants to check out the competition, but it would also be an opportunity to ask some questions and . . . what's wrong? Can't you dance?"

Flustered at the prospect of being surrounded by numerous locals, he hesitated before responding. "Oh, I can dance fine. That's not the problem."

He could not explain that such sustained contact with a pre-space travel population was strictly against regulations and he could get into a lot of trouble for just thinking about participating. However, circumstances as they were, he could see her logic, and it wasn't as if he wouldn't fit in because the two races were visually identical. Plus, he hadn't danced in quite some time and was intrigued by the opportunity to observe another culture's activities—as long as there was the opportunity to further his mission.

He shrugged and added, "I'm just not sure about your local customs. I wouldn't want to embarrass or anger anyone."

"You don't have to do anything but arrive with me. I'm sure you'll be welcomed, especially by Melli and Gelwood. They're Taryn's parents, and they're friends of my family." "What's left of it anyway," she added in a whisper. She sighed and continued, fingers running across the reader in her hands. "I haven't been to a dance of any type since before my mother died. The last one was after the Northern Blade Ring Championships. There's always a dance afterwards. Do you have them in Southern?"

"Of course, though I haven't attended one in a while either," he said, aware of the ploy to get him to reveal more information.

He sincerely hoped that Southern did hold dances after competitions. His own Lrakirans loved dance and singing contests. The best dancers and singers were often honored more than athletes, and an athlete who could sing or dance was held in high regard. Though he was among those athletes who danced and sang, few knew he was talented in all three activities. To avoid the excessive attention that had threatened to derail his career choice, he had made it a practice to sing and dance in his home district and compete in the blade ring only in the biannual capital events. He'd often wondered why he'd been so blessed. His mother had said, "The Stones have a purpose for you. Live well and true to you and your talents and you shall not disappoint either Stone or self." Perhaps now was the time to show what he was good at, especially if it would get the information he needed.

Ani glanced at Kela, then at Renloret. "Do you sing, dance, or play?" Her look flicked back to Kela, who rolled his eyes and moaned before flopping on his side, tongue rolling out over his teeth.

"As I said, I dance, but I may not know the local steps or rhythms. I can carry a reasonable tune, and as for instruments, I didn't think I'd need any on a rescue mission."

"Right. I'm sorry," she said looking down at her hands.

He decided to change the subject. "You mentioned Taryn wanting to check out the competition. What competition?" He was delighted with her blush.

"Oh, he's a bit overprotective, but he also knows I can take care of myself. He's just a friend, not competition for you or me. I've beaten him in the ring, though I needed his help to win on the dance floor. He's an excellent dancer. There's no competition at this gathering, if you're concerned about that. It's just to celebrate the arrival of spring." The blush had stayed, highlighting the bronze tones of her cheeks.

"What happened today with that Dalkey fellow?" Renloret asked, though he was much more interested in what had happened between Ani and Taryn.

"In brief, the *general* tried to defend his behavior at my mother's funeral last year, I got mad and threatened him, and he left. No bloodshed. Everyone left of their own accord, which in itself is a bit odd. I may have trouble in the future with Dalkey. He's had it in for my family for a number of years. I don't understand why, but . . . he's crazy . . . I think."

She pasted a bright smile on her lips and shrugged. "So, I'm hungry and there's a dance coming up. You need to find some names and I need to put some food on the table. Let's get to it."

As she set about preparing the eve meal, Renloret returned to the reader in his hand. He scrolled through dozens of garbled data lines before finding a first name and rank—no surname. He sighed and continued searching the info-vial.

A food laden plate and mug of tea were placed at his elbow. He nodded his thanks and watched Ani settle on the couch with one of the contour maps spread across her lap. She sipped tea and ate without looking up from the map.

Again shaking his head at his luck, he turned back to the reader. The Stones be praised he had not crashed on the southern continent. His search may have come to an abrupt end if that had happened. At least he was a good enough pilot to crash as near to the chosen location as he had—only twenty of their miles away. And he now had an invitation to an event that would, with continued luck, connect him with the missing members of the research team. Then, maybe, he'd be able to save his world.

He found a partial list of the crew. Using the Teramaran script provided by the bio-teacher, he carefully wrote three of the names. He did not include Commander Chenakainet because he was already on Lrakira. It was then that Renloret realized he did not know the commander's brother's name, and none of the names he'd found so far resembled Chenakainet in any manner. He wondered why there were no references to S'Hendale until he remembered the commander telling Diani that the crew had not known her real identity until after arriving on Teramar. The crew manifest would not have listed her real name. But what name had she used? He had no idea. He continued to scan the vials.

Several chimes of silence from Ani caused him to look up. Ani was no longer studying the map in her lap. She stared into the fireplace, her hand caressing the base of Kela's ears. Kela's head was on her lap, his eyes closed in obvious pleasure. The warmth and closeness of their companionship brought a smile to Renloret's face. When he returned to Lrakira, at least she would have Kela—not a biped, but certainly someone who loved her. He observed a smile flick across her face, then a frown furrowed its way between her eyes. Her hand stopped moving.

Kela opened his eyes and stared directly at Renloret. They held each other's gaze until Renloret had to blink. He shifted to look at Ani. She continued to focus on the flames. The frown faded as a half-smile drifted into its place. Even from across the room Renloret felt the heat and lust from her eyes, though she looked at the fire and not him. Oh, how he wanted her to look at him. What was she thinking? To get his mind off such topics he turned back to the info-vial in the reader.

I'm telling you, it's not normal, Kela. I can't be this attracted to someone I met just a few days ago. It's just not like me. She frowned. *He makes me see green. He's in my dreams. I want . . .*

You want him so bad you'd take him on the table right now if I weren't here. And he'd be more than a willing participant if my observations are correct. Which they are.

You're overconfident, my friend. But her frown softened to a lusty half smile and her eyes became smoky with desire as she related her fantasy of Renloret, not Taryn, on the desk at the lake house.

Half listening to Ani, Kela opened his eyes to Renloret's stare. Kela held the gaze until the pilot looked away. *Yes,* he thought, *this man would be more than willing.* But there was more at work than two love-struck people. Ani's comment about seeing green matched the pilot's. Kela wondered about an outside force. He'd have to be on guard. He saw no problem with the possible match. However . . .

Ani chuckled in his mind.

Good thing you broke up that near kiss on the porch. I almost embarrassed you with what I wanted to do. Once started, I'm not sure I'd want to stop. She sighed. *I've got to keep on track, no matter how he makes me feel. All the hells of Teramar, I've known him less than a week and I feel like I've known him all my life. I wish Mother was here. She'd explain everything. Even Uncle Reslo would be some help. Maybe this is just a rebound fling.*

Perhaps, Kela replied. His eyes closed again to concentrate on the waves of emotion and words from her. *Did you conclude things with Taryn?*

Yes. Her answer was firm, without a trace of hesitation.

Satisfied, Kela brought up another concern. *What's the real story about your meeting with Dalkey?*

Ani recited the details of the encounter. When she finished he told her that she was correct in not killing the general and correct in thinking they would have to watch for him in the future because he was trouble. Her fingers worked their way from the base of his ear to under his chin. A soft growl of pleasure rumbled in Kela's throat.

Dalkey is gone, for now anyway. I'd like to move on to other things, like helping Renloret and the valley's sing and dance. Since I'm introducing a friend, I'll have to dress appropriately, and I haven't worn a gown in over two years!

When Kela began to ask about the one she'd worn at her mother's funeral, she dismissed him. She needed something more than a dress in funeral colors for the dance. Kela suggested she wear the green one, knowing that it was a bit revealing and also knowing that she would understand what he was suggesting.

An angry oath from Renloret shattered the silence as the pilot slammed the reader onto the table. He got up, both hands wrapped in his hair. Ani and Kela remained motionless as he stalked out of the cabin, then they both followed him. The two watched Renloret pace the clearing, tramping in and out of the band of light from the doorway, the tone of his foreign words providing a clue about his despair and frustration.

What's with him? Kela asked.

I don't think he's told us the whole story or how vital it is that he find these people. I think the radio signal Dalkey picked up may have come from his aircraft, perhaps an automated distress signal.

But this was not her only concern. Kela listened intently as she expressed concern about how soon after the crash Dalkey had arrived. She wondered if he had been forewarned or if it was just a coincidence.

Kela sat, his tail wrapped around his front paws, watching the pilot continue his ranting. *Maybe you should confer with your uncle. When did you last speak to him?*

Two weeks ago, before I left the university.

Why don't you send him a message? And mark it urgent, though it may still take him days to respond. You don't know where he is on Southern or what kind of trouble he's into.

They continued to watch Renloret pace across the clearing. He came to an abrupt stop in the middle of the light and turned to the cabin.

He stretched his arms toward them, pleading, his mouth working several times before the correct language arrived on his tongue. "I . . . I do not know how to do this . . . this saving of my people. I am just the pilot. Sharnel and Kiver had all the information. They told me nothing. All I was asked to do was get them here and then return them all home. Everything will be fine if I return with all of them."

Ani started down the steps but stopped when Renloret put one palm towards her. Words continued to tumble out, the accent heavy. "The problem is . . . is every info-vial is damaged. How am I supposed to proceed? Even if I *can* locate them, how will I get them home? My ship is in pieces. There was nothing wrong with the coordinates or my ship. I should not have crashed." Obviously frustrated, he dropped his hands to his knees and shook his head. "I should not have crashed. And now, they will all die."

"Not if we have a good plan. There is always hope," Ani said taking the last steps off the porch. He looked directly at her. Nodding once, she reached out a hand to him.

Renloret looked up when the whistlepot sounded off and watched Ani fill their mugs. "I apologize for my outburst, but there's just not enough information here." He waved his hands over the vials spread across the table. "I get partial words, perhaps only a few letters. I'm wasting time I don't have."

Ani placed the tea on the table. "No apologies needed. I think this dance will be the perfect opportunity to gather information from a large portion of Star Valley residents without having to talk to everyone at one time. Taryn will be a great help as well. As sheriff, he has access to different information sources than the villagers. With his help, you and your people could be on your way back to Southern in the next day or so. You'll like Taryn. He's very protective of everyone in Star Valley, including me. He protects us from all sorts of invasions, from General Dalkey to aliens from other planets."

A smile twitched at the edge of her mouth. She sipped from her mug and picked up one of the vials, missing Renloret's sudden stillness and hard stare until she looked up at him. "Oh, I'm just teasing about the aliens, though Dalkey seems to think they're everywhere. Have no fear, Renloret. We'd know if aliens were here, 'cause we all know they have four arms, scales, and three eyes. They would have a difficult time blending in."

Kela whined. Ani shushed him with a tap on the top of his muzzle. Though the pilot was aware of Kela's intense scrutiny, he shook his head and grinned. He'd never seen an alien of that particular description. Scales, yes, four arms, yes, three eyes, yes—but not all on the same species. He knew he couldn't tell her she was wrong about aliens. Not only was it against protocol, it would be dangerous to do so. But he was relieved he blended in so well.

They decided to call it a day, but Ani insisted on looking at the stitches in his leg before they retired. He dutifully sat again and placed his leg on the footstool for her examination.

She was silent as her fingers probed the long line of stitches. A soft clucking sound preceded her whisper. "I don't understand how you're healing so rapidly. They look two weeks old instead of five days. I could take these out tomorrow if you want." She looked at him with raised eyebrows.

"It's in my nature to heal fast," he explained, hoping that would satisfy.

"I wish we all had that nature. It would sure help in the ring or in battle."

"Do you think the continents will go to war?" He had been surprised at that possibility just a few moon-cycles after Commander Chenakainet had stated that there was a solid truce between the continental governments and war was unlikely. What had changed?

"Oh, I don't know. Politicians are such children. They need a set of parents to discipline them." She finished her examination and gathered the mugs for washing at the sink.

Renloret waited for her to continue.

"Even though I've trained recruits this past year, I don't believe anyone is ready for a real war. It's been too long since there was more than feints and jabs. Neither government has an understanding of what could be accomplished if they actually communicated." She laughed and then added, "It's an old idea that may work if both sides would listen to each other. Communication is the key to avoiding conflict in any relationship."

She finished washing the mugs and placed them in the wire drain next to the sink. "Better get some sleep. We could work out a bit in the morn and then plan how you want to get information at the dance."

"Sounds appropriate." He stood and moved to the blanket wall. "We say, 'sleep deep.'"

She nodded. "Sleep deep, then, Renloret." She turned her back on him as he slipped through the corner of the blankets.

Renloret worked the muscles of his shin by flexing and pointing his foot slowly to avoid cramping them. The stitches were indeed almost ready to come out. A little stiffness greeted his testing. More stretching in the morning combined with a workout and he would know whether he was combat ready again. He heard Ani's soft laugh and wondered what had caused it. Perhaps it was the canine. Commander Chenakainet had not mentioned anything about highly intelligent animals in his reports. Kela was not merely a pet, he was a companion and friend who seemed to be able to communicate with Ani. As such, he warranted closer scrutiny and study.

A shadow on the ceiling caught his eye and mesmerized him. Ani was combing out her hair. He considered getting out of bed and watching from the crack between the hanging blankets, but remembered Kela, who might have a problem with him peeping through the curtain. He shifted to ease a cramp out of his back—where he'd landed earlier that afternoon—and grinned at the shadow, looking forward to the offered workout. Instead of being caught off guard by a girl with a stick, he would have a chance to see if she deserved a championship title. He turned away from the shadow, away from temptation. As he drifted into sleep, he thought he heard a familiar tune, again.

A damp, cold nose on his neck brought Renloret awake the following morning. He pushed at Kela, but the dog kept his cold nose near Renloret's ear. A giggle made him open his eyes. Ani stood at the corner of the hanging blankets wearing dark brown pants and a tan short robe knotted about her waist. She was barefoot.

"Kela," she said as she flicked her head. Kela dropped off the bed to sit on the rug. "Good morn, Renloret. I have fruit and tea ready. Here's a training robe and pants for you. I hope they fit."

Smiling, she tossed pants, robe, and belt on the foot of the bed. Her smile deepened until her eyes glowed and she abruptly turned away. "Come eat. Then we can stretch."

Renloret quickly donned the training garb, leaving his boots in the corner, and joined her at the table. He greeted Ani and Kela, then looked with interest at the three different fruits on his plate. One of them looked like a small ball with thin blue skin. It had been cut in half and showed a purplish pulp. Another was tube shaped. Its red skin had been peeled back a bit to reveal bright yellow meat and flecks of reddish seeds. The third was a cluster of pinkish grapes. He took a sip of cinnamon tea and delayed his eating until he could observe any special methods necessary so he wouldn't make a fool of himself.

"Here," she said, pointing to one of the blue ball halves. "You may not have had these before and they just came into season. I don't know if they grow in Southern. You have to turn them inside out." Picking one from her plate, she demonstrated and sucked the pulp into her mouth.

Renloret followed her example. It was very sweet and had a thick, creamy texture. No juice dribbled, though his saliva threatened as the pulp melted on his tongue. He nodded and swallowed. "Mm, sweet."

Nodding, she said, "Gnediums are best first of the season. They get more tart as summer approaches. They're my favorite spring season fruit. What's your favorite fruit?" She picked up the other half of the gnedium and began sucking the pulp.

Without thinking he answered, "Whis'jeras."

Ani stopped in mid suck and asked, "Whis . . . what?" She looked perplexed. "I don't think I've heard of a fruit by that name."

Renloret mentally searched the database the bio-teacher provided for something close that perhaps came from the southern continent. He was startled to find a plausible entry and then took a sip of tea before commenting. "It's a nickname from my childhood for a rare fruit that only comes into season every three years, whirjerata. I was always wishing for them and my mother kept telling me, 'Not until next year.'" He flashed a convincing smile over the mug of tea and wondered how she'd gotten him to slip on that? He dropped the smile as the remaining information from the bio-teacher arrived in his consciousness.

The Lrakiran whis'jeras had the same life cycle as Southern's whirjerata and both could only be found south of the equatorial line. Could they be the same? That was impossible of course, but it was another distraction to add to the growing list of things that could keep him on Teramar instead of fulfilling his mission. He reminded himself that if he didn't complete the mission no one would be eating whis'jeras on Lrakira.

Ani looked at Kela, then shrugged her shoulders and said, "My uncle mentioned having them a couple of times." She paused to finish her gnedium. "I'll get some bread to spread the plantains on."

She cut two slices and offered one to the pilot. Their fingers brushed as he reached across the table to get it and they both flinched. The meal was concluded in silence.

"Meet me out front when you're done," she said, her tone terse.

Though her exit was rushed, Renloret noticed the blush coloring her face. Had she read his thoughts? Was that why she'd blushed and left so suddenly? He grinned a little and sighed, reluctantly pushing away the rather sensual imagined scene. Kela appeared from under the table, his knowing expression taking Renloret by surprise.

"What are you looking at? I didn't do anything. Did you?" he said, sounding defensive. The canine actually winked at him.

As he cleaned the dishes, Renloret realized that he was thinking in Teramaran, not Lrakiran. That was good. The bio-teacher was doing its job and his language was beginning to sound more natural. He left the dishes to dry and joined Ani in her warm-up routine.

He did his best to match her movements, and they flowed through the complicated series twice. She was silent the entire time, though he caught her studying him once, an unreadable expression on her face. When they finished, each took a cleansing breath. He stopped the urge to laugh. It was fascinating to find the advanced stretching routine to be so familiar with only a few differences from the patterns taught by his blade-master. Ani turned and placed her right fist high in front of her left shoulder and bowed her head. He did the same, though on Lrakira it would have been the left fist to the right shoulder. She smiled.

"Okay, you've surprised me. That's an advanced warm-up and you hardly missed a beat. Now let's see how you do in hand-to-hand."

Her eyes flickered toward Kela, who sat on the porch, apparently an avid spectator.

Renloret took another breath. Hand-to-hand with her? He'd often watched female fighters when they competed or trained. Frequently, they seemed more intense and unpredictable when fighting against their own sex, but his experience had shown him that when opposite sexes did face, everyone, especially the men, seemed to hold back. Ani had said she'd won against men and she was not stocky or rough. He decided to be careful and hold back until he could gauge how good she was. Then he would give as he got. But he could not afford to hurt her. She was his only assistance to completing his mission.

She nodded and shifted her position; he returned the nod. Her smile was so seductive that he was caught off guard at the flurry of her attack. He backed up several steps before doing more than block her punches. He kicked and was rewarded by her sharp exhale. Her smile disappeared—as did his decision to hold back.

They fought intensely for several minutes, occasionally muttering oaths as they punched, kicked, and struck one another. Finally, Renloret tried ducking under a double kick as she twisted, but his head rocked as the second foot connected. He dropped to the grass, vision blurring, but he knew where she was. And as she recovered and moved to check on him, he struck out, hitting her at the knee. She cried out and buckled down next to him. They lay side by side, sucking in air. Renloret was aware—and knew that she was, too—that this ending was similar to that of their previous, much shorter bout. Kela remained on the porch, scowling.

Renloret was soaked with sweat and ached in a dozen places. He looked around. The trees were blurry. He squeezed his eyes shut then opened them. Still blurry. The echo of her hit still vibrated in his head. He flexed his leg, testing the stitches she had somehow missed throughout the bout. This girl deserved a championship rating if she was a year or more out of practice and still this good. He would have bruises and sore muscles. Shaking his head to clear his vision, a wave of dizziness swept over him and he realized he felt worse than he had when he'd regained consciousness. So much for healing quickly.

A muffled voice from somewhere about his hip asked, "Where'd you learn that? All the hells, you almost broke my knee."

"I think I made it up," he replied with a chuckle. Focus was still a problem. "Oh, thanks for the knock on the head. It definitely has done something to my vision." Long hair tickled his face.

"Sorry. I forgot. I was trying to be careful. But you were doing so well and I was having fun. I forgot about the concussion. Open your eyes."

He opened them. Concern was etched over her face. With gentle hands, she checked the stitches in his scalp and then held his head still to study his eyes. He stared into her eyes. Her lips were so close. He considered wrapping her up in his arms and kissing her.

But she was all business. "No unevenness in the pupils."

A growled mumble from Kela seemed to comment as he arrived at their sides.

"Shut up, Kela. I know. He's fine." She cast a disgruntled look at the canine. He sat down, moving his head from side to side.

"Your knee?" Renloret asked from between her hands.

She grimaced as she unfolded her legs to sit next to him. "I'll live. Might limp for a few hours, but a good stretch session and maybe a hot soak will fix a lot of that." She stood and offered him a hand.

He considered not taking it, remembering the last time she'd offered a hand.

A soft laugh accompanied her words. "I promise."

He took it and was pulled to a sitting position. His head

threatened to wobble off as his vision, which had been clearing up, blurred again. "Oh, blades," he whispered.

"Stay here."

She stood and, limping, made her way to the cabin. When she returned with a cup of water, the limp was already less noticeable. He took a sip. It was more than water.

"It'll help," Ani said.

He drank it all. Indeed, it did help settle his stomach and clear his vision.

He remained seated until the trees were sharp and he could change his focal point without any problems, then moved to his knees and slowly straightened. He studied the slender girl in front of him. Had he been bested by her? Not exactly, but he thanked the Stones they had not used blades. If they'd been enemies, he'd most likely be dead. Then where would Lrakira's people be? He'd taken chances during their workout he never should have.

"I should not do that again unless I am forced to," he finally said.

Few opponents had managed to cut her or even throw her while she was training for the competitions, and now this pilot had thrown her hard, twice. Throwing herself wholly into the mock combat had tested both of them. She'd proven Renloret would make a better partner than Taryn and doubted anyone else on Northern would beat them if they entered the pairs' competition.

The idea of matching her previous title lit a latent competitive fire.

"Want to be my partner?" she asked as she stretched the leg he'd hit.

"Your what?" he asked looking confused as he gingerly stretched his back.

"My partner, in the blade ring. There really is a regional competition next month, and I am positive there are no rules against a Southerner entering a Northern competition. We'd only need a few weeks to perfect a strate . . ." She stopped in mid word as she remembered he had a mission to complete. He wouldn't have time for her or the blade ring until after the mission. She raised her hand, palm out. "Sorry. I know we need to concentrate on finding those people. Let's do that first, then, if time allows, we can talk about the blade ring."

"Time," he said. A frown wrinkled his brow. "Time is important. When is this dance?"

"Tonight. We need to plan what we're going to say and make sure we have as many names as possible before we leave for the dance." She looked at the high sun. "And we need to have a meal and then stretch again."

Back inside the cabin, she stretched one leg with the heel on the edge of the table. A grimace wrinkled her forehead as she flexed her toes. He raised an eye brow in concern.

"Cramp," she explained. "Could you get the bread and cheese from the cooler?" She flicked her chin sideways to indicate the cooling box at the end of the counter.

Renloret retrieved the items and put them on the table, then filled cups with water and offered her one.

"Definitely need a soak," she muttered, massaging the calf with both hands.

Renloret looked around the cabin.

"Not here, at the spring. I'll show you in a day or so. Your stitches should be removed and scabs gone before you use it." She glanced at Kela.

The hot spring? Kela asked.

Yes, but not until I'm more sure of him. It provides access to parts of the mountain no one else knows about. And I don't want anyone near the blade chamber.

Kela huffed deeply. *Why not? He's as good as you.*

She turned to look at Renloret. *Probably. I think he has fought against women before because he is neither afraid nor intimidated by me. Southern is apparently not just training men and women, but training them together. That will be to their advantage if war comes. I don't believe Northern can train enough women to respond in kind. Most men still assume women are less than men in all ways. But with Renloret at my side, I could prove them wrong. And if he completes this mission then he'll be more likely to come back and stay. Hells, I'd give a lot to have him for a partner.*

In more ways than the blade ring, Kela replied, scooting out of the way as she swatted at him.

"Out, Kela." She motioned to the open door. "Go find a hopper to chase." She sat down as Kela slipped out to the porch, turned, and settled in the doorway to watch. Ani rolled her eyes and sighed in exasperation. "A mind of his own."

After breaking a small loaf of bread in half and handing one to Renloret, she drained the water and held it up for refilling. "A student always keeps his trainer's cup full," she said with a mischievous smile.

Renloret returned the smile and saluted her. "I am at your command, Master."

She giggled. "Oh, I like the sound of that. But you're not even a real student. How about 'partner'?"

Kela harrumphed loudly from the open doorway.

Renloret hesitated before answering, "How about just Ani?" He refilled and handed her the cup.

She dropped her gaze to the cup. "Right. Sorry, Renloret."

Grabbing one of the mechanical readers, she inserted a vial and said, "Show me, Renloret. I'm a fast learner."

They spent the remaining hours of the afternoon reviewing the vials. Ani delighted in her ability to use the readers and pick up some of the language as Renloret translated parts of the individual logs. They concocted a plausible story of Renloret doing medical and genealogical research on his family as well as being a potential blade competitor at the regionals in preparation for upcoming Southern championships. He'd come to Star Valley to locate possible connections because old family letters had mentioned the valley and its reputation of being in the forefront of medical research. The blade training he could get by working with her was a bonus.

It was as close to the truth as they could get without mentioning the crash. Ani noted that he was particularly intent on finding a woman with a young daughter. Apparently, the unknown pair was the key to solving the medical problem in Southern. Ani could not place any current family in that circumstance, but new people were always moving in or out, so someone else might recognize the situation.

Hours later, Ani pushed away from the table, realizing the need for more light as the sun sank just below the tallest trees. She stretched and muttered about the inadvisability of overusing muscles during the morning workout and then being almost completely immobile all afternoon. Renloret agreed.

The names he had been able to recover constituted a short list. He'd admitted that he didn't know how many people had been on the original mission but guessed at eleven. And he'd expressed frustration again at knowing too little about the original mission. Ani studied the list again. Five full names. Not quite half but better than none. This was a long knife throw, but Renloret seemed to think it would garner the information he sought. Presenting Renloret to the residents of the valley was perhaps the quickest way, but it certainly was not going to be the most comfortable.

Taryn was already suspicious, as usual. Perhaps telling him about the crash would not be a good idea. She shook her head and pulled her bottom lip between her teeth. Better to keep him on the same page as everyone else unless it was absolutely necessary. With that decided she could think about the dance itself. She wondered if Renloret was as good a dancer as his talent with blades indicated. She smiled at the prospect of finding out.

A groan interrupted her musing. Renloret had moved to the wall and was step-stretching his calves. He didn't favor the injured leg. She nodded. She retrieved the first aid kit and pulled the footstool in front of one of the chairs.

Renloret looked up from a drooping blossom position.

"Want them out?" she asked.

"Yes, please." He sat and placed his leg on the footstool.

She took the lantern from the table and set it next to his leg for the best lighting. Scissors in one hand and tweezers in the other, Ani clipped and pulled until she had a small pile of thread. She was pleased with the results. No sign of infection reddened or puffed the skin. Slathering scar reduction cream across the line of bird-track scars, Ani realized they resembled the delicate blade championship patterns on his wrists. She considered asking about them but decided it was too late to start that conversation.

"There you go, Renloret," she said, handing him the tube of cream. "Put that on them each eve and morn for the next couple of days and at your rate of healing, no one will know."

"My thanks."

She stood and pointed at the blanket wall. "Now, go choose what you'll wear tonight and put them in one of the backpacks. We'll head down to the house so I can get a dress, and then we drive to the dance."

Uncertainty crossed his face. "Will I cause you any trouble?"

"What trouble? We've a plan and, hopefully, you'll get enough information so you can get your people back where they belong in time." She hesitated. "Then you can return and we'll see how much real trouble we can stir."

CHAPTER THIRTEEN

For the fifth time, Taryn adjusted the platters of bread and cheese. He knew it was not necessary, but at least it was distracting him from staring at everyone as they entered the hall. He reached for the blue-streaked brahman cheese and moved it back to its original position.

"Stop it, Taryn," Melli said. She had snuck up to him from the kitchen carrying a bucket of hot water and a dozen rags. "Your father needs you more than the cheese needs to be moved again." She pointed her chin to the back door.

Gelwood and the other band members were arriving. They juggled instrument cases and music folders. One of the folders escaped and scattered sheets fluttered across the floor. Someone cursed mildly and was shushed by the others. Taryn nodded to his mother and went to rescue the music for the evening's dance. He shuffled the pages together and hopped onto the stage to place the folder on the stand. The main door opened. Music hit the floor again as Taryn glanced away from the stand to see who

153

had entered. He frowned. Would she come?

"Who are you waiting for?" Eteel asked. He had braced his instrument against the stage's back wall and appeared next to Taryn with the sheets of music, which had slid under the keyboard bench.

"No one special," Taryn said, embarrassed. Snatching the lead sheets from Eteel, he glanced at the door again.

"So, Ani's not special?" Eteel shot a wink in Gelwood's direction.

Did everyone know? Taryn glared at his father.

"Oh, I told him she was in town, but nothing else," Gelwood said while busying himself with examining the keyboard's interior mechanism as if it were the first time he'd ever seen it. The two older men shared a chuckle.

Trying not to be indignant, Taryn started for the edge of the stage as the main door opened for another group of families. He almost stepped off the stage, but managed to control the near fall to sit, hard, on the stage edge. The entire band laughed. This was going to be a long eve.

Taryn looked around the hall. It was filling quickly, the noise level gradually building as more families arrived. Children were dodging and laughing as they hurried to wipe dust off chairs being set up. As Melli was handing out rinsed rags in exchange for cold dirty ones, she caught his eye and waved to him. He stayed on the stage.

His mother leaned close to the child at the front of the line. He watched seven-year-old Ryken stand straighter and give Melli a broad smile. A front tooth was missing. The girl dipped her hand into the bucket, retrieved one of the rags, squeezed it out, and handed it to the next child. Melli patted Ryken on the head and marched across the hall to stand next to him.

"What did you promise her?" Taryn asked.

"A loaf of my spice bread."

Taryn nodded, knowing that a whole loaf of Melli's spice bread was highly prized. He remembered racing classmates to finish cleaning the hall so he could get that first loaf of hot bread. It didn't feel that long ago.

The door opened again. Taryn frowned.

"You invited her and she said she'd come, didn't she?" Melli asked.

Taryn was glad she was watching Ryken hand out the rags.

"Yes," he said. Glancing at the door again as it opened for another group of families, he added with a hint of dejection, "But, she's not coming alone."

When he started to move away to assist the arrivals with their platters, Melli held him back with a touch on his arm. "Others can help." Placing both her hands on his shoulders, Melli turned him away from the door. "So, she's bringing a friend? Good for her."

"We'll see if he's good for her."

Melli clucked her tongue, chiding him. Taryn barely heard the mantra about how their relationship was as it was meant to be, something he was trying to understand. Perhaps this "friend" would make her happy.

"I know. She says he's just a student, newly arrived for private training," he said with a long sigh.

Melli patted his shoulder. "You've met him?"

"No, not in person. I saw him on the cabin's tel-com. He's tall, a little on the thin side, but muscled well enough to be the blade fighter she contends he is. He had a cut above his eye. Ani said it had happened during a practice session."

"That's my observant sheriff showing through," Melli said, nodding.

Taryn smiled a bit then turned solemn. "Mother, he's been here for less than a week, and she acts like she's known him a lot longer. And you should have seen her face when she talked about him. She was glowing about this new student, and not just about his ability with blades. Mother, I know it's ended between us, but does she have to get over me so fast?"

His mother clucked her tongue again. "Son, she's been trying to get over you for years. You've been too smitten to see. She relied on your friendship to get her through her mother's illness and death." Her voice softened. "And you kept her from killing herself. The bond between you is stronger than a blade-oath. You'll always be a part of her life." Melli hesitated.

"And . . . what else?" Taryn asked.

She seemed to change her mind. She took a breath and said, "Perhaps by training again she'll start living again." Her eyes flicked past his shoulder to the back of the hall. "Now, grow up and remember your best friend is the better half of the reigning Continental Blade Pairs Champion and she's back in training." She winked and turned him smartly by the shoulders to face the back door as Ani, dressed in dark green, reached behind the door to pull her friend into the hall.

Melli moved past Taryn, spreading out her arms to the tall blue-eyed young man behind Ani.

"So, who's this, my dear Ani?"

She pulled him down to her height and squeezed his broad shoulders, then planted a motherly kiss on his cheek. Taryn noted the blush and flustered glance at Ani. His mother was in fine form this eve. Melli released the man and swung Ani into her embrace.

"Good to see you. It's been months. And the dress! Excellent choice. It matches your eyes. Now answer me before I pester this handsome thing."

"Melli, this is Renloret, a student of the blade and possible challenger for this year's title." Ani gave the ritualistic introductions in serious tones then appeared to struggle to suppress a giggle as Melli faced Renloret and executed a proper blade salute. "You don't forget a thing, Melli! It's been years since you've held a blade."

"Oh, hush, youngster. It hasn't been that long." To Renloret she said, "Her mother and I were best friends, though I was not as well suited to competition. But watch out when it's dark."

An adjustment in her stance brought a look of recognition to the man's face. He answered with a tentative smile and solemn salute. "You honor me, Mistress."

"He's also looking for possible family ties in our area, for medical reasons," Ani said.

Taryn noted the subtle undercurrent of warning. Dipping his chin in acknowledgment, he reached out to clasp the forearm of his apparent rival. "Good eve, Renloret. Do you dance?"

"A little. Ani tells me she was your partner for competitions a while back. She claims to be rustier with the blade than the dance. If she is, I'm in bigger trouble after the thrashing I received during our first practice session." His eyes slid accusingly to Ani, who smiled wanly.

"It was only a stick and I didn't hurt him," Ani said, holding up both hands in defense.

Melli pointed to the expertly disguised bruise above his eye. "Any others?" she asked.

"None that were caused by our training. A slight concussion resulted from the stick, but I have recovered sufficiently. We will see how I do on the dance floor. I will need some time to observe before trying anything, with your permission."

Taryn tried not to snort. Ani punched him lightly on the shoulder.

Ignoring Taryn's rudeness, Melli entwined her arm around Renloret's arm and began moving him out onto to the floor. "Don't worry. The moves are simple enough at the beginning. By the middle break you'll have the way of the rhythms we do here." She patted his arm and batted her graying eyelashes. "Now, tell me, Renloret, you're not here just to win a blade contest. What brings you to Star Valley and where do you hail from?"

As his mother led the visitor across the floor, Taryn noticed the admiring glances from every female in the hall. "Oh, for cripe's sake. You really know how to pick 'em, Ani."

She smacked him harder this time, and they watched as Melli maneuvered the guest toward the food table, snatching two hand-sized loaves from the tray being brought from the kitchen by Ryken. Renloret acknowledged the youngster at Melli's introduction. Ryken grinned and actually dipped a curtsy in response.

Taryn harrumphed. "That pippin of a girl has never done that before."

"You're not jealous of a handsome stranger, are you?"

Before he could take a breath to answer she continued.

"Listen, Ryken's known you her whole life. She wouldn't curtsy to her cousins or even to her classmates, but someone like Renloret, that's another matter."

Oh, yes, he was definitely another matter. Taryn observed the glint in Ani's eyes as she watched Melli introduce her "student" to the group of older girls. *She* ought to be performing that function as his instructor. Evidently, she had realized her error in manners because she began to drift away from his side, her eyes never leaving the pair.

One of the musicians began playing. Another joined him and they quickly brought their instruments into tune. Stepping quickly after Ani, Taryn pulled on her elbow, bringing her up short. A hint of anger flashed across her face. He put his fingers to his lips to stop the impending outburst he was sure was building. With arms crossed tightly, she glared at him.

He nodded towards his mother and her captive guest. "Since the music is starting and he is otherwise occupied, I ask for the first dance. I'm thinking it may be the only one I get this eve. Please?"

The musicians began a familiar tune and people moved from the edges of the hall into long lines of facing couples.

After another look at the pair on the other side of the hall, Ani sighed and placed her hand in Taryn's. "Thank you. I'd be pleased to dance with you," she said, curtsying.

"So formal?" Delighted with her acceptance, Taryn reciprocated with a bow of his own.

"Why not? We should remember our manners and you have honored me with the first dance."

As they maneuvered through the crowd to join a set looking for another couple, the eve's prompter and tavern owner, Mroz, announced the name of the first dance. Dancers applauded and cheered his selection though everyone had known by the music which dance it would be. Signaling the band by moving his hand fluidly, the prompter whispered the count. The musicians began playing the two-bar introduction and Mroz issued the first command. The repeating prompts gradually died out and soon the dancers were on their own, moving in time to the music. The final time through, Mroz prompted a slight change to the figures and deftly set up the next dance formation.

With hardly a phrase of music to resettle the dancers, Mroz called them into the next dance. It was still simple, but quicker in tempo and with ever changing figures, so the dancers were kept on their toes and moving.

Taryn had always enjoyed these variable patterns more than the set ones, though his true favorites were the couple dances when he could invent moves and combinations as the music and mood demanded. Though appreciating the opportunity to dance, he looked forward to playing with the band as well. This eve Mroz had planned a well-balanced program. As the mixing of figures created flowing designs in his head, Taryn could not stop himself from thinking of alternate phrasings and descants to the music. In a particularly inventive moment he missed a call and his set scrambled to repair the hiccough in flow. Laughter from Ani brought a grin to his face as she shook her head and corrected his placement.

"Stop letting the music distract you. Just dance," she said while passing by his shoulder on her way to her next partner.

He had always wondered how Ani could hold down a conversation with several people while in the middle of a variable patterned set. Multitasking was her forte. A gypsy turn allowed him eight counts to respond. "I'll be good and listen to Mroz instead of the music."

They melted into a swing. For sixteen counts he relished her in his arms. Ani again curtsied with a wide grin on the last note. He returned it with a deep bow. They thanked their fellow dancers and then made a path toward Melli and Renloret.

"But none of the figure names are the same. I don't want to be a fool or step on your lovely feet," Renloret said to Melli.

"Oh, hush. Make an old lady happy. I'd like to be the first one to dance with the handsome Southerner," she said, pulling him past Ani and Taryn.

Renloret waved and linked arms to escort Melli to the forming sets.

Ani grinned and called after them, "Relax, you'll do fine. She's a wonderful lead."

Taryn and Ani seated themselves on the vacated chairs while the dancers again formed long lines of facing couples. Mroz announced the series of figures to be used and walked the dancers through one time, then motioned for the band. They began a hornpipe and Mroz called out the figure. Everyone in the set that included Melli and Renloret helped pull or point the newest dancer through the figures, though the walk-through had obviously helped. By the third time through the sequence Renloret didn't need much directing.

Taryn leaned close. "He's a quick learner. Did I hear Mother say he was from Southern?"

She nodded, her eyes staying on her student. She seemed intent on observing her student's attempts. Taryn knew she was analyzing his movements, balance, ability to learn new things, and sense of rhythm. She would later use all this information while training him in blade work.

Taryn found he was analyzing the man dancing with his mother as only a sheriff would. Would he, in ways other than personal jealousy, be a problem? He considered the Southerners he'd met over the years. There were not many because Star Valley was a distance from any metropolitan area. And though out-of-towners often came up for holidays or semester breaks to hike, camp, or just to escape the heat of the plains, Taryn could only name Ani's family and the few assistants who had arrived with them decades ago as being from Southern.

Though the continental governments were frequently at odds, people were still allowed to move between continents with relative freedom, unless they were as contentious as her uncle. Even so, at least to Taryn's knowledge, her uncle had willingly moved to Southern just after the funeral. Taryn also knew that

Northern's government had been all too happy to see him go. Twenty years of pestering, experimenting, and challenging the Northern ideals had forced her uncle's "retirement" to Southern. But at least there he enjoyed more open-minded support of his exotic endeavors. Taryn suspected that Southern hoped to use the renegade scientist to beat the more conservative and larger Northern into the depths of space. Obviously, they had succeeded with the launch of at least one satellite.

Taryn wondered how much influence Reslo Chenak had had on that, even while he had still been on Northern ground. Unfortunately for Ani, because he was unwelcome in Northern, any contact between her and Reslo was kept secret and infrequent. When was the last time Ani had mentioned hearing from him, anyway? Weeks or months ago? He should ask.

Applause from the floor interrupted his thoughts as the musicians held the final note just the right length. The dancers either changed partners or moved to the side, making room for fresh feet. Taryn shoved sheriff-type thoughts of Ani's uncle aside and tugged on her hand. She looked startled at first, then smiled and joined him in a four-couple grouping for the next tip.

A baritone laugh brought his attention to the couple at the top of the set, Renloret and Melli. Seeing Melli so thoroughly enjoying herself made Taryn smile. For once her partner was not under ten or over seventy. Gelwood's injury made dancing almost impossible, so he played in the band and Melli partnered with anyone available. This eve, Melli's partner was the talk of the hall. Renloret flirted with every female in the room without seeming to raise the ire of any of the men, except for himself.

He squeezed Ani's hand possessively. She looked at him as he tried, unsuccessfully, to hide the jealousy. She squeezed back as Taryn's father turned a page and set his fingers to the keys in a warning tremolo that hushed the crowd. He stood, leaning on the keyboard frame in a stance that belied his crippled leg.

"Welcome to all this good eve. Star Valley welcomes Ani back from the university."

She raised her hand in acknowledgment of the applause.

Gelwood continued with the announcements. "Star Valley welcomes Keci and Nonnash's newest little one, Brenlee, another girl."

There was laughter around the hall as Ryken jumped up and down pointing at her two-month-old sister bundled up in a carrier at her mother's feet.

Gelwood continued. "Welcome to those who provide us music to dance and sing with, The Star Valley Bashers!" He waved his arm toward the other musicians on the stage. Cheers and whistles accompanied the loud applause as band members took their bows. "We welcome also Renloret, a traveler from Southern, guest and blade student of Ani. We understand he is hoping that training with the first female Northern champion will give him an advantage in the Southern competitions later this year. Perhaps he will stay and enter our Northern regionals next month to test his theory. He is also researching distant family history for medical reasons and searches for information and community ties, looking to us for assistance."

The Southerner gave a short nod of his head in acknowledgment. He seemed surprised at the speed in which his quest had been taken up. Taryn knew that before the eve was done, Renloret would have as much information as was available. Family was very important to the valley's populace.

"By special decree, this eve's after-party entertainment will include songs from our long-distance guest and his supporter." A mischievous smile curled Gelwood's lips as the pair exchanged startled looks. Ani's was concerned and Renloret's was full of questions. "Melli and I will assist in their choices. After the next dance please avail yourself of the breads, cheese, and fruits while the band takes a break." Without further comment he seated himself and looked to Mroz, who stepped to the microphone and stroked out the tempo for a jig.

The hall jumped at his prompting. After the final notes Ani moved toward Melli with determined steps, shaking her head and pointing at Renloret.

Melli just smiled, nodded, and patted her partner's arm. "I've already spoken to him, Ani. He is agreeable to at least one song. Now, for your part, I'd like to hear my favorite if you please."

Renloret nodded. "I'm fine with this, Ani. If I can gain support by sharing a simple song, I think it would be good."

Her sigh of acquiescence surprised Taryn.

A tapping from the stage interrupted, and they all turned their attention to Mroz. His announcement of the next dance was greeted enthusiastically. Dancers haphazardly left plates of food and chatting groups to join the five couple sets. Everyone knew the dance, except Renloret. Melli directed him smoothly through the first fifth of the dance. All the figures had been taught earlier, and once he figured out the order, he moved through them without prompts. Everyone was laughing and breathless as the last notes carried them into ending bows.

"Your pardon, I need to speak with Melli," Gelwood said. He had sidled up between his wife and Renloret. As manners dictated, the Southerner backed away to give the couple some room.

"Renloret, why don't you choose some partners for the mixer? They will come to you if you hold up your hand. I suggest taking the first two," Melli said, laying her hand on Gelwood's arm to be escorted towards the punch bowls.

Taryn eyed his parents as his father whispered in Melli's ear. She looked over her shoulder, then back to Gelwood, a grin on her face. Their heads together, they wandered down the tables popping fruit pieces and bits of cheese into each other's mouth. What were they plotting now? After a few more surreptitious glances at the Southerner, Taryn was confident of the discussion topic. Well, leave them to their gossip. Another dance was forming and it called for groupings of three people. Without a word to Ani, Taryn scanned the crowd and waved at Ryken and her older sister who were looking for a third person to fill out their trio. It was best to be out of sight when his parents were conniving.

A few minutes later, Gelwood clambered onto the stage and clapped his hands to get the crowd's attention. "If Taryn would join the band please, Eteel has a new piece we'd like to hear. This will be a free dance, so choose your partner well. We'll let Taryn familiarize himself with the music for a minute or so, then we'll begin."

Taryn arrived on stage pulling the strap of his twelve-stringed cyralist over his head, sat down in the central chair, and looked over the sheets Eteel placed on the stand. He fingered a few bars here and there, eyebrows rising in surprised approval at the rhythm and tune. "When did you write this, Eteel?"

"I finished it a month or so ago," Eteel replied. "I wrote it with you in mind as the soloist. We've been working on it since then for this eve." Eteel grinned at the rest of the band.

"And you just now thought to let me look at it?" Taryn asked as a gentle laugh rippled through the crowd.

"I suspect your first sight-reading will be better than our month of practice. We'll try to keep up. Watch the key change in part B. Do what you do and I'll change the score to match later." Eteel moved back to his upright bass, settled on the high seat, and nodded at Gelwood.

"Everyone has a partner? Let's dance." Gelwood checked over his shoulder at the band and at the crowd forming pairs, then marked the timing and struck the first chord.

While waiting for his first entrance, Taryn watched the dancers, especially Ani and her partner. He saw the light in her eyes and the uncertain smiles as they stepped into each other's arms. Taryn studied the score again noting where some alterations could prove to himself, and to Ani, whether or not this Southerner was worthy of her. Then he turned back to the one pair of dancers that mattered to him. Their eyes were focused on each other, already in their own world, the music directing their movements and, perhaps, their thoughts. Taryn smiled. With this piece, Taryn knew he could show them the truth of their dance.

The exotic lilting rhythm soon had the dancers moving around the hall. Laughter filtered from the dancers to Taryn as a few feet were stepped on, apologies accepted, and the dancers resettled into the rhythm. The band swung into the main part and Taryn hugged the bulbous hourglass shaped cyralist to his waist and began picking the over melody, a smile on his face as he planned how to modify Eteel's markings.

In his peripheral vision Taryn noticed that some of the dancers had stopped to listen to the captivating melody. Soon the floor was freed up for the advanced dancers who experimented on their own. A few measures rest allowed Taryn to observe the few remaining couples.

With a twist of his hand over his head, he signaled an increase in the tempo. The melody grew more seductive. A murmur of approval whispered its way onto the stage. Taryn glanced away from the music. Only one couple remained. Taryn smiled and checked the music again. An upcoming solo would allow him to truly play with the melody. He set his fingers to match the dancers' movements when it arrived and brought them to a crescendo of spins before releasing them. Ah, the Southerner was indeed an excellent dancer—far better than Taryn expected. Deciding that he had proven the mutual attraction between them as only music and dancing could, Taryn allowed them to slow. As the last note faded, the entire audience seemed to hold their breath, not wanting to break the spell cast so beautifully by musician and dancers.

Renloret and Ani finally seemed to realize they were the center of attention and that the music had ceased. Ani straightened her dress in quick jerks, her hand halting high on her thigh where the Southerner's hand had rested. They both blushed in response to the applause.

Taryn watched what his playing had created. For a moment he thought he had been unfair to Ani—or to himself. He saw her eyes glowing with desire at every slip of a glance at her guest. Oh, how he wished it was him she looked at, not this Southern intruder. But she'd warned him, more than once, that her mind had been made up. Had he really heard her? He remembered her parting words when she left for the university. "It just doesn't feel right, anymore. So much has happened. I've changed. I have to change my life. I need time." He had let her go then, thinking she would realize that nothing had to change. His heart would not change. But hers had. Now Taryn watched the pair in the middle of the hall falling in love.

While the attention was focused on Ani and Renloret, Taryn set the cyralist to the side and shuffled the sheet music together. Even knowing he had played into fate's opportunity and to his own ego, he tried to blame the music for the outcome. But certain things had changed. He hoped he was mature enough to be satisfied with being her friend. For that was what he *had* to be. And to be that friend he would have to get to know this Southerner. He hoped Renloret would be worthy. If he was, Taryn would stand next to him as a friend; if not, he'd just kill him. He smiled to himself. Yes, he could do either.

Continued applause roused him from his thoughts. He nodded acknowledgment as the audience turned from the dancers to include him in their appreciation. Taryn waved Eteel forward and clasped his forearm. "Nice piece." He cleared his throat. "I apologize for letting my fingers go off the page on the last solo, but they had a mind of their own. And it *is* one of your best. I will enjoy playing it again."

Eteel shrugged off the praise. "You are a true master, young man. I'll have the solo rewritten by next week. Perhaps we could discuss presenting it at the summer festival. I've had my eye on that trophy for many a year, and we'd win for sure with you playing with us."

"I'd be happy to play with the band. Come up with more pieces like that and you'll be a wealthy composer by year-end."

Eteel smiled at the praise. "After that performance I need a drink. Let's go shake some of this from our system. We still have the after-party sing." He jumped from the stage and headed for the beverage table.

Taryn waited until all band members, including his father, had exited the stage before following. He wanted to observe the Southerner from a more neutral spot. He really didn't want to be seen as the instigator of the whole scene, especially when he had no prior knowledge of that particular piece of music. Grabbing a plate, he pretended to concentrate on his choices of cheeses and bread as he moved toward the punch bowls to eavesdrop and observe.

Eteel turned to Gelwood with a punch filled cup. "Did you ask if he could sing?"

"Says he's competed in locals, so it's a fair bet he carries a tune well enough," Gelwood replied.

Eteel raised his voice and addressed the pilot. "Southern, can you share a lost-love drinking song, kind of sad, but not too sad, perhaps with a bit of humor? Do you have any like that down there?"

"What?"

Taryn thought Renloret sounded confused by the question.

"A drinking song, perhaps humorous. Do you know any?" Eteel tried again.

"Um, yes, I do know a few."

"Good. Now finish that drink and come with me to the stage."

Taryn put down his plate and moved through the crowd without looking back. It wouldn't do for him to be caught eavesdropping, even if he was the sheriff. And he had to get ready for his part of the duet. He pursed his lips at the coming irony between song and real life.

Taryn watched his father use the crutch for support to raise his good leg high enough to gain a seat on the stage surface. The twisted remains of the injured leg hung limply. Gelwood clapped his hands three times.

At that signal the murmuring crowd grabbed chairs and quickly created a large half circle facing him. When all were seated and the children shushed, Gelwood waved to Renloret, encouraging him to approach.

"Since we've been blessed by an eve of good music and dancing, we'll commence with the singing. First, we'll have the duet that won the regional two years ago. They should have taken the continental prize as well, but we all know the modern tastes of the city judges. Then second, our Southern dance-man, Renloret, will treat us to one or two of his own songs, giving us an opportunity to share and enjoy a different culture."

Light applause and appreciative smiles from the audience bespoke agreement to the plan.

"Then we'll look to our visitor's list of names one last time and see how helpful we can be in thanks for the entertainment tonight. Now, the duet."

CHAPTER FOURTEEN

Renloret smiled back as Taryn gave him a challenging grin on his way to the stage. Then he leaned back against the stage as ready as the villagers for more music from this obviously talented young man. Would his singing be as good as his playing?

Renloret straightened with interest as Taryn began in a minor key, his tenor evoking sighs from most of the ladies in the hall. He sang of a young man's lost love, questioning the eternal powers of love and the emptiness its loss had left in his heart.

An alto voice answered his questions from the back of the stage, startling only Renloret, who'd been concentrating on Taryn's performance and had not seen Ani slip onto the stage. She seemed fully recovered from their dance and had eyes only for Taryn, her character's former beloved. Renloret watched her, fascinated by the unexpected depth of emotion in her voice and actions as she eased off the stage to stand behind Taryn, pleading with him to stay alive and find new love, for she was not worth a finite ending.

Taryn turned into her arms as their combined voices rose in agreement that the painful heartache would heal with time and patience. Ani's character suggested new love was possible if the heart was open and willing. Taryn's character answered affirmatively. The last notes were as tender as the touch of Ani's hands on his face before she turned away, a tear on her cheek, to seek her own new love.

Applause and cheers were accompanied by the crowd rising to their feet. Ani ran back to Taryn, hugging him fiercely and wiping more tears off. She whispered something and he nodded and placed a kiss on her forehead. Smiling, they turned to the audience, hand-in-hand, accepting their adulation. Renloret added his appreciation. The song would have won many competitions on Lrakira. He now knew that these two were multitalented in extremes and would bear watching. Who knew all the talents that lay hidden under the surface within this race? He suddenly wished they were space travelers. Teramar would be a wondrous world to share with his fellow Lrakirans.

Gelwood waved everyone into their seats, wiping tears from his own face. "If you'd done it that way at the competition there would have been no question about the title. Perhaps this year?"

Taryn shook his head, hugging Ani into his shoulder, kissing her dark hair lightly.

Renloret was surprised by the sudden desire to pull them apart and plant his own lips on her. He pushed the impulse away. He had to stay focused. Being impulsive and jealous for no reason would not get him what he was there for. He needed to be accepted by these people. His own advanced technology had let him down and he was now risking everything by asking natives for help. Important questions remained: Would he find those left behind? Could he return everyone to Lrakira and save his world? Even with all that on his mind he couldn't help glowering at the still hugging couple.

Ani pulled away from Taryn's embrace and answered Gelwood's question. "Circumstances are not the same, Gelwood. Many things have changed. Let others sing for the crystal chalice. It was politics and history that landed us with second place. My family made this valley home and I prefer to stay here, even though invitations and challenges in music and the blade ring are intriguing. I'll never leave of my free will. Star Valley has been and will always be my home. The entire valley is my family now."

The crowd applauded their support. Ani faced Renloret and said, "Now to a better topic. Let's hear the songs my student, Renloret, has promised." She flashed a grin at him and clapped her hands together. The audience joined her.

Renloret nodded and came up onto the stage. He draped an arm cozily over Gelwood's shoulders and gave his eyebrows a suggestive raise, which brought a smattering of laughter from the attentive audience. He could play a part as well as anyone on Lrakira.

He drew a full breath and became the new love interest of a well-endowed older woman reputed to have had more men than lived in the local region. The song complained of not having enough "energy" to keep up with his love, and he sought advice from other men as to how they handled her attentions. Hoping that the audience would assume his native language was a Southern dialect, Renloret sang in Lrakiran. It was a brash ploy and he hoped no one had enough knowledge of Southern to question his assumed nationality. It had been the tone and melody of the song he'd been going for, not the words. Completing the song by repeating the refrain, which had a catchy tune and simple words, he heard descants being hummed, the foreign words being tasted or sung by several members of the audience. They added a pleasant harmony to the ending lines. He straightened up, grinning as he patted Gelwood's shoulder in thanks. During the applause he chose a second song.

"Now, for a slight change of pace, I offer a song for the littlest ones as they head off to slumber." He moved smoothly into a short lullaby, his baritone soft and calming. Ryken and several other youngsters settled at his feet as he sang to them, their attention adoring and appreciative. A satisfied applause answered the last note.

Gelwood offered his forearm in a wrist-to-wrist grip, the firmness of which surprised Renloret. He made direct eye contact and answered with equal pressure. Gelwood pulled him close and whispered, "Take care of her. If you hurt her you'll have to deal with the entire valley.

"Our thanks to you, Renloret, for an entertaining evening," Gelwood said to Renloret with a nod, then turned to the audience and addressed them. "Before you leave, please look over his list of names. If you recognize any, please let us know. And now, may all who have attended Star Valley's spring dance rest well and be at peace. Safe journey."

Adults gathered up children, coats, and empty dishes as the

undercurrent of conversation slipped on and off the newcomer. The list was perused by each before they left.

Renloret looked across the crowd. Where was Ani?

"Renloret!" Taryn waved to catch the pilot's attention. Two men approached with Taryn. "I want you to meet Tezak, Star Valley's remaining doctor, and Mroz, whom you saw directing the band. He is also the valley's part-time mortician. They both recognize two of the names on your list."

Renloret instantly focused on the men. Tezak extended his arm for a firm wrist grip greeting. He was slender with grey tinting his neatly braided black hair, and his eyes twinkled below graying brows.

"I can't stay too long, Southern. After that dance and those last songs, my sweet Azzoli is expecting a longer night. Your pardon, I digress." He gave a conspiratorial wink then straightened. Pointing at two names on the list, he said, "I treated both of these individuals some twenty years ago for wounds received in the ransacking of the medical center. Neither survived, in spite of the treatments tried. Mroz here knows where they be buried."

Mroz cleared his throat. "As part-time coroner and mortician, I assisted in the preparation and internment of Romack and Navidi. There were differences in spellings of the first names, but I'm sure of the surnames. Tezak and I can take you to the cemetery in the morn if you want."

"Yes. And you can fill me in on this medical center, too? Perhaps there's more information to be found there. Some of my family worked in the medical field. Are there any records available on those who may have worked there?" Renloret had trouble believing his search might be successful.

Tezak looked thoughtful. "I'll have to do some digging, but I might have some in the storage area that weren't destroyed in the fires. I'll see what I can come up with after we check out the cemetery. Now, if you'll excuse me, my Azzoli is at the door with my coat."

He crossed the floor with hurried steps to the waiting woman. She helped him into the coat, slipped her arm around his, and accepted a light kiss on her cheek. The invitation on her face was seen by all still in the hall. Laughter drifted about as the couple ran out the door.

Mroz shook his head and winked at Renloret. "Amazing what a simple dance can do to some people. I've a mind to search out an old friend or two, myself." He placed a hand on Renloret's shoulder and squeezed briefly. "We'll meet at Gelwood and Melli's home about 9:00. Hopefully, Tezak won't be too late." He bowed and took his leave.

Taryn tapped Renloret on the other shoulder. "I should arrest you right now."

"Why? What crime have I done?" Renloret asked.

"Well, how about indecent exposure?" Taryn said.

"For dancing?" Renloret asked. What kind of excuse was that?

"For dancing." Taryn nodded apparently accepting Renloret's question as an admission of guilt.

"But everyone was dancing tonight," Renloret said.

"Not the way you danced with her," Taryn replied.

This sounded like jealousy to Renloret. He parried back. "What about the way you played? We just danced to your music. Which came first, the dance or the music? Who should be arrested?"

After a brief pause, Taryn grinned. "Since you put it that way, neither of us."

"You love her."

"More than she'll let me, but enough to let her go," Taryn admitted.

Renloret only nodded. The sheriff was apparently reevaluating his relationship with Ani.

"Where did she go, anyway?" Taryn asked, obviously covering his discomfort.

They both searched the hall for signs of the dark green dress.

Several older girls bustled out of the kitchen carrying trays. Their laughter settled quickly as they noticed the sheriff and southerner watching. Ani appeared behind them with an armful of coats and wraps. She seemed to herd the girls toward the last of waiting parents. Ani gave each girl a quick hug and handed off coats so they could exit.

Renloret turned his attention back to Taryn.

"So you'll be leaving soon if the information in the cemetery is helpful?" Taryn asked. His straight-faced question earned him a sharp smack on the shoulder from Melli as she arrived from the kitchen. "Ow! Why'd you do that?" He turned to face his mother.

"You know. Now, son, behave yourself." Melli rapped him again.

Taryn rubbed his shoulder with an unconvincing wince just as Melli reached out to rap him again but managed to dodge the blow.

"Okay, okay," he said, laughing as he held out both hands palms out, fending off another smack before leaving to assist Gelwood with moving the keyboard to the back of the stage.

Melli had the following day already planned. He and Ani were to stay at Ani's lake house rather than the cabin so they could attend the morn meal with Taryn's family. The two men, Mroz and Tezak, had also been invited. Renloret somewhat reluctantly agreed. He was sure that prolonged contact with the natives would increase his chances of making blunders in Northern etiquette or first contact rules that could not be repaired. But if this trip to the cemetery would garner needed information, then he had to go against protocol and just do his best.

A few of her statements revealed just how closely knotted the two families, Taryn's and Ani's, were. Concern etched itself on Melli's face when she spoke of Ani's mother's passing the previous year quickly followed by the apparent abandonment by her uncle when he escaped to Southern to further his own scientific research. Renloret was surprised at the amount of personal information Melli poured forth. She had not struck him as the gossiping type. Perhaps it was her method of warning him that Ani might reject him in spite of the feelings the dance seemed to have roused in her.

When Taryn stepped away for a moment, Melli said a few things to Renloret that suggested a relationship between him and Ani. And when he protested, she whispered that there was no reason for Renloret to be jealous of Taryn. According to Melli, they were only friends and that was as it should be. Ani was ready to move on and was more than available if Renloret was interested.

As Renloret tried to cover his surprise at her comment and support, Taryn returned and Gelwood approached jangling a set of keys from his fingers. Relieved that the conversation was interrupted, Renloret escorted Melli to the door. Gelwood pushed Ani and Taryn out onto the hall's porch and locked the door before taking Melli's hand and heading to their hover-car.

Silence was quick to surround the trio.

"Well?" Taryn and Ani spoke simultaneously. They both laughed. Taryn offered his forearm to Renloret, who clasped it with like firmness. "I'll see you at my parents. We should be at the cemetery by mid-morn, so don't over sleep."

Renloret watched as Taryn pulled Ani to him and whispered in her ear, then pressed a light kiss on her cheek and made his way to the last hover-car on the street.

CHAPTER FIFTEEN

"Here she is, General." Private Damron Meryth's handlight illuminated the carved double grave marker. He read the inscription aloud. "Shendahl Chenak. Released from the physical world and debilitating disease on 23 Piron 1028. Doctor, Level Four Blade Champion, and friend to all. Mother to her daughter, Anyala Chenak." He moved the light to the other side of the marker. "Hey, listen to what they say about the man. 'Yenne Chenak. Released from the physical world through wrongful government action on 35 Leigha 1009. Leader in medical research, dreamer of great futures. Father to his daughter, Anyala Chenak.'"

General Dalkey snorted in disgust at the cause of the man's death. He muttered, "There was nothing wrongful about our attack. They *were* consorting with aliens. If we hadn't destroyed their laboratory they would have released the aliens amongst us and we'd all be victims of their 'medical research.'"

Private Meryth shifted uncomfortably and licked his lips.

"I know the answer is here. That daughter of theirs should be praising my efforts to keep our world safe—*her* safe. Her parents had no right to expose her to their insane notions of aliens and space travel. Who in their right mind would want to go to the moon or even to Kriswren? What could live in places that have no air to breathe? They had no right!" He struck the headstone. "She was such a pretty little thing back then with big green eyes. Five or six years old she was. I almost had her safe. But her parents didn't love her." He shook his head. "They just needed her blood to feed the aliens they kept hidden in the med center—"

"You were there?" Private Meryth asked.

"Yes. I raised the alarm and stopped her mother from taking her to the ship. No one else saw the ship leave. They were so intent on the burning building they didn't even look up. I saw it. If I'd been able to capture one of the aliens, I would have gotten the honor due me." He stabbed his chest with a fist. "Me. Then I waited almost twenty years. Kept my mouth shut for twenty long years. Didn't say anything when her uncle started encouraging women to compete in the ring. I didn't say anything two years ago when that little girl unfairly won at the championships."

He turned knowing eyes on the private. "It was all a hoax you know, perpetrated by this whole cursed valley. I figured when her mother died I'd come and get my answers. I'd show everyone. Didn't get here soon enough though. They were putting her in the ground. Had to break open the box to show 'em she wasn't there 'cause the aliens had taken her away—like her husband. There's no one under his stone either." He pointed at the left side of the headstone.

A predatory howl from a local canine interrupted his monologue. Private Meryth snapped his gun into his shoulder, scanning the graveyard to the limits of the lantern light.

Dalky laughed. "Meryth, I thought you said you weren't afraid of any old bones? You're going to let someone's hound scare you into revealing what we're out here to do?"

Meryth licked his lips again. "No, sir, but can we just get on with this? The longer we're here, the more likely we're to be found."

"They're too busy with their little dance to come to the graveyard, so don't worry about them. What are you hoping to find? Bones or nothing?"

"Does it matter, sir?" Meryth asked. "If there are bones, we'll both know everyone was speaking the truth, and you're headed back to the hospital. If there are none, then everyone was lying. You were right and the investigation will start. And I'll be at the best point—an eye witness either way, sir." He kept his eyes on the darkness at the edge of the light.

General Dalkey grinned. "I like the way you think, Meryth. But I *am* right." He motioned to the shovels. "Get to it then. I'll keep watch."

Meryth set the gun against the headstone and took up a shovel.

Dalkey was patient as his private dug away. He'd waited twenty years to finish what began with a simple inquiry into the almost magical medical breakthroughs coming from the little known research facility located in a secluded, backward part of the northern continent. He'd been a mere sergeant at the time, assigned to accompany and report on anything the investigating medical observer might miss. Dalkey had assumed his superior didn't fully trust the observer and had charged Dalkey with observing the observer.

Both Dalkey and the medical observer were surprised at the advanced technology available at the research center. The observer quickly became enthralled with the lead researcher's mission and participated unreservedly in numerous experiments. Dalkey closed his mind to all but the extensive security surrounding the facility, which he found excessive and unusual. He wondered why it was necessary. He took his observations to his superior, who dismissed his concerns because, he said, they were merely expected business practices to protect the research center's proprietary information. When some of the technological and medical practices developed in this insignificant valley had been released to the public, their eager acceptance and implementation in both military and civil society had astounded and disturbed Dalkey. Now, in hindsight, Dalkey had to admit it was to Northern's advantage to have such advances because politics had definitely soured with Southern and tensions between the continents were escalating to possible military conflict.

After his attack during the funeral, he had been confined to a mental ward. Then, recently, his haranguing about aliens had been brought to the attention of his superiors again at the discovery of more indecipherable radio-like signals emanating from the region—curiously, with Star Valley at the center. Though the communication advances had improved enough to detect these faint signals being sent out, it was the interception of an answering signal arriving from outside Teramar's atmosphere that had generated fear and sudden interest in Dalkey's ramblings. Dalkey was removed from the isolated asylum, given the title of general, and instructed to locate the exact source of the signals and anything that smacked of alien life forms or communications with such.

He knew he was violating his military directive by being in the graveyard, but he couldn't think of another way to elicit the desired response from the valley's community. And, perhaps, someone would give up information leading to the source of all the signals aimed into space and why they were being answered now—after twenty years of silence. After being thrown off the Chenak property, Dalkey decided to move more directly, by digging up what he felt was the source.

The dull thunk of the shovel hitting the casket brought a leer to Dalkey's face. He jumped in the hole with the second shovel, scraping and tossing the remaining dirt from the wooden surface, and ran his fingers across the deep crosswise cuts that scarred the wood. Using the edge of the shovel, he pried at the lid of the casket. It cracked and objected loudly to his intrusion. He grinned and worked the shovel deeper under the lip, rocking it back and forth. The lid popped loose. Now he would know. His laughter rolled across the cemetery.

CHAPTER SIXTEEN

Renloret noticed the reflection of the ringed moon in her eyes. There was pain there as well. "Are you correct?

She blinked at his misspoken word then answered, "Am I okay? Yes, sure. What time do we have to meet in the morn?"

"Nine bells, but after breaking fast with Melli and Gelwood."

"Bells?" she asked sharply.

He jumped at her intensity. He'd made another mistake. That was not how time was indicated here. Now he couldn't remember how it was stated on Teramar. "Um, I think of time increments as when I was small in my village. There was a bell tower that rang out the time. I grew up counting the rings of the bell. This village reminds me of home more than I realized." He paused as he recognized the truth of his statement. Yes, he did feel at home. He was going to miss it when he left.

"Oh, I like that. It sounds so relaxed," Ani said.

"Not if you're always late."

"You, late?" She turned her head up to look at him.

He was very aware of the reflection of the haloed moon's light in her eyes. "Always. My commander even started telling me different bells and chimes so I would be on time to meetings, though I missed the opening of the meeting where I was selected to pilot this mission."

"Miss anything important?" Ani asked as she stepped off the porch.

Renloret followed. "I don't think so. But certain people didn't like Trimag's choice of pilot and tension was tight until we left."

She slowed her pace until they were side by side. "Were you the only one available?"

He hesitated, the warmth of her nearness again clouding his thoughts. "I doubt it. Trimag just said I was the best, but even the Singers were reluctant until my 'interview.'"

"Singers?" She turned her head up to look at him again. "What would singers have to do with rescuing lost personnel?"

"It is a bit complicated. Suffice it to say that one of those missing is related to one of the Singers." He felt some explanation was needed. "They are leaders of an ancient religion of sorts and, while it helps to be able to sing, I do not think it is part of the job anymore. But the title remains."

"Do Southerners worship music?" Her question seemed serious.

They had arrived at her vehicle. She pressed a small button near the vehicle's handle to unlock both doors. He slid in and strapped on the safety belt she had insisted he wear.

"Well?" She closed the door and turned to look at him.

"I shouldn't discuss it. But, no, we don't worship music. A long time ago we used music to communicate with our . . . gods.

It's not the same anymore. The people may have forgotten about the gods, but music is still important to village society. We have contests, like you."

"Mroz thought you sang well." The vehicle's engine rumbled pleasantly.

"Well enough. I have not competed in either song or dance since entering pilot training." He thought of all the good music and the fresh, new dance figures he'd learned and would forget by morn. "I apologize for stepping on your feet."

He watched a blush darken her face in the low light from the instrument panel and was glad she was driving because he couldn't take his eyes off her.

"It wasn't *my* feet you remember stepping on. You didn't miss a stroke…a beat." She coughed lightly. "I'd like to know the translation of the song you sang to Gelwood. It was fun and you seemed to have a good time singing it. Everyone enjoyed your performance."

It was his turn to blush as he reviewed their dance and the song he'd sung. Then he cleared his throat. "I cannot translate it appropriately at this time. It is rather suggestive." He shifted into a more comfortable position as Ani chuckled.

"I gathered that from your actions. You'd do well in the operas here. Your voice is exceptional."

"It would be inappropriate to accept that much of a compliment. You and Taryn would have won more than a fair share of the contests on Lra . . . Southern." He slid over the slip of tongue. He was not at home and he had to be careful. He had to stay focused, but she was so close he found it almost impossible. Remembering Melli's comments about Ani's uncle, he changed the subject.

"Melli mentioned that your uncle now lives in Southern. Where?"

Ani blinked several times and released a deep sigh. "I don't know. He moves around a lot. He contacts me by tel-com when he's in a town, which is not often. He's happier down there. Doesn't get into trouble for his beliefs. In fact his ideas are well supported."

"What kind of ideas?" Renloret asked.

"All he'll tell me is that it's groundbreaking research in areas that will change Teramar's entire way of thinking."

"In what areas?" he asked. Any topic that distracted him from her allure was going to be helpful and, perhaps, he could fill in some of the missing information about the people of Teramar.

"He's never been too clear about that either, though he was pleased when Southern launched their first satellite a few years ago. That's one of the reasons he left so soon after Mother's death. He said, 'If I can help them, they'll have to help us.' So he left. I couldn't stop him. He was devastated when Mother died and kept raging about the incompetence of politics getting in the way of progress. He still blames the military for her death."

"Why?"

"Because they let certain idiots decide what kind of research could be done, when and where it could be done, and whether or not the results got to the public. It was considered unlawful to perform experiments on people even after all other forms of testing had been outlawed. Some in the government, I'm sure, were thrilled when my mother became too ill to carry on her research, even though she helped so many."

Ani was quiet for a time.

The road continued to wind up and through the trees to the turnoff. She slowed to maneuver the sharper washboarded turns.

"I still haven't figured out how Dalkey got so involved. Or why he keeps insisting aliens have anything to do with my family. It's the alien thing that's laughable."

"Not entirely," Renloret said. He wondered if she really was unwilling to admit to the possibility of extraterrestrial life.

She turned wide eyes to him during a short straight stretch. "Really? You believe in aliens?"

"Why not? Statistically, with so many stars, how could ours be the only one with planets and forms of life?" All he could do was state the obvious. Though he'd been a pilot for two sun-cycles, he'd already been to dozens of planets and had encountered several of those "nonexistent" aliens. These people were losing out on so much. They would provide a cure for his people and not even know about them.

"That's what Uncle keeps on about. I want to believe him, but beliefs like that create a lot of conflict. I don't want to be a part of that anymore. I just want to be normal so people like Dalkey will leave me alone. All I need is my blade and Kela, though I'd really like Uncle to come home. I miss him."

Nodding, Renloret remembered Melli saying the same thing. But she'd also said something about that changing. He was intrigued and decided that before he left, if he ever left Teramar for home, he would have a long conversation with Melli.

The vehicle's lights illuminated the broad, pillared porch of the house as they came out of the trees. Though the building was immense, it fit its surroundings, nestled amongst the trees. Ani turned the vehicle into the single lane on the side of the house and aimed it at a smaller, separate building. The door lifted. Renloret speculated they had passed some sort of sensor that triggered the action. Ani drove straight into the center of the building. She unclipped the restraint system, stepped out of the vehicle, and waited for him at the door.

When he joined her, she placed her palm on a pad on the wall next to the door. The pad glowed and the massive storage door lowered while the vehicle rotated to face the front of the building. He shook his head and chuckled.

"What's so funny?" she asked.

"I didn't expect such technology so far from a large city, especially after the basics of the cabin."

"You may have launched the first satellite, but we're not as backward as you Southerners would like to believe." She glanced at him over her shoulder as she headed to the back door of the house. A large pool shimmered in the moonlight.

"I didn't say you were backward." He ran to catch up. "Speaking of my people, do you think this cemetery search will connect me with any of them?"

"I don't know. I hope so, I guess," she said, hesitating as she slipped off her shoes.

Renloret's next question caught in his throat as the slit in her skirt revealed both legs to the top of her thighs. Defensively, he closed his eyes and inhaled deeply. Blades, he wanted her. Why hadn't he just . . . .

"Renloret?"

He opened his eyes. She stood a few feet away, barefoot, bathed in the moon's brightness, shoes dangling from one hand, the other hand unbraiding her hair. He tried to speak but his throat had dried up.

"Are you all right?" she asked.

Her hand finished its travels down the length of her hair. He tried to clear his throat.

"No," he whispered. He felt hot in the cool late night. Was he sick? He closed his eyes again and managed a shaky breath as he forced away the vision of her in the moonlight and tried to remember why he was there. He needed to remember his purpose, remember that his people were relying on him to locate the research team, remember that he must find and return the child. His body and mind began to cool. He couldn't get distracted. He had to refocus. Ani was too beguiling. He drew another breath.

"Renloret?"

When she touched him, the warmth of her hand seared through his arm. He jerked away.

"Can't," he whispered. Would this desire for her ruin the mission or would this mission ruin everything? Which was more important?

"Can't what?" she asked.

Why did she ask impossible questions? He forced himself to look at the concerned face that was just inches away. He wanted to fall into those eyes and hold her as he had at the end of the dance. He ached for her.

"Can't what?" she repeated.

"Let you distract me," he confessed in a whisper. He had to

choose his world and mission. He could not have her. Lrakira and her millions of people were far more important than what might happen between them. He was insignificant as long as his world needed him to find and return the child. He looked back up at the moon and saw five distinct rings, all different shades of green. He was beginning to dislike that color, except for her eyes. When he looked back at her, she seemed vulnerable and lost, eyes looking at the ground, lips moving but words imperceptible.

With a short nod she turned to face the house. "Kela says to come in."

Renloret stood, rooted in place. When he looked back at the moon, its rings snapped to their real colors of rose, pale blue, and yellow against the moon's creamy white.

"Kela says what?"

"Come inside."

It wasn't exactly an order, more of a request. She turned at Kela's arrival from around the corner of the house. What had happened? Renloret had lost the context of his surroundings. How had he messed up this time? Renloret looked from the girl to the animal and back again. She had opened the door.

"Are you coming?" She watched Kela slip through the opening.

Whatever mood had been present was irretrievably altered. Feeling like a child being sent into the house to be punished for some unknown crime, Renloret followed her.

She appeared to ignore him as she set a spouted kettle on the stove and took down two large mugs from a wall rack. Renloret sat on one of the tall stools and watched as she prepared the tea. When the kettle whistled she retrieved it, poured water over the small metal balls filled with loose tea that she had placed in the cups, and touched the front of the stove to turn it off.

Renloret thought he should say something. He chose a safe topic and cleared his throat. "Why don't you have this technology at the cabin?"

"The cabin is my retreat. This is my parent's home." She shrugged as if that should explain everything.

"Choose." Her eyes stayed on the cups.

Renloret started to reach, stopping just before his movement would indicate his choice. "Is this a test?"

"Perhaps."

No smile, no shift in her eyes. Her breathing was slow, calm— almost dangerous. He felt like he was in the blade ring facing an unknown opponent. She raised her eyes from the mugs to his face, and he fell into the smoky green of them as the mingled fragrance of the teas intertwined in the air. He imagined the music of the dance. She blinked; the connection broke.

She unhooked the ball from one of the cups and put it on a small plate, then wrapped her hands about the cup, lifted it to her lips, and sipped carefully. Renloret followed her example.

Kela whined. Ani's eyes flicked to him and his ears flattened as he removed his paws from the counter and headed into the next room. She tilted her head toward the exiting animal. "He wants to know what happened."

"He wants to know what happened?" Renloret took another sip and the hot piney liquid spread through his body. Again he wondered if Kela could talk or understand what they said. And recent experience with Kela seemed to prove just that. It was not impossible, but wouldn't the team have been informed if there were telepathic capabilities on Teramar?

"Come, I'll explain," she said as she got up and went down the hall.

Renloret followed, trying not to appreciate the swaying hips as he trailed her through the doorway.

The wide hall emptied into a spacious foyer edged with a staircase and three sets of double doors. He pointed at the central doors. There were gouges and cuts on either side of the latches and splinters of wood on the floor.

"Front door damage courtesy of General Stubin Dalkey," she said in reply to the unasked question.

"Was anything else damaged?" He remembered her dash from the cabin to meet with this General Dalkey.

Her eyes flicked to the set of doors on the left. "Not that you need to know about."

Renloret raised a questioning eyebrow, wondering what kind of damage was behind those doors. Then he noticed the doors themselves. They were carved in great detail, reminding Renloret of the doors to the Stone Chambers on Lrakira. He moved toward them to examine the carvings, but Ani turned to the right and opened the third set of similarly carved doors.

"Lights," she said, and the room became illuminated as ceiling light fixtures came on.

An ornate rug covered much of the patterned wood flooring. Two long couches angled away from the rug to frame a stone fireplace. A wide mantel held framed images of people and vases of dried plants. All these drew the observer's eye to the crossed set of swords in the center.

Renloret walked past Ani to look more closely at the swords. Each blade was etched and they appeared to be identical except for the metal-studded wood grips, one larger in circumference than the other. He reached for the larger.

"No." Her voice stopped him. "That one belongs to my uncle. The other is mine. They were personal gifts from the continental commander in thanks for our services with training troops after the championships. He, at least, appreciated my uncle's training methods and was impressed enough with my efforts to offer me a position at the university when I declined a military posting. I think his intent was that I train his son, who was a first year then, though he managed to convince my uncle to work with the older noncollegiate recruits until Mother died."

She nestled into the couch on the right side, one leg tucked under her. "But Uncle is down on Southern now. He never explained why he didn't take his sword. He just left it here, maybe as a reminder of some kind." A pensive look crossed her face as she appeared to study the swords. After a moment she shrugged. "Enough about the past. Kela wants answers."

The animal appeared from behind the other couch to sit between Ani and Renloret.

"You'd better sit down," Ani said, pointing at the couch across from her. Her voice was grave, her expression serious. She nodded at the canine. "He's mad at us."

"Mad at us? What did we do?" Renloret settled in the cushions, directing his questions at the canine.

Kela looked accusingly at Ani, who blushed and then giggled.

"He wants me to state aloud everything he says to me. He says you can take it." She sipped her tea and poked Kela in the chest with her toes.

"Ah, so he *does* understand the spoken word and you can hear him in your head."

"Well, yes. You don't seem surprised."

"Well," he said, hedging, "I try to have an open mind about all sorts of things. I believe telepathy is not impossible." He'd been exposed to several species that did just that, but he couldn't let her know. "My mother always said to expect the unusual and learn how to deal with it. Only then would we be able to survive in the future."

Ani nodded and took another sip. "My mother said something similar. 'Only by evolution and flexibility will we surpass our forefathers and remake our world.' Perhaps it's a saying from Southern?"

Again, he avoided a direct answer. "More likely just two intelligent, open-minded women. My mother is a biologist."

Kela whined and pawed at Ani's leg.

"Pardon me. Kela asks if you're all right with him knowing all of what you have said since waking."

Renloret considered what he could remember saying aloud in Kela's presence. If Kela was intelligent enough to ask such a question, he was capable of revealing Renloret's alien status. "So long as he doesn't . . . embarrass me. Can he lie?"

Ani looked at Kela, who winked at her. She smiled. "Oh, I'm sure he does when it suits him."

"Can he communicate with anyone else?"

"Not that we know of. Our ability is unique, and only my uncle knew, until now. I'd appreciate your keeping it that way."

The pilot nodded. He was delighted that she was comfortable enough with him to share this unusual ability.

She shifted, stretching out her long legs, and swallowed the last of her tea. "Kela believes he understands you and how important your mission is. He wants to help in any way he can." A quizzical expression crossed her face. "He goes no further than that and wants an answer from you."

Kela turned his ice blue eyes on Renloret. The pilot shifted under the scrutiny. Renloret remembered saying all sorts of things about being an alien in the animal's presence. He'd expressed frustration about the crash and self-doubt about his ability to complete the mission. Kela continued to stare. How could Renloret find out how much Kela understood without revealing his own alien identity to Ani? He decided a simple answer would have to suffice until they were alone together. He faced Kela. "I accept your assistance," he said.

Kela rumbled an answer deep in his throat.

Ani smiled. "Now that that's over, how about some sleep?" She stood.

Kela pawed her thigh.

Ani turned to him and answered, "Yes, some of the names were recognized. Mroz and Tezak are going to take us to the cemetery tomorrow morning. They think two of the people are buried there. I'll take some flowers for Mother and Father since we'll be there, even if it is a week early."

"A week early for what?" Renloret asked as he stood.

Ani glanced at the crossed blades, the smile gone. "The anniversary of her death." Her chin trembled and tears appeared.

Renloret stepped closer, daring to run his hand down the side of her face to brush the tears from her cheeks. He did not know what to say.

Biting her bottom lip, she looked at him and whispered, "I think we'd better not get distracted from your mission."

She did not twist away as he expected, but remained where she was, almost in his arms.

"You are correct, Ani. You should know that I, too, have lost a parent and understand such things." He remembered the yearly celebration of his father's passing and began to wonder why so many of the traditions were similar between the two planets. It was a topic worthy of discussion—if he could find the child and return her to the home she'd never seen.

The combined heat of their bodies, so close yet not touching, began to take a toll on their resolve to not get distracted. Ani moved away, picked up her cup, and headed for the foyer. "I'll show you the guest room."

Renloret let himself admire her walk to the door before sighing and picking up his own cup to follow.

Ani laughed. "Shut up, Kela."

Renloret wondered what had been said, but refrained from asking as she led him up the staircase to the second door on the right.

"This is the guest room. There's a robe hanging on the back of the door and a private bath. I'll be in my room across the hall." She nodded at the door a few paces further down the hall.

"Since Melli is expecting us to break fast with them, we should rise at six 'bells.' I'll make sure you're not late. Melli has a real problem with late risers. She's a morn person. I'd prefer not to be up so early, but we have a mission to accomplish." Her smile was tentative.

"Thank you, Ani. I hadn't planned on relying so much on the locals. Kiver and Sharnel were supposed to know where and who to look for. I hope this excursion to the cemetery will bring up connections so I can be away before you have more conflicts because of me." He moved past her to enter the room. "Lights." He grinned as his command illuminated the spacious room.

A wide thickly-padded bed was covered with an embroidered spread patterned in flowers and animals. Renloret thought Lrakiran botanists would be delighted to examine the spread as representative of local flora and fauna. Matching tables offset the carved headboard. Real paper books were stacked on the shelves along the right side of the room, framing a large window with a bench seat decorated with several embroidered pillows. A rocking chair with a knotted shawl or coverlet thrown over the back sat next to a large six-drawer chest to the left of the private bath.

Renloret crossed to the bathroom door, which slid into a wall pocket. The light came up as he entered, unannounced. He guessed there was a movement sensor. A large tub was surrounded by striking cream and blue veined wood. The double vanity in the same wood followed the left wall to end in a series of shelves filled with what promised to be thick, soft, absorbent towels. There was a separate walk-in shower room and a second sliding door revealed the toilet.

The accommodations were on the side of luxury if he compared them to hotels, inns, or even some of the mansions of the wealthy he'd been in. It was such a contrast to the cabin's rustic feel that he was curious about why Ani felt more comfortable away from all the finery. He returned to the main room.

Ani had remained in the doorway watching him prowl, a small smile gracing her lips. "Adequate?"

"More than. Thank you," he said with a bow. He wanted to talk more but she held up a hand, palm toward him, shaking her head.

She bade him good eve and closed the door.

"Curse all the blades and hells, I want him," she whispered. She backed away from the door, biting her lip again. She mentally shared the dance with Kela as she slid down to the floor, her head in her hands.

Kela knew she had fallen in love from their first long stare, and now the memory of the dance proved it—to both of them and the entire valley. He was surprised that she was not taking it very well. He wondered how Taryn had reacted but decided not to ask.

Her sense of loss almost overwhelmed Kela, and he snuggled closer. He could feel her pushing away the feelings, rejecting them in an attempt to help this pilot, to center herself and not distract him from his mission. She wanted someone to be happy, someone to have family again. She stood, brushed away her tears, and entered her old room. She changed to sleep wear, slipped under the sheets, and stared at the ceiling a long time. He could feel her dancing the dance as if it would be the last one.

She would give up a possible future for herself to assist the pilot in his quest of an impossible rescue. If only Kela was sure who he was and who he searched for. The names on the list were similar to names he'd heard mentioned years ago between her mother and uncle. He didn't know enough about the original team. He'd been developed to be Ani's companion and protector long after her father disappeared. Their telepathic link was a unique design. For her to so freely admit that link to Renloret had revealed how deeply she trusted this pilot. What would be seen as more alien than telepathic communication with an animal? Even Taryn didn't know, and they had grown up together. She'd known this pilot five days and she was sharing the deepest secret she knew with him. Ah, love. How dangerous it was. Kela settled down between the two rooms in the center of the hall.

What would happen to Ani if this was not the rescue mission Shendahl and Reslo had so long waited for? What if it was?

CHAPTER SEVENTEEN

After they had cleared the dishes from the table, Mroz pulled Renloret and Ani into the sitting room to show them the map of the cemetery and the location of the two graves with names he and Tezak had recognized from the list. Tezak had called earlier saying his presence was unnecessary and Mroz was more than capable of leading them to the graves. All but Ani and Renloret had a good laugh at the lingering effects of the previous eve's dance.

In the kitchen, Taryn glanced at Melli and Gelwood. Waving a hand toward the sitting room he said, "I can't believe this. After last night, can you?" He dropped the last plates into the sink, splashing soapy water over the counter.

"You mean Ani and Renloret?" Gelwood asked with a chuckle. "Now, Taryn, what's there to complain about? They're in the public eye. Realize the position they're in."

"I know what position they should be in. They should have come into the house holding hands or least looking at each other.

Instead, they come in separately, as if they had actually arrived separately, and they sit at opposite ends of the table." He shook his head as he hung the dish towel on the hook beside the sink.

Melli poked her husband in the ribs. "I agree. They said hardly a word to each other all morn. And they certainly haven't made eye contact. They're acting like they had a fight and are only here out of necessity." Melli shooed Taryn towards the trio in the other room. "Go find out what happened."

"Me? Why not you?" The look she gave him changed his mind. "Fine." He slapped the swinging door open to the sitting room.

Mroz looked up at Taryn's entrance. "Ready?"

He shook his head. "Excuse me. I need to speak with Renloret, in private." He jerked his head toward the porch.

Renloret raised his eyebrows but complied.

As soon as the door was shut, Taryn turned to face Renloret. "I can't believe I'm saying this, but you didn't take her when you had the chance. You wasted the dance, didn't you?"

"I do not think that is any of your business. What happened last night after the dance is between Ani and me."

Taryn stepped forward, backing Renloret to the closed door. "You wasted the music, the dance, the whole thing . . . for what?" He was trying to imagine all sorts of reasons. He couldn't come up with one that would have kept him from her under similar circumstances.

"My mission." Renloret answered.

"Your mission? You abandoned that dance and that girl to find dead people?" Taryn was incredulous.

"Again, that is not your business, and I hope they are not all deceased. Besides, why do you care?"

Taryn cocked his head. Why should he care? That was a good question. He considered his answer. "Because she's like family and she deserves to be happy. She doesn't want me, she wants you."

"Are you so sure?" Renloret's confidence was obviously not complete, even after the dance.

Taryn took a step back. "I was last night. Any other man on the continent would have died to have been in your place last night, dancing with her, holding her. Did you even see how she looked at you? In all the hells, what did you do that was such a drastic cool off, anyway?"

"When we got to the house we had some tea and talked about her family and my mission. Then she showed me to the guest room. To be honest, Taryn, I expected a slightly different end to the night myself, but she shut the door." Renloret shrugged.

"*She* shut the door? After what I saw last night, that's nigh on impossible. She was ready to . . ."

Taryn reviewed the events of the previous night in his mind. "Ha! We were set up. She figured out we were all set up."

"We were set up? By whom?" Renloret asked.

"My parents," Taryn said as he saw his father duck behind the window curtain. "My conniving parents couldn't ask straight out how Ani felt about you because they knew how Ani would answer. I bet the whole thing was planned, even the new piece for me to debut to keep me out of the way so the two of you could dance. I'm guessing this was Mother's idea and the others went along with it just to see how right she might be." He reached for the door latch. "I wonder how much money passed."

Renloret was smiling when he blocked Taryn's hand. "I cannot believe that piece of music was written just for that purpose, but it was convenient. I am guessing you took it far beyond what the composer had written. Do not blame the music or your parents. They could not have planned ahead that far. They did not even know I was coming. They are looking out for everyone's best interests. They obviously see Ani as a daughter, so of course they'd be interested in the person she chooses to be with, just like you. To be honest, I do not know why I am so attracted to her. That fact was on my mind before the dance and I can hardly keep it from interfering even now."

Renloret sighed. "I need to find these people as soon as possible. After I find them, perhaps there will be time to see where other things might lead. Until then, my own desires must take a distant second place. That is what we discussed."

Taryn mulled over the pilot's statements. He'd never had a conversation like this with anyone, and he was amazed to discover he was not as angry with the Southerner as he was with Ani. He did want her to be happy, and if her expressions and tone of voice last night were any indication, this man would make her more than happy. The sooner Renloret found his family, the sooner the two of them could get together. And then *he* could get on with finding someone to make *him* happy.

"All right, I believe you. But you two are acting like you had broken blade promises and blamed each other. I don't know how you're going to stay focused, but if you're any kind of blade ring fighter, you'd better be more convincing. It won't be easy with her hanging around all the time, but someone has to make it difficult, hey?" Taryn knocked his fist against Renloret's shoulder for emphasis.

"Mind if we come out?" Ani asked, poking her head out the door.

The young men exchanged glances—each understanding the other. They nodded in unison.

"Well, let's get on to the cemetery and dig up some roots." Mroz motioned to the carry-all.

The cool morn air was warming up and small animal noises from the heavy trees at the edge of the cemetery added cheerfulness to the surroundings. It was all in opposition to the mood that hung about the four people staring at the pair of headstones.

"I don't know how this is going to help you locate your other relatives. Did they work at the medical center?" Mroz asked.

The headstones were plain in comparison to most in the cemetery. One stated, "Rikoret Navidi. Released from the physical world and wrongful government accusations on 4 Sewtra 1009. Assistant in medical research." According to Mroz, the date was five days after the attack on the research center. He had taken five days to die. The other read, "Terhani Romack. Released from the physical world and wrongful government accusations on 3 Sewtra 1009. Assistant in medical research, level three blade." Terhani had taken four days.

"Probably," Renloret replied, disheartened. "I was hoping there would be an indication of relatives or where they were from so I'd have a chance to locate the others."

"Oh." Mroz shook his head. "Not much to go on then. Sorry. As far as I know neither had any relatives. The ones from Southern didn't talk much about their homes. But they did a good job of fitting in with us and were welcome additions to our valley."

Renloret shrugged. "It was worth a try. Thank you." He paused, then pointed, curious. "This Terhani Romack, it says he was a level three blade. What does that mean on Northern?"

"A couple of years after they arrived some of the Southern workers began entering the blade-ring tournaments as a way to stay in condition and get to know the community," Mroz replied. "I think it helped them feel more at home. There were five or six of them and they were very good. I remember Romack. We were about the same age. He'd been competing for about two years and was moving up in the standings. We'd celebrated his third level about twelve days before the attack. The whole valley threw him a party." Mroz paused, as if remembering. "At the time, he was my sparring partner. Even though he had reached level three, he taught me a lot—enough to get me to level five the year after he died. I did it for him, but I haven't competed since."

Renloret glanced at Ani, who stood next to the headstone, and wondered what level came with the continental championship title. Now was not the time to ask. He'd ask later. Glancing at the headstones again, he rubbed his stomach, which cramped every time he looked at them. Something was wrong, but he couldn't pin a blade on the feeling long enough to figure it out.

"I'll have to keep looking I guess, maybe in another valley nearby." He looked beyond the cemetery to the mountain that separated Star Valley from the next valley over. Ani claimed that had been his true landing target. He tried not to look at the headstones. They made him dizzy, almost sick.

Ani removed two of the flowers from the bouquets she held and placed them on the stones. "I'll be back in a bit." She moved off to the other side of the hill.

Renloret forced himself to read the stone in front of him again. Something about it bothered him, like he should know something or recognize the name. A sense of danger tickled at his nerves. He shivered in the mid-morn sun as the uneasiness escalated and looked away from the stone. A sudden need for Ani to be in sight, to be safe, filled him. "Where'd she go?"

Taryn pointed and answered, "To her parents' graves. Why?"

"Something's very wrong." Renloret began walking to the crest of the hill. Taryn and Mroz followed.

A keening cry stopped them. Taryn and Mroz exchanged knowing looks. Then they ran. Renloret removed the blade he had hidden in his boot and Taryn unbuckled his waist blade. They topped the hill and were brought up short by the scene below.

Flowers were scattered in a line from the top of the hill to where Ani was, on her knees in front of a gaping hole surrounded by piles of soil, the last of the flowers dropping from her hands. She began rocking.

Renloret scanned the graveyard from his vantage point as the three men renewed their run to Ani's side. He saw nothing.

"Ani?"

She continued to rock, staring at the headstone.

Mroz put his hand to his mouth. "Curse them. Who would have done such a thing?" Renloret was aghast at the desecration of the grave site. He tried to get Ani's attention. Her eyes were wide with grief and her keening harmonics grated on his spine, but no tears fell.

His head began to ache and his eyes were drawn to the writing on the headstone. His blade slipped unnoticed from his hand as he read. He couldn't breathe. He stared at the name. This was impossible.

"This is Ani's mother's grave?" Renloret asked.

"Yes. We buried her last year," Mroz replied. "I think I know who did this."

Renloret's voice shook as he said, "Shendahl Chenak is Ani's mother?" He pointed at the gravestone with one hand and ran the other hand through his hair.

"Yes," Mroz said simply as he put a steadying hand on the man's shoulder. Renloret caught his arm and turned to face him. "Shendahl Chenak is her mother?"

"I said yes, man. Didn't you hear me?" Mroz placed both hands on Renloret's shoulders, shaking him slightly. "Are you all right?"

"Yes and no." Renloret ran his hands through his hair again, the color beginning to come back to darken his face. "I . . . I heard you but I am not . . . all right." He looked at the double headstone again, reading the lines aloud. "Mother to her daughter, Anyala. Father to his daughter, Anyala." He looked at the girl on her knees at the edge of the desecrated grave. "Anyala . . . Ani."

It began to form in his mind. S'Hendale had named her daughter after the Anyala Stone. The savior of his people was not a five-sun-cycles-old child. He fought off the wave of nausea as he realized that even though he'd been late for most things in his life, he'd never been this late. How many years had passed? He couldn't remember how old Ani said she was? Had she ever said? How could this be? He couldn't grasp the reality of his predicament. He pointed at the keening girl. "She's Anyala?"

"Yes," said Mroz. "Didn't you know her name? You danced with her and you don't know her name?"

"She said it was Ani, just Ani. No surname, no parent names, just Ani." He realized that during the entire trip to Teramar, no one ever bothered to tell him the child's name. S'Hendale had given another name to get on the ship, so her name was not on the roster. He had assumed she would maintain the alias and, therefore, he had not put her given name on the list he had passed around.

He gestured at Ani. "She's supposed to be little." He waved a hand at mid-thigh height and then stopped himself.

Mroz wouldn't understand; no one here would. He wasn't sure *he* did. He was supposed to bring back S'Hendale and her young daughter, but Ani was no child and S'Hendale was dead. He stumbled mentally. S'Hendale was dead. Commander Yenne Chenakainet was going to be devastated. The names on the headstone were just enough different, syllables shortened or blurred to achieve a pronunciation acceptable on Teramar. What about the child—now a grown woman? Without her mother's cooperation or explanation, what was he going to do? How was he going to rescue someone who didn't know she needed to be rescued, didn't know she was the only one who could save an entire species from extinction, and didn't know *she* was an alien?

He looked beseechingly at Mroz, wanting to tell him everything, but knowing he couldn't. They didn't believe in aliens here. How could he tell them some of their most honored citizens were aliens? How could he save his world?

It was supposed to be a simple rescue mission. All he had to do was fly the crew to a hidden valley, wait for them to gather the ones left behind, and return everyone to Lrakira. That's what the Anyala Stone had said. "Return all and all will be well." How could he return all if S'Hendale was dead? How could it have gone so wrong? Could he convince Ani to go to Lrakira if he could even find a ship to fly on a pre-space flight world? Even if he managed that, would there be any women left to save? How many years had passed? How had that happened? Too many questions; too many answers he didn't like or want to hear. Tears began to sting his eyes. He was the Stones' hope, his world's hope. Had he failed everyone? Had he failed an entire world? He choked back a sob.

Mroz forced him to sit down. "Renloret, I know this looks terrible, but it's our problem and we'll solve it. We'll also help you find those relatives of yours. It's two different things. Let's get Ani over to Taryn's parents' house. They'll keep watch while we try to figure this out."

Renloret wanted to shout. *It's not two different things—it's the same!* How was he going to straighten this out? He put his head in his hands.

Mroz gripped his shoulder, offering wordless support, then retrieved Renloret's blade from the dirt. The blade was exquisite. Almost as long as the bartender's forearm, it had keen edges and a handle carved with symbols similar to designs blade champions often had tattooed on their wrists. Mroz twisted the knife in the sunlight, bringing out more of the designs etched into the metallic blade, and grinned at Renloret.

"I've got my own hunches about who did this," Mroz said, still examining the blade. "We could use a good blade when we find him, too."

He offered Renloret's blade to him, grip first. "Better keep that blade to yourself. Everyone in the valley would want that blade. It could be better than Ani's or Taryn's, though not better than Shendahl's. Those are the best blades in the region. Ani's uncle made them. He's from Southern, you know. Who made yours? I could use a few like it. I can afford to pay."

Renloret was speechless as he slipped the blade back inside his boot. How could Mroz talk about blades when Lrakira was dying or already dead? But, of course, Mroz had no idea what was happening on Lrakira. Nor did anyone else here. His head seemed to burst with pain as he thought about blades. S'Hendale's blade? He sat up and took a deep, slow breath as he remembered the rumor of the missing Stone Blade. His tone was tense as he asked, "You said Shendahl had a blade?" He slurred the first and last syllables to make it more like how Mroz pronounced it.

Mroz nodded.

"Was it made of a green crystal?"

Mroz nodded again. "How'd you know? Sharpest blade on the

planet. Reslo said it never needed sharpening. I asked once how it was made. He was pretty vague but said it was from a very rare crystal. He spent a lot of time looking for similar material here in Northern. He said he had a feeling there was the right kind of crystal around, but he couldn't find it here. Then shortly after the funeral last year, he took off for Southern, saying he had a better chance of finding it down there. You're from Southern. Do you know the source of the crystal?"

Renloret considered this information. He answered, "Yes, and it is very rare indeed. You say her uncle made it and was looking for more crystal to make others?"

"At least that's one of his many reasons for going back to Southern."

Both men glanced at Ani and Taryn. The sheriff was trying to gather her in his arms. She had quieted, for now.

"She's really Anyala?" Renloret asked.

"Yes. Why do you keep asking? Why is that so important? Her name's not on your list and neither are her parents' names."

They were interrupted when Ani elbowed Taryn sharply in the face, knocking him into the empty grave. She jumped to her feet and bolted up the hill, moving so fast Mroz couldn't stop her.

Renloret had a better angle and tackled her before she could get three body lengths. As they tumbled, Ani aimed vicious kicks and jabs at his face. All the while, she was absolutely silent. He grunted after a particularly well aimed knee to his groin shoved all air from his lungs. Managing to get on his feet, he held her off with one arm and then threw a short punch to her jaw. She dropped into a pile.

He began cursing in Lrakiran, raising eyebrows from Mroz and Taryn as the bartender helped the sheriff out of the hole. Blood dripped from cuts on Taryn's cheek and mouth.

Renloret had almost run out of expletives and was considering changing to a more colorful language, perhaps one of the Gartainian dialects, when he realized the other two men were staring at him. How could he explain? He couldn't tell them he'd just knocked out the one person who could save his world.

CHAPTER EIGHTEEN

General Stubin Dalkey stared at the black box on the desk. Did he dare open it? He was sure the legendary crystal blade was inside, but what else now resided with it?

When he'd opened the casket, she'd looked so alive, as if she were sleeping. But when he really looked her body was thin, sickly like he imagined a corpse would look shortly after dying from some ravaging disease. Even so, after a year in the ground, he'd not expected to see a recognizable body. At most, he'd expected a partial skeleton. But there she was, almost breathing.

He'd looked at her for a long time, studying her, trying to reconcile the thin, frail body with the strong, vital woman he'd kept from joining the aliens by holding her daughter. That had been so long ago. Twenty years. He almost regretted her death, but that had not been his fault. He'd been stuck in supply support since the raid on the medical center had not yielded any aliens, and it wasn't until he'd seen the news reporting her passing that he'd even known she'd been ill. Then there had been the funeral and, well, the hospital stay for almost a year until someone realized their mistake and got him out to find proof of aliens on Teramar.

The box he'd found under her hands was just a plain black box, about two hands long, the perfect length for the perfect blade. Envy had rushed through his body. He could own a crystal blade that never needed sharpening and no one else was allowed to touch. It was said that after her first pairs title with her brother-in-law, she'd never been without it. He hadn't realized the blade had been buried with her body. The first time he'd tried to touch the box his hands hit a glass-like barrier that, after a brief examination, seemed to surround her entire body. It had taken both shovels to smash through the barrier. Then he pulled the box out from under those thin, long-fingered hands.

Private Meryth had started yelling then, pointing at the body in wide-eyed fear. They had watched as a green smoke-like mist rose from the corpse's hands. It had almost danced out of the body, sensuously making its way toward the box. Then Meryth had pounded on his back, again pointing at the body. This time it seemed to be melting away from the skeleton as if being drained by the mist. Before their eyes, the entire body had disappeared. The clothing lay in the bottom of the casket. That was all there was left of her. The box had heated up as the mist disappeared inside until it was so hot that Dalkey had dropped it back into the casket, his hands blistered. There was no smell or sound, just the green mist and the hot box.

Meryth had exchanged looks with him, clearly as terrified as he was. When Meryth asked him what they should do next,

Dalkey had handed him a pad of paper and a pen and told the man to write down what he'd seen when they opened the casket.

Now General Stubin Dalkey looked at the pages on the desk next to the box and smiled. He had an eyewitness account. It was a comfort not being the only one who believed. Jubilant that there was no longer a body, he could now prove the wonderful doctor and celebrated blade fighter had been in cahoots with aliens. The reason for her sudden illness and death was still a mystery. The important thing was that the body had "disappeared" into the box he now had on his desk.

What did the box really contain? Should he open it? Could he even open it? Visually, there was no indication of a lid or seam anywhere on the box. It had burned him every time he'd touched it with his bare hands. He wore thick synthetic gloves now as he picked it up again to examine it. Even with the gloves, he could not open the box. Curiously, it did not emit heat or burn unless touched with bare hands. It was truly something of alien manufacture. But who could he tell? Who would believe him, even with Private Meryth's written account? He'd have to think about that, but he had lots of time to think.

He wondered how long it would take for the locals to notify that so-called sheriff of the grave robbery and how long it would then take to connect General Stubin Dalkey to the act and find him. He smiled again as he congratulated himself on his obscure hiding place. He thought it would take weeks before anyone would even think of looking for him in the ruins of the medical center—if they ever thought to look there at all. That infuriating sheriff would have been an infant when Dalkey had first been in the valley, twenty years ago. The sheriff would never make the connection, and soon this minor incident would all be forgotten and the valley residents would go back to living their boring little lives. Then Dalkey would leave unnoticed and show his superiors the box and explain once again why they shouldn't ignore him. He smiled and set the box down, giving it a pat. It would prove he was right about aliens invading Teramar.

CHAPTER NINETEEN

The tavern had just opened when Taryn stepped into the cool, dimly lit interior.

Melli had kicked him out of the house saying, "She doesn't need the two of you hovering over her. You can take turns. Taryn, you leave now. Go for a walk, a drive—anything except stay here. Go see how Mroz is. She'll be fine."

So Taryn left after making sure Renloret knew he'd be back, that he'd always be there for Ani. Renloret had been holding her hand to his forehead, whispering in his native language. It had sounded apologetic, so Taryn had let well enough alone.

"Good eve, Taryn," Mroz said, greeting the sheriff with a nod. "The usual?"

"Have I gotten predictable, Mroz?" Taryn slipped off the black jacket and hung it over the back of the chair before he sat.

"Let's see," Mroz said. He paused to count on his fingers two and a half times over both hands. "Yup. Saltren gin, a dash of cinnamon, on the cold stuff. When you do come in—and that is as predictable as your drink choice, except for today—you have the same thing." He was already shaking in the brown spice. It glinted darkly against the golden yellow of the gin. Mroz dropped in three ice cubes, shuddered the glass to settle them, and slid it to Taryn. The tavern's lighting accentuated the beginnings of a marvelous bruise around the cut on the sheriff's cheek.

"How's Ani?" Mroz asked.

"All right, I guess. Renloret really does care for her." Taryn swirled the ice cubes, watching the patterns change in the cinnamon, remembering how close Renloret sat to the edge of the bed, holding her hand and whispering in that incomprehensible language of his. Taryn hesitated, then swallowed half of the drink. It burned its way to his stomach. He shook off the shiver. "He hasn't left her side since we got her to my parents' house. She's still in shock, but at least she's conscious now. I don't think she'll do anything while he's with her. She got pretty quiet after we told her what happened and who hit her. She still hasn't said anything, just nods every other sentence." He looked at Mroz. "How are you?"

"Outside of a rude ending to what started out to be a positive morn, I'm fine. That's a beaut of a bruise you're gonna have." He put a few cubes of ice in a bar towel and handed it to Taryn.

Taryn put the cold pack on his cheek and thanked him.

Mroz leaned over the counter. "I've been thinking about his reaction. It's like he didn't know who she was until he saw the headstones."

"I didn't notice. I was a bit occupied at the time." Taryn swallowed the other half of the drink. He ignored the burn and shiver that followed, remembering holding her next to her mother's grave—again.

"He was in a state of shock, himself, when he figured out she was 'the' Anyala Chenak. Do you suppose she didn't tell him?" Mroz asked.

"Probably. She doesn't mind winning, she just never liked being in the spotlight. That military commander pressured her into training at the university even though her mother was ill. To fulfill that commitment she missed the last year of her mother's life. She'll never forgive them or herself for going along with it." He set the towel on the counter and offered his glass to Mroz.

The bartender added more gin and cinnamon to the glass and handed it to Taryn, who finished it in one swallow—no shiver.

"How're you doing?" Mroz asked as he rinsed and dried a glass.

Taryn shrugged. "I've lost the love of my life to a stranger from another land. A crazy general is pestering the valley. Someone has spirited away a body from its grave and aliens have supposedly landed again." He stared at the glass, wishing it were full. "Normal for Star Valley, wouldn't you say?"

"Not exactly, Taryn. It could be worse." Mroz grabbed a clean cloth from under the counter and began wiping moisture off the bar. "The aliens could be real." They shared a chuckle.

"Did you hear how he pronounced her mother's name?" Mroz asked.

"No, I was concentrating on her, not how some Southerner pronounces a name."

"It was sort of disconnected and I got to thinking that the names on his list were written phonetically to his way of pronouncing them. That's why we only recognized those two surnames. I want to sit down with that list again and listen to how he says them."

"You might be right. The Southern accent is different." Taryn lifted his empty glass and tipped it to the bartender. Another drink might help.

Mroz shook his head. "You don't need any more. You need to think about all this. It's your job—start doing it, Sheriff."

Taryn set the glass down.

"I'd suggest you put that badge of yours back on and take a few steps away from the personal side. You need to talk to Renloret. He knows a lot more than we all think he does."

"What do you mean?" Taryn sat straighter and reflexively brought out his notebook and pen. The tone of Mroz's voice had awakened the sheriff in him.

"That's more like it." Mroz continued to wipe down the bar with a smile on his face.

"Well?" Taryn had his pen ready.

"He asked about a green crystal blade, but he's more interested in finding this woman with a young daughter, right?"

"Yeah, so? We don't have anyone like that in Star Valley or in Sweetwater Creek. I checked."

"We did twenty years ago."

Taryn leaned over the counter. "What are you getting at?"

"Just that maybe he's looking for Shendahl and Anyala," Mroz said.

"But . . ." Taryn stopped. He held up a hand to keep Mroz quiet while he thought. Twenty years ago he'd just turned five. The raid on the research center had happened after accusations that alien experimentation was the source of the medical breakthroughs instead of the true research being conducted. So many people, including his father, had been injured or killed in that raid. Anyala's father was presumed dead, though his body had never been found, leaving Shendahl alone with a five-year-old daughter.

What about the blade? Why would someone from Southern know about it? It had been a personal gift from Shendahl to Ani after her continental championship. Then Ani had insisted that the blade be buried with Shendahl. Where was the blade? He was sure he'd have noticed the long black box if it'd been there. He'd put it there himself just before Ani's uncle had secured the glass cover. Had it been taken with the body? He hit the counter with his hand.

"Taryn?" Mroz asked, jumping at the sudden slap.

"Thanks, Mroz. For some reason, that makes sense. I've got to check the grave site for the blade and then have a talk with Renloret." Taryn put the notebook in his pocket, grabbed his jacket, and hurried out the door, heading to the cemetery, then back to his parents' house.

Once back at his parents' house, Taryn paused to dust off the traces of dirt from his knees and hands before stepping into the house. "Father? Mother? I'm back." His mother came from the kitchen, drew him into her embrace, and kissed him on the cheek. "How is she?" he asked, eyeing the stairs.

"They've been quiet since you left. I assume they're fine." Melli lead the way up the stairs, to Taryn's old room. She knocked softly and when she got no reply, she opened the door.

The midday light snuck through the crack in the middle of the heavy curtains to fall softly across the two forms snuggled on the bed. Taryn saw a hand rise and wave in acknowledgment of his arrival. He quickly buried the impulse to charge in and pull the Southerner away from Ani. Mroz was correct that he should think like a sheriff instead of a spurned lover.

Renloret untangled himself and glanced back at Ani, who appeared to be sleeping. The three went downstairs and Melli left the two men in the front room with a warning look at her son.

They stood on opposite sides of the room, silent, eyeing each other. Melli returned with a tray of fruit and two mugs of cinnamon tea. Shaking her head she said, "Sit down, both of you. It's been a harrowing morn. You've both done what you needed to do. She's asleep now. So talk. Help each other. Help her. She needs both of you working together to solve *this* mystery first, before you help Renloret with his search." Then she turned and left the room.

"Good, she left," Taryn said as he took a seat and reached for a mug. Renloret followed. Taryn jumped straight to the impossible. "Ani's the little girl you're looking for, isn't she?" Saying it aloud made it less scary, more reasonable, more controllable.

Renloret nodded with a surprised look on his face. "She's supposed to be about five, not a grown woman." He glanced toward the staircase.

"How is that possible?" Taryn asked.

"I don't know," Renloret admitted. "Keep an open mind."

Taryn nodded in response and let him continue.

"It has to be a time shift of some sort. That could even account for the crash."

"The crash?" Taryn asked, skipping over the time shift comment.

"Yes, I crashed my ship in the canyon above Ani's cabin."

"Oh, hells. He was right," Taryn said.

"Who?"

"General Stubin Dalkey, of all people, was right. There *was* a crash on the Chenak property." Suddenly he didn't want to think about the implications. "Wait, wait, wait. Let's start at the beginning. As the sheriff, I need all the facts and I don't want to prejudge you or the reasons you're here. I'm less critical than some, so don't spare me and don't lie." He hoped that would be enough to get the Southerner, if he *was* from Southern, talking.

Renloret took a deep swallow of the tea and winced. Taryn knew it burned all the way down. Renloret twisted the cup, appearing to gather courage. He finally looked up and leaned across the table, his expression earnest.

"My people are dying. This plague kills women during pregnancy or within a sun-cycle after they give birth. It took us almost a decade to understand that it affects only women. Our search for a cure led us beyond our boundaries. One of our teams was sent to Northern. Their efforts to maintain a degree of secrecy was marred by government interference that resulted in only one member of the team coming home. It is my understanding that he returned with research pointing to his five-sun-cycles-old daughter as being a possible cure. There was also the fact that her mother was still alive when he left and in good health. Once the child is returned home, the research will be verified and a vaccine prepared. Without this child, my people will be unable to propagate within one generation. We will become extinct."

"I have a few questions," Taryn said. He was trying to put the information into some type of order. "First, is a *sun-cycle* equivalent to a year?"

"Sorry," Renloret said. "I forget some of the terms you use. I apologize for making this more difficult. Yes, a sun-cycle is equivalent to a year." He twisted his cup again and took another swallow.

"Second, beyond your boundaries? How far beyond? Surely Southern's medical community can find a cure. Why haven't they contacted us?"

Taryn noted the hesitation from Renloret.

"Farther than you imagine. And the only medical community that knows about this is one your government doesn't approve of or believe in," Renloret said softly. He glanced at the door to the kitchen.

"Okay, but why were you chosen?" Taryn could see the pilot was uncomfortable revealing so much. But he also knew Renloret understood that revealing so much was necessary to solve the multiple problems before them.

"The Stone chose me."

"The Stone?" Taryn asked. He was now totally confused.

"They're our leaders, for lack of a better explanation you'd understand or accept. I didn't think I was qualified for such an important mission, but the Stone insisted. I had to accept. It was supposed to be a simple in and out. I wasn't supposed to have any contact with natives. We were not to attract any attention or disrupt your world in any way. We planned to be back before the plague could progress beyond recovery."

Taryn studied the man on the other side of the table. He knew Renloret was not lying and also knew there was a lot more not being said. Rocks as rulers? Natives? A reference to Northern as "your world"? And if a plague of some sort was threatening any part of Teramar's population with extinction, surely everyone, no matter where they resided, would have known about it, wouldn't they? He decided to work on all those questions later. "Okay, I can accept that on principle. So, if Ani is supposedly this little girl, explain to me how you arrived more than twenty years later."

Renloret abruptly stood, running his hand through his hair again, looking everywhere except at Taryn. "I cannot. That is what has been bothering me. Little signs have been telling me time is different here and I don't know why. It shouldn't be. At most, it took us less than one moon-cycle to get here. She should still be a little girl if her parents are S'Hendale and Yenne Chenakainet."

"Mroz was right. It's the way you pronounce the names that's so different, but I can hear them as we say them. Shendahl and Yenne Chenak. Mroz said he wanted to listen to how you said the names and compare them with how we might. He's the one who suggested that Ani and her mother are the pair you're looking for. But neither of their names was on your list. Why?"

"Shendahl traveled under an assumed name to escape her own mother's plans—but that's a long story to be told much later or not at all. I was not told which name she used once they landed, so I figured she kept the alias. Commander Chenakai—Chenak— was alive on Lrakira when I left him one moon-cycle ago."

"Her father is alive?" Now that was news worth hearing.

However, if he'd understood the pilot, there was another problem. "*On* Lrakira?" All the hells, did he really want to know?

"Yes, on Lrakira." Renloret nodded in seeming defeat.

Taryn sighed. It was almost too much too quickly. "I do know my geography and no place on Teramar has a name remotely similar to Lrakira. So he's not *on* Teramar, is he?" He kept his voice soft, knowing his parents were trying to listen in from the other room. He was trying not to judge, but the only answer didn't make sense. And he knew he didn't want it to.

"No."

Taryn stood up, resolved to face the impossibility laid before him. So the pair in the kitchen couldn't hear, he whispered, "So I guess what you're trying so hard not to tell me is that General Dalkey was right again. Ani's parents were involved with . . . aliens." He paused to digest the word. "I can't believe I just said that." He rubbed his forehead.

"Not just involved with aliens. They *are* the aliens."

"They're aliens?" Now Taryn sat down. "Aliens? They didn't look like aliens." A thought crossed his mind. "Are *you* an alien?"

"Yes. I promised not to lie, Taryn. I am sorry."

"But you don't look like an alien. You look just like us. Anyway, you don't have tentacles, or extra eyes, or scales or . . ." He coughed, embarrassed. "Look, this isn't getting us anywhere on the current problem. If we all look alike, I'll have to accept that. And we won't be able to tell the difference between us and the others."

"Let me clarify. We don't look like all aliens. Some do have tentacles, scales—some even have wings. But this instance, where two worlds so far apart have nearly the identical bi-pedal populations, is very rare. I can't even imagine how rare. I suppose that's one reason why Teramar was chosen as a possible planet for a cure. Don't ask me why we're so alike. I don't have the answer. I was not supposed to have contact with anyone except the rescue crew. Imagine my surprise when I first saw Ani—who was the first person from Teramar I laid eyes on."

"Does Ani know?" Taryn asked.

"That I'm an alien? No." Renloret shook his head.

Taryn smiled and sat back in the chair. "That's gonna be a problem isn't it?"

Renloret nodded. "I'm working on how to tell her. My intuition says right now is not the best time. Plus I need to recover S'Hendale's remains and the blade, if possible, in order to verify Ani's identity. So could we get on with doing that first? Then I can work on telling her why I'm here . . . and that she has to go back with me."

"Renloret, that's another problem. How are you going to return? We don't have a *spaceship*. We have some high altitude aircraft and Southern just launched some satellites, but that's about it."

"I will cross that chasm when I need to. Lrakira may have been notified of the crash with the distress beacon by now, so another ship could be on its way."

"A beacon? Could that have been the signal General Dalkey was talking about?" Taryn took out his notepad and starting writing.

"I do not know. When I got close to Teramar I sent a special transponder signal and received an answering one, so I would know where to land. You were not supposed to be able to detect the signal—not for several decades at least. That was just before the crash."

Taryn kept writing. "Apparently, several decades have passed. But here's the deal, Renloret, let's solve one problem at a time. Let's get the scum who stole Shendahl's body and the blade first. Then you and I can explain things to Ani and start looking for a way to get you off my planet. We obviously have to adjust for the time problem a bit. But with luck, all will be well anyway."

"You're being awfully good about this. Why?" Renloret asked with a frown.

"I guess I have a bigger imagination than most," Taryn replied, "and, well, I guess I've always thought there was something else out there. We can't be the only ones. That doesn't make sense. Life is so varied here on Teramar, why couldn't there be other planets with life of some sort?" He rubbed his chin. "Outside of that, a crime happened at the cemetery and I'm the sheriff, so I'm going to solve it. In reality, it doesn't matter to me if it involves aliens or real people."

"We're all real people, Taryn. We usually *look* a bit different, though here on Teramar that's another mystery to solve later." Renloret drained his cup and stood.

"Agreed. Let's go back to the cemetery and do some looking around. Mroz thinks he knows who did it, and with the information you supplied, I think I do too. Mother and Father can keep an eye on Ani. She won't go too far. They'll let us know if she tries to leave."

Renloret headed for the door. "I want to check on her one more time. Her blood is the key. I cannot lose her or I will lose any chance to save my people."

Taryn watched Renloret finger the clear crystal-like shards that remained of the casket lining before tossing them out onto the piles of dirt.

"I can't believe this," Renloret whispered. "This is a burial stasis unit."

"A what?" Taryn jumped into the grave.

"I didn't know this planet was so advanced." Renloret tossed another handful of shattered crystal out of the grave.

"So advanced? It's just the glass lining Reslo had made."

Renloret stopped and turned to Taryn. "Who made this 'lining'?"

Taryn tried to step back but the dirt sides of the grave held him. "Reslo Chenak. He's Anyala's uncle, her father's brother."

"Stones! No one bothers to tell the pilot anything. Just a simple rescue mission. Fly in, wait for everyone to be picked up, fly out. No one sees us. No one on Teramar knows how important the girl is. No one knows, no one tells anyone anything—least of all the pilot. Me!" He glared at Taryn. "Least of all me!" He jumped up to sit on the edge of the grave.

Taryn considered asking questions and taking notes but decided letting him rant was too interesting to interrupt it. So much could be learned by letting people vent. He nodded in sympathy, encouraging Renloret to continue.

"The child is a woman. Her mother is dead." He indicated the empty casket with upturned hands. "The body is gone. The blade is gone." He ran both hands through his hair. He turned glazed eyes on Taryn. "The child is a woman. How can I be so late? She's supposed to be a little girl, not that woman. What's happened on Lrakira? Is there anyone left to save?"

Silence wrapped around them as Taryn joined the pilot on the side of the grave. They stared at the broken, empty casket for several minutes.

"There are reasons, Renloret. It's all connected, but I don't know how. Let's solve the most obvious problem first."

Renloret nodded.

Taryn placed a hand on the pilot's shoulder. "I've got one question before we continue. Why did Reslo's name set you off?"

"I let my frustration show. I apologize. It was not the actual name, it was the connection. He is the commander's brother, which no one from Lrakira seemed to think I might need to know. Reslo—or rather Reschlo—is a short name for R'schlonick, which is one of the names on the list. I did not have a surname with that one. I agree with Mroz about pronunciation or dialect differences. With the exception of Anyala's parents' names, the names on my list were retrieved from files found on the ship after the crash. The rest of the team knew everything and they're both dead. I was only the pilot."

"I think you are much more than the pilot," Taryn said.

"I have to be now. I am not sure where to begin or how it will end."

Taryn squeezed his shoulder again. "Well, you *have* started and you're not alone." He jumped back into the grave. He held out his hand to the pilot. "Let's find Shendahl and the blade."

When Renloret took his hand, Taryn knew that they had sealed an unspoken bargain, and there was trust between them.

"You said you might know who did this," Renloret said.

"Yes, and you said this crystal lining was a funeral stasis chamber. Care to explain the stasis chamber part while we look for clues?" Taryn held up a forearm length of the glass-like material. The edges were deadly sharp. He could keep some of the larger pieces to add to his weapon arsenal. All they needed were grips and sheaths. He placed the sliver on the grass and bent to examine a piece of fabric caught on the edge of the casket. He carefully collected it and put it in his pocket.

"We have two different types of stasis chambers, essentially one for the living and one for the dead." Renloret picked up a small grey device from inside the casket and handed it to Taryn. "This one is specifically for the dead. That control node and the thickness of the crystal indicate a funeral stasis chamber. It keeps a body from decaying for decades or until the ceremony of passing is conducted."

"Ceremony of passing?" Taryn studied what looked like script on the thumb-size control node. Instructions? He put it in his pocket to study later.

Renloret turned to sift through the center of the casket, carefully lifting the silk burial robe. "I'll explain some other time."

"What exactly are you looking for?" Taryn asked.

"The blade box."

"It's not here. I already searched for it. You make the box itself sound more important than her body."

"It is, now." Renloret folded the robe reverently. "Perhaps I should explain the ceremony of passing now instead of some other time." Het held out the folded robe. "This tells me a passing has occurred."

"An empty burial robe? Maybe the robbers just wanted the body."

"No." He paused and stared at Taryn as if deciding what to say. "Well, maybe that's what they thought they wanted. If the stasis unit was unsealed and the blade was present, then a passing occurred. The only thing left to take from the casket would have been the box that contained the blade . . . because the body would no longer be available."

"*What?*" Taryn leaned against the edge of the casket not sure if he could take much more.

Renloret joined him. "Do you want me to continue?"

"I'm writing this down so I can read it later and know it was not my imagination. I'll keep it out of the official report."

Taryn pulled out his notebook and poised the pen expectantly.

CHAPTER TWENTY

"She's gone," Melli had said, and the look on her face had been one of pure defeat.

Renloret knew what that felt like. He was feeling pretty defeated himself at the moment. Somehow Ani had slipped out while he and Taryn had been at the grave site. But why? It appeared she'd gone out the window and down a tree that was just inches from the roof's edge. Why sneak off?

Gelwood and Melli were barely holding it together as they answered Taryn's questions. For his part, Taryn seemed to have stepped into the role of sheriff, jotting down notes as his parents relayed exactly what had happened. There wasn't much to tell. Ani had been safely ensconced in the upstairs bedroom and they hadn't heard a thing. He and Taryn had been gone no more than two bells and Melli had just gone to check on her when they returned. She'd run down the stairs in a state of panic as they walked through the door.

Now they all stood in the abandoned bedroom, just trying to figure it out.

Melli, who had been pulling at the twisted braid of her hair in an absent sort of way, seemed to come to life. "Oh, hells, Taryn! She must have figured it out. She knows, Taryn. She's going to kill him this time."

"Kill who, Melli?" Renloret stepped close and turned Melli toward him so he could study her face.

"Dalkey," Taryn whispered. He seemed confident.

Melli and Gelwood nodded in agreement.

"Come on, we've got to find her." Taryn turned and ran down the stairs, not bothering to see if any of them followed.

Renloret paused and hugged Melli and Gelwood. "We'll find her. If you find out where she might have gone or see her, contact Taryn."

They both nodded and Melli pushed him to the stairway. "Go."

There were no signs of anything unusual at the house when they arrived but the place seemed eerily quiet except for Kela's growling and scratching at the back door. Kela was clearly concerned; his claws had done a significant amount of damage. Renloret was happy he knew where the back door key was hidden. Kela dashed through as soon as the door was cracked open. The two men followed him into the front room. A desk drawer near the window hung open and its contents were scattered across the floor and desk top. Kela paused, nosing through the piles of small office items. Then he turned to look at the fireplace. Taryn followed the canine's gaze and cursed.

"She has the sword."

Taryn snatched the remaining larger weapon out of its brackets. "Do you know how to use one of these?"

"Yes, though I am better with the hand blade." He held his hand out.

Taryn tossed it across the couch hilt first. "Did you know she's a champion in hand blade and sword? Not that it matters, of course, but she should be considered extremely dangerous."

Renloret hefted the well-balanced masterpiece with an awed expression on his face. "I have never held a weapon of this caliber. I am honored. Is there a scabbard?"

Taryn opened a panel to the left of the fireplace, retrieving a scabbard and several smaller blades, which he laid out on the table. He tossed the scabbard to Renloret and removed his jacket to buckle two of the small blades to his arms.

"Do you think she knows where that Dalkey fellow is?" Renloret asked as he peered into the compartment that had yielded the weapon supply, opening and closing the panel several times. "Intriguing storage unit." He came back to the table and surveyed the remaining blades.

Pointing at a small handle, Taryn pressed one of the designs carved into the ivory-colored bone. Renloret jumped back as a narrow metallic double-edged blade sprang out of the tip. The sheriff touched a different pattern and the blade disappeared. "It takes getting used to, but it is quite formidable, especially in close quarters." He rolled up his sleeve, baring a similar weapon strapped to the inside of his left forearm, the blade-end just above his wrist. "Ani wears her flick-blades so she can open them as she throws. Be glad she's not wearing them."

"How do you know she's not wearing them?" Renloret asked.

"That's one and the other is on the shelf in the closet." Taryn tipped his head toward the hidden panel.

"How'd you know where to find these?"

"Our families are very close." Taryn turned a serious face to the pilot. "It was also the first place she went after her mother's funeral. She almost got away from me then, intent on killing Dalkey, though he didn't know it. By that time he was under guard and safely on his way to the psychiatric ward. I agree with Melli and Gelwood. She's figured out who took her mother's body and the blade." He headed for the door. "I just hope we can catch her before she catches Dalkey. He won't survive."

Kela barked at the men and they turned their attention to him. Kela tugged on the heavy rug between the couches, and Renloret rolled the carpet to the side with Taryn's help. Then Kela scratched at a particular place on the floor. The sheriff knelt and ran his fingers across the intricate patterns laid bare by the removal of the rug.

"Hmm, I didn't know about this." He stared accusingly at the dog. "Sometimes I really think you understand us. This is a shortcut to the cabin, isn't it?"

"What are you talking about? What shortcut?" Renloret asked.

Kela wagged his tail and pawed at the floor again. Taryn chuckled and pressed on three of the inlaid dark wood pieces. "This design is a copy of a puzzle game we used to play when we were children. It had something to do with secret passages and buried treasure." A handle popped up. Taryn stood and pulled on it. "I'll bet you anything this will lead us to Ani." Several sections of the flooring dropped downward and slid out of the way. He laughed. "Well, well. Stairs."

Kela brushed past him and disappeared into the hole. Taryn started down after the canine and Renloret followed on his heels.

The faint light from the room above them ceased as they neared the bottom of the stairway and the floor panel closed automatically. Taryn cursed.

Renloret smiled and said, "Lights."

Soft lighting appeared at shoulder height, evenly spaced following the curving path of the stairs. Taryn's call of thanks echoed back as he double-stepped the stairs. Renloret touched the handrail for balance and followed the canine and sheriff.

The stairs emptied out to a large oval landing. Another set of stairs rose on the left. A barred door scowled at the pair as Renloret joined Taryn. Renloret estimated they were at least one hundred feet below the house. The lighting remained steady and the air supply did not lessen. The sheriff squatted, peering intently at the floor, but Kela was nowhere in sight.

"Where's . . ." Renloret stopped the question as Taryn pointed to the slight disturbances in the dust.

"He almost took the hallway but changed his mind and went through the door." Taryn shook his head as he studied the barred exit. "Now how'd he do that?"

"More secrets?" Renloret asked.

"Every family has secrets and even the best of friends don't know them all," Taryn replied. "I didn't know Ani's family was from another planet, so I shouldn't be surprised, now, to learn new things about them."

"Don't forget that Ani doesn't know either," Renloret said as he ran his hands over the doorjamb. His attention was drawn to the dusty residual paw prints on the surface of the door itself. He laughed. "Hah, a method used by my family to secure certain areas. It's based on an optical illusion designed to keep people from going through the door in either direction." He shoved at the door below the bar and it swung away. "But in reality, it still allows us access to the other side while appearing to be blocked."

He ducked low and entered. Taryn followed. The low door swung shut without a sound, cutting off the light once again.

"Lights," Renloret said again, expecting illumination to appear at his command.

"It's still dark," Taryn said.

Renloret could hear the sheriff shuffling around, evidently trying to find a switch or something to ignite the lights.

The pilot snorted. "Lights," he said again, louder.

"Still dark."

"Shut up. *You* try."

"If there's not a switch on the wall and a verbal command doesn't work, then how are we expected to turn them on?"

They both flinched and covered their eyes as the area was flooded with light.

"Very funny," Renloret said. "Try turning them off."

Darkness once again surrounded them.

"Funny indeed. Cover your eyes," Taryn said. "On." Light blazed hotly. "Off." Blackness blanketed them. "On."

"Stop that, Taryn. It's too bright." After thinking a moment, he said, "Dim," and the intensity lessened to a tolerable level.

"All right, now what?" Taryn asked.

The space was actually a hall with Kela's paw prints in the dust, showing the way. They shared a shrug and turned to follow Kela's trail, chasing a series of echoing barks.

The frantic canine brought them to a halt. They watched Kela as he prowled between a pair of doors, sniffing at the minute cracks at the bottom edge. He barked in frustration as he pushed against the lower panel of one of the doors.

"Did she go through that door?" Renloret asked.

Kela stopped pushing and shook his head. He sat and looked expectantly at Renloret.

"Why ask him?" Taryn asked. "There're no boot prints in the dust, never have been. Besides, he can't answer like that." He stepped to the other door and tried pushing on the lower section. It did not open.

"He just did," Renloret pointed out. "He's more intelligent than he looks." Renloret tried to formulate a question Kela could answer without telepathy.

Kela tipped his head and raised both eyebrows. He barked again, turned to push at the door he had chosen, and growled at the unmoving obstacle.

"Taryn, maybe it's stuck from disuse or something. Maybe we can get it loosened up if we lean on it together."

Taryn switched doors and joined Renloret. Their combined steady pressure did not swing it open. An unspoken decision caused them to change to a series of forceful shoulder lunges.

"If this . . . doesn't work . . . how're we going to get it . . . open?" Taryn said between each push.

Both men fell through. Kela dashed over their sprawled bodies to vanish into the pervading darkness and the door closed.

"Let me guess. Use a different password, like 'open,'" Taryn said drily.

The door opened and they both laughed.

"So, Renloret, do you have technology like this?"

"Motion sensors usually, but a lot of things can be attained through verbal commands. Research is being done on telepathic commands." He looked down the new hall as far as the light from the previous room illuminated it. Kela was gone again, no doubt ahead of them.

Taryn blocked the door with his body as it tried to close and ran his hands over the walls. He seemed to find what he was looking for and soft glowing yellow tubes at the floor and ceiling lit up the hall. Not too far down, the walls ceased to be a smooth prefabricated material, showing the rough surface of rock and earth. The vertical light tubes were spaced several paces apart until the curve of the hall hid them. The floor continued in a downward slope as well.

"Fascinating," Taryn said with a shake of his head.

"Seems the job is unfinished. Just the lighting was continued. Any idea who built this?" Renloret asked as he probed the clean division between natural rock and the prefabricated surface.

"Haven't a clue, Renloret. I could assume Ani's parents, but I know Ani doesn't know about this. This would have taken years to complete, so whoever did build it never told her. Otherwise we would have been exploring every bend and stairway as we grew up. Ani would have told me or I would have noticed a difference in travel timing between the lake house and wherever these go. She's too curious to keep stuff like this from me."

He pulled at Renloret's arm. "Come on. I don't know how or why, but Kela seems to know where these go and he's showing us the way. Let's go."

The air was noticeably cooler and damper as they passed into the raw stone and dirt tunnel. Renloret wondered how much longer the tunnel was and whether Kela was leading them to where Ani had gone.

They picked up the pace and ran.

CHAPTER TWENTY-ONE

The troop carrier was hidden amongst the trees. It was empty, as she thought it would be. By cutting the lid off the pressure valve, she disabled it. She hadn't been to the old research center since her father disappeared, twenty years earlier. And though time had softened the physical harshness of the explosions, she flinched as memories flooded back. The bitter smell of burning flesh, the concussions from explosions, the screeching of metal as the building's entranceway tore apart. It all rolled through her memory, again and again, in blinding clarity, as if happening all over again.

The debilitating fear of loud, sudden noises had kept her from serving in the active military. She shook her head to clear it, demanded her racing heart to slow, and concentrated on breathing as she leaned against the troop carrier. Its presence had proved her hunch, however unlikely. The stolen body and blade were somewhere in the wreck of the research center. Ani didn't know why she knew she'd find them there, she just did.

She didn't remember what had awakened her and galvanized her to escape the safety of Gelwood's and Melli's home. She had used the window and tree to leave without notice, like she had so many times to make late night visits to Taryn. Running the miles to the lake house had not calmed her.

The sword had practically leapt into her hand when she reached for it. It would be fitting to use the championship sword to regain her mother's body and the green crystal blade. Ani knew who had them, but where they were had been the unknown. Out of frustration she decided to go to the least likely place—the research center where her father had died. It had been almost a shock to see the transport parked amongst the rubble at the entrance.

Kela's incessant thought-questing was a major distraction and Ani had to split her concentration between keeping him out of her head and focusing on her mission. She knew she'd slipped several times but didn't know when or what information he'd gleaned from the slivers of her thoughts. She brushed aside his attempts to dissuade her and built a mental wall, closing him out, though his presence lingered.

She had locked the doors of the house and covered her exit in case Taryn came looking. He would come, but he would not know where she'd gone and would be hours behind her. There would be plenty of time to show General Stubin Dalkey exactly how thieves should be dealt with. She smiled, her breathing now smooth and deep, the memories hidden once again. Pushing off the carrier, she entered the shattered lobby of the building to begin her search.

"Tunnel ends," Taryn whispered as he skidded to a stop and flattened his back to the stone wall. After a few breaths of silence he nodded at Renloret to move into the huge room.

A brief survey showed it empty. The pilot was smiling as he walked directly to the console with keyboards and screens along the opposite wall. He lay the sword down, pulled out a chair, and began tapping on one of the keyboards. He seemed familiar with the instruments. Taryn still hesitated at the edge of the tunnel until Renloret waved him in.

Taryn made it to the middle and looked up. His jaw dropped as he took in the height of the room. Few buildings in Northern's largest cities were as tall. It must exit near the top of Keshler Peak. He brought his attention back to the depths of his location as the alien pilot's mutterings rose to a round of now familiar curses Taryn remembered from the cemetery.

Renloret slammed a fist on the console and Taryn could see some small lights flicker.

"Work! I need you to work!" The flickers brightened and became steady. The screen in front of Renloret glowed fuzzily, slowly resolving itself to some type of text. A relieved look settled on the pilot's face. "Yes. Now let's see what happened here."

Taryn moved to stand behind the pilot. He watched Renloret's fingers fly over the switches, diodes, and large keyboard with two sets of keys—one familiar to every Northerner, the other filled with unrecognizable symbols. Renloret concentrated on the larger, unfamiliar keys. The screen rapidly flipped between graphs and text.

"What is the current date?" Renloret asked as he focused on the screen in front of him.

Taryn stumbled mentally. It was not a question he expected. "Uh, twenty-three Hutia 1024."

"You are sure?"

"Of course."

Renloret straightened and pointed to the screen. "The last time this launch tower was used was 35 Leigha 1009."

"That's the same date on her father's headstone," Taryn whispered.

Renloret nodded. "So what does that tell you about Anyala's father?"

"He didn't die on Teramar?" Taryn answered.

"He didn't die at all, Taryn. He returned to Lrakira over one moon-cycle ago. At the meeting, the commander said his five-sun-cycles-old daughter was the cure, and the medical team was testing a vaccine on one of the two female crew members. I'm assuming it was not Shendahl because she had already survived the birth of Anyala. Commander Chenakainet had most of the notes with him but not any of the results of those tests. After reading the notes, it was agreed that my people will be virtually extinct within one generation without his daughter's blood. I need to find her alive and take her home to Lrakira."

The enormity of the pilot's mission finally clicked for Taryn. "But she's not five, is she?"

Renloret turned around and leaned against the console. "No, she's a very grown-up *twenty*-five. Oh, Stones, how can I be twenty years late? Where is she, Taryn?"

The sheriff turned a critical eye to the walls of the launch tower, or whatever it was. A door was ajar. He moved to examine the jamb. Several canine hairs were caught in the door frame. "Well, Kela went through here," he said.

Renloret nodded. "I think he is leading us to her."

They slipped through the door and found themselves at the bottom of a stairway.

As they stepped upward, Taryn whispered, "I agree with you about Kela. Sometimes I think he can understand every word we say. But I wish Kela could talk."

The sound of a door closing several flights above them brought three fingers to two pairs of lips, each hushing the other. They backed up close to the wall and listened intently.

"It's just another stairway, General."

"There's more to this stupid research center than I imagined, and I was here for over a year. It must be built halfway into the mountain. Yes, more than enough room to hide a couple of aliens and a spacecraft, Private. And don't contradict me after what you witnessed. Plus, I know what I saw twenty years ago. There's plenty of time to explore more thoroughly. The locals will never consider looking here. Right now I'm hungry." Boots scraped and the voices disappeared.

In the silence, Taryn raised his eyebrows in recognition of the second voice. He whispered, "General Stubin Dalkey. I thought so."

Renloret nodded in agreement. "What did he mean by 'twenty years ago'?"

"When we find him we'll have to ask, I guess," Taryn said.

They continued moving up the stairs until they reached a landing where the door was not quite latched closed. Light showed through the cracks. Voices blurred and echoed metallically from the other side, fading farther and farther away until there was no sound.

The pair eased through the door. The hall was well lit. Taryn studied the sign next to the door, which showed a simple graphic of a stair set with unfamiliar symbols above and below. Pointing to them, he raised questioning eyebrows at Renloret.

"The top line says 'launch tower.' The bottom says 'control room.'"

Taryn leaned against the wall, his knees weak. "I'm still having trouble believing all this alien business." He tipped his head toward the sign. "Rakian words?"

"Lrakiran," Renloret replied, correcting him. He placed a firm hold on Taryn's shoulder. "It will be all right. We just have to find her, the crystal blade, and another ship. Then you can pretend this never happened."

"Sure, not a thing to worry about," Taryn muttered. "Just find a grief-crazed girl I've known my entire life, who's really an alien, who's going to kill an insane general who's stolen her mother's body and blade from the cemetery. Then help locate and use a spaceship to get them home to a planet I shouldn't know exists so they can save an entire alien race, which, by the by, looks exactly like us."

"Yes, it is simple when you say it straight," Renloret said as he squeezed Taryn's shoulder in sympathy before edging down the hall. "Just one Stone, one blade, and one fight at a time."

Taryn followed. "Is that some sort of advisory saying on your planet?"

"Yes."

"Sounds reasonable, but I don't know about the rock part."

Renloret grinned at the Teramaran sheriff. "I'll explain when there's not quite so much at stake."

"Okay," Taryn said, "but I want to hear you explain all of this to her." He grinned at Renloret, then pointed down the hall. "Let's find your wayward little girl."

A sign on the wall showed them what direction led to the cafeteria, and since the general had mentioned he was hungry, they headed in that direction.

Two turns later Renloret pointed to the double doors on the right side of the hall. "That should be the cafeteria."

They bent low, took positions on either side of the door, and peeked in the head-high windows.

General Stubin Dalkey sat alone at a table on a low stage with several bowls of food arranged in front of him. He was heaping his already full plate with a pale yellow mash. A line of uniformed men waited for him to finish. When he set the bowl down they moved forward to take much smaller servings onto their plates. They scattered about the room, sitting in companionable groups, leaving their commander to eat in solitude.

Taryn whispered, "They must be using the center's kitchen to prepare the meals."

"Where are they getting the supplies?" Renloret asked.

"Most likely brought in with the troops," Taryn said. "Dalkey seems to have planned a longer stay than I thought or he let on. That indicates trouble for the entire valley."

"How so?"

"Dalkey won't be able to keep all these men here for too many days. They'll be itching to move about and mix with the locals. So far, I've heard no rumors as to their presence in the valley, but then, I don't think anyone would have thought of using the research center as a base." He snapped his fingers. "That's why Kela led us here. He knew where they were."

"Where is Kela now?"

They shared concerned looks.

"He'll show up when we least expect him," Taryn said. "He has a knack of knowing when people need the interruption."

"That is so true," Renloret said, blushing.

Taryn chuckled. Apparently the pilot knew from personal experience, and Taryn could imagine what the nature of that personal experience might have been. He peeked into the cafeteria again. "Looks like the general has something to say. Shall we listen?"

"Of course."

General Stubin Dalkey noisily cleared his throat a third time. The troops put down their utensils and turned to see what their commander had to say.

"I want to thank you for following orders on what most of you assume is an insane venture. However, I have definitive proof that aliens have been and are currently amongst us on Teramar's surface."

There was nervous laughter as the soldiers shared winks and head nods.

Renloret winked at Taryn and pushed the door open a crack and yelled, "What's your proof, sir?"

Taryn pulled his blade out of its boot sheath, glaring at Renloret's audacity. They waited for the clatter of chairs and rush of running boots. No one turned to see from where the voice had come.

"I don't see any aliens, sir," an anonymous voice said.

"Unless you're one of them," a voice from the nearest table said softly. The group nearest the double door smothered more laughter.

The general's face shaded in a flustered blush. "I have documented proof with this box." He held a long, narrow black box over his head in a gloved hand.

"If an alien is small enough to fit in that there box, we have nothin' to worry about, sir. You have obviously captured it already."

"That's it, Taryn," Renloret whispered, pointing at the box, which was a forearm in length, at least two palms wide, and a palm deep.

Taryn shifted to get a better view. "I recognize it from the funeral. Why's he holding it in a glove?"

"The Stones are very particular about their blade owners. I've heard many stories about how they defend themselves."

"The blades defend themselves?"

"I'll explain later."

Dalkey put the box down. "If you think this is an ordinary

box, come forward to examine it? You'll find it quite alien in nature. I realize my word alone, even if I am your commanding officer, will not convince you. Some must witness or experience this to understand what we are up against."

A wave of murmurs accompanied several men as they approached. The first reached to pick up the blade box.

"He stole that from my mother's grave."

All eyes turned to the kitchen at the back of the room.

"Damn the hells, it's Ani," Taryn hissed. "Let's go. Stay behind me and don't get in my way. Understand?"

Taryn pushed his way through the double door, pulling free a second blade from a sleeve sheath. Then he paused briefly to make sure the pilot was in a desirable position before edging along the left wall towards the kitchen, keeping his eyes on Ani.

Striding toward the general's table, she held the sword ready. Cold, metallic green eyes pinned the still cursing officer in place as the rest of the troops melted out of her way. Taryn eased around several of the tables, trying to get closer, and waved the troops toward the cafeteria door. Obeying the local sheriff over their commander, they moved efficiently past Renloret. Would they leave the premises or gather their courage and return to defend their commander? He hoped for the former but knew he needed to be prepared for the latter as he moved to one side of Ani.

"I've come to retrieve my mother's body," Ani said, her voice tight with anger. Her eyes never left the general's face as she maneuvered the box to the edge of the table with the sword. "Where is she?"

"There's no body, at least not anymore."

The sword slipped upward causing Dalkey to tip his head back, out of the way.

"You destroyed her body?" Ani's voice cracked and the sword trembled.

Dalkey winced as the tip nicked the flesh beneath his chin and a thin line of blood trailed down to be absorbed by his sweaty uniform collar.

"No, it just disappeared."

A terrible laugh came from Ani. "Disappeared?"

The sword squiggled another design; more blood seeped. Dalkey shut his eyes.

"A body doesn't just disappear. What did you do?" Ani asked.

Taryn found a small amount of respect for the general surfacing as he watched him stand firm under Ani's pointed inquiry. He was not sure he'd be able to stand still with that sword at his throat, though he would never have let her get that close in the first place.

"Where is the body?" Ani repeated, her voice twisting between anger and grief.

"It's in the box. I saw it disappear into the box."

Dalkey's watery eyes wavered away from Ani, and Taryn found himself eye to eye with the general.

"Sheriff, this is unacceptable treatment. I came here on an official assignment to examine an aircraft crash site, and you can see how I'm being treated." He cleared his throat and tried to maintain eye contact with the slow moving sheriff.

"I demand to—"

"You'll demand nothing, Dalkey," Taryn said as he kept his

eyes on the girl, knowing she was the more dangerous of the two in front of him. "No crash has been reported and you've had several days in which to verify one even occurred. Instead, you have entered a private home without permission *and* ransacked a grave. The item on the table was stolen from the casket of Miss Chenak's mother. It would appear that you stole it. It matters little to me what you think it contains. I know what's in the box because I watched Miss Chenak put a crystal blade in it. She placed the box under her mother's hands before the casket was sealed. The casket itself was not out of my sight from that moment until the last shovel of dirt covered it—after you tried to destroy it. You have no rights to either the box or the body. Now, as Miss Chenak has already asked, where is the body?" Did he really want to know? Probably not, but he was the sheriff and a crime had been committed. Hopefully, he could bring about a solution without anyone getting killed.

"I told you, it's in the box." Dalkey leaned toward the box but backed away again at the closeness of the sword tip.

"Show us." Taryn inched closer.

"It won't open," Dalkey said, spreading his arms to foolishly expose his chest to the sword.

A tear slid down her cheek as Ani asked, "What do you mean it won't open? You just said you saw the body go into the box. Did you cut it up? Burn it? How'd you fit her body in the box?" She blinked and flinched with each suggestion but she held the sword tip steady.

"I didn't do anything to the body. It just sort of dissolved into smoke and the smoke went into the box." Sweat was now pouring down the general's forehead.

"What kind of an idiot do you take me for, General? The body turned into smoke and entered a box that won't open? You're asking me to believe a simple stage trick?"

"It wasn't a trick, I swear. It just . . . changed," Dalkey said. Sweat trickled over his eyebrow and into his eyes. He blinked but kept his head still at the pressure from the sword tip. "Why would I lie about something like that?"

Taryn maintained his composure but realized that the general's comment about the body's disappearance had just supported the pilot's explanation of a passing. Strangely, rather than being troubled by this confirmation that there was, indeed, an alien presence on Teramar, he found himself feeling excited and curious.

Ani lowered the sword tip to General Dalkey's ribs. "You would lie for the same reason you lied about my mother protecting aliens or even being one herself."

Taryn sent Renloret a pained look. He wanted to get the general safely away from Ani's sword. He could not imagine what Ani's reaction was going to be when Renloret told her exactly who—and what—she was.

CHAPTER TWENTY-TWO

"Well?" Ani asked, her voice slipping upward to mania. "Even back then I was protecting you, they were up to something and it wasn't right." Dalkey's tongue wiped sweat off his upper lip.

"What? Who are you talking about?" Ani stepped back, the hysteria replaced by deadly calm. The sword tip remained aimed at his chest.

"Your parents."

For the first time, Ani took her eyes off the general. She looked at Taryn quizzically. "My parents? What do they have to do with this, outside of the fact you took my mother's body from her grave?"

"They kept taking your blood. They were sacrificing you to keep the aliens alive," Dalkey stammered.

She shook her head. "What are you talking about?"

"You were such a little thing back then. You couldn't have been more than five, but they used you anyway." He stepped to the side and the sword followed. He sighed but continued talking. "I overheard them talking about how important you were to their research. Just a few more tests and they'd have it all figured out as to why you were the cure. They said all they needed was your blood and everyone would live. They were going to send you away to a place called Rakia or something."

"Lrakira," Taryn said, pronouncing it correctly. Both Ani and Dalkey turned to look at him. He shrugged. "My mother once told me that was the name of the village in Southern near where your parents were from."

"There's no such place in Southern, you idiot. It's in another galaxy," Dalkey said in frustration as he tried to move toward the sheriff. He was halted with Ani's sword.

"Actually, General, the name of the village is Awarna, and it's in a small province called Lrakira," Taryn said, his voice confident.

"How come it's not on any map?" Dalkey challenged.

"How come Star Valley isn't on any map of Northern?" Ani asked, her smile deceptively sweet.

"She's got a point, General," Taryn said. "You'd have to get a very detailed local area map to find us. Have you ever seen a detailed area map of Southern? It's a big continent."

"But, but," Dalkey said, sputtering spit. Frustration darkened his face.

Ani waved the sword. "Back to the point. How do you know what my parents said when I was five?" The tip flicked out and blood beaded in a thin row just under Dalkey's nose.

"I was here, under orders from someone concerned about how

this no-name place was suddenly coming out with all sorts of breakthroughs in medicine and technology. It was disrupting other plans, ruining careers."

"Who ordered you to do what?" Ani asked.

"I gathered information—names and such. I had almost enough so he could bring the center down or get control of it when I overheard your parents. I realized they were doing all this research to keep aliens alive," Dalkey answered, skipping over who had done the ordering.

Taryn shook his head and stepped forward. "You thought aliens when it was a little village on Southern."

"I know what I heard," the general replied. His tongue flicked moisture from his lip again. "I told him everything. He didn't laugh at me. He told me to do whatever it took to stop the research. He sent in his private army."

"A private army?" Taryn asked. "So this group you're leading now isn't the continental army like you claimed?"

This time Dalkey grinned. "Oh this group is the real army. The private one didn't work out so well back then. He spent a lot of money and time convincing someone a bit higher up that any sort of contact with aliens was a threat to our planet. When the crash was detected, all he needed was someone who'd been here before. He chose me. Got me out of that hole of hells hospital, and here I am protecting you, again." He bowed his head to Ani. "I kept them from sending you away then, and I'll keep you from them now."

"You're avoiding the issue at hand," Taryn said. "Open the box and show us that what you've said is true. If the body is there or there's smoke inside, I might believe you. If it's only a blade, I'll let Anyala take care of you."

Ani grinned at that.

"I told you it won't open," Dalkey said with despair beginning to show in his voice.

The long sword blade flashed, taking everyone by surprise. Ani flipped the box off the table and into her left hand and had the sword point back at Dalkey's chest before a breath was taken.

"It'll burn your—"

"Burn my what?" Ani interrupted.

"Hands. It's too hot."

"Feels cool enough to me. How about you, Taryn?" She tossed it.

Taryn freed a hand by putting both blades together and caught the box, seemingly without problem.

"Burn my hand? I don't think so. It didn't last year at the funeral, why should it now?"

"But the blisters?" Dalkey mumbled as he started to raise a gloved hand. He gulped audibly and stopped as Ani shook her head and pressed the sword point into his shirt.

"Open it, Taryn," Ani ordered.

"As you wish, Champion," Taryn replied. He grinned as Dalkey flinched at the reminder of Ani's blade ring status.

Ani watched as Taryn pressed the box's corners rapidly, knowing he was aware that one particular series would actually trigger the mechanism.

The lid opened without further coaxing revealing a green crystal blade set in a silver pommel and grip. Light danced across the glyphs etched into the grip and the blade seemed to glow.

"Sorry, General, no body, no smoke," Taryn said. He smiled wickedly and placed the blade box on a table and rearmed both hands, just in case.

"They took your father," Dalkey said to Ani, evidently trying a different tact.

"What?" Ani asked.

"The aliens took your father when we stormed the center twenty years ago. They almost got you and your mother, but I caught up with her and took you. She had to come back. She wanted me to take her and let you go. I'll never forget what she said. 'Without Anyala, millions will die. Are you willing to accept that responsibility?'" He cleared his throat. "I'm not responsible for killing anyone. It's the aliens who've done the killing. I couldn't let them kill a little girl or my planet."

The sword shivered and Ani pressed her free hand to her forehead. "You were there? You were the one who kept us from following Father? You destroyed my family for your alien delusions!" Anger rose once again in her voice. "I remember the noise, the explosions ripping apart the building, and the people. You killed hundreds of good people, all because you thought aliens were on Teramar, here in Star Valley?"

Ani drifted off for a split second, memories of that day surfacing. Her sword tip wavered and Taryn called out to her, alarmed.

"Ani!"

Dalkey threw his large frame off the platform and scrambled toward the double doors to the hallway. His way was blocked as Renloret stepped in front of him, his boot blade held ready.

Renloret shook his head and gave Dalkey a tsk-tsk. "You kept a child from her parents?"

"I saved her life! Who are you?" Dalkey was clearly confused, having just noticed Renloret's presence in the cafeteria.

"It doesn't matter." He twirled the blade. Dalkey's eyes widened. "Let me get this straight. You kept Ani from joining her parents twenty years ago. You tried to break open her mother's coffin during the funeral last year. You dug it up yesterday and removed the contents. You say the body turned into smoke and entered the blade box, which you say burns your hands and won't open."

Dalkey nodded, the spinning blade holding his attention.

Ani was about to relieve Renloret of his momentary captive, intent on killing the general right then and there, when Taryn came up behind her and whispered in her ear, attempting to calm her. She kept her eyes and her attention on Dalkey and Renloret.

"I am inclined to agree with the sheriff," Renloret said. "I do not care what you think you saw or heard twenty years ago. You are in the wrong no matter which continent you are on. Would you like to see how we deal with your type in Southern?"

Dalkey held both hands palms up, showing that he was unarmed, as he edged toward the kitchen doors.

Renloret shoved his chin towards Dalkey. "Sheriff, I do believe he needs a blade. I don't kill unarmed beings."

"It's *my* family he's torn apart with his delusions," Ani said, her voice calm, her eyes on Dalkey. "If any killing happens, it'll be by this sword, for my mother's honor."

"As you wish, Champion," Renloret said. He saluted, Northern style.

Dalkey paled as he gingerly turned from Renloret to face her. Then his eyes shifted to the sheriff, still standing behind her. "Tell the man with the blade to step away and keep her away from me," he said, nodding towards Ani. "And I'll surrender to you."

"I think they're doing a fine job all on their own. Wrong move on your part and my job's over. No paperwork," Taryn said with a shrug of indifference.

"No problems explaining a general's maiming or death at the hands of a crazy girl?" Dalkey asked, incredulous.

"Crazy? Anyala?" Taryn scoffed. "Haven't you heard what the Southerner said? You even filed a false aircraft crash just to antagonize Miss Chenak on the anniversary of her mother's death. Do you call *that* sane?"

"I didn't file a false crash report. I was told to come and investigate a possible alien aircraft crash. Imagine my surprise at discovering it was on the Chenak property. My boss gave me all the authority I needed. Talk to *him* if you have problems."

"Oh, how convenient that someone else is responsible, not you," Taryn said. "Ani, Renloret, I want him alive."

"I don't think so. Sorry, Taryn." She kicked a table out of the way and jumped forward, a predatory gleam brightening her eyes.

Dalkey backed into the wall near the kitchen, again raising his hands high. "I'm unarmed," he said in protest.

"I was unarmed and five years old when you kept me from my father. You held a knife to my throat to get Mother to come back."

The fury in Ani's voice echoed into the hallway as she raised the sword.

Kela rushed past Renloret, throwing himself at Ani's body and knocking her to the floor as a beam of yellow light followed his dash from the double doors. It laced across the canine's back, scorching hair on its way. A second beam pierced the general's neck, searing the sword blade cuts. Stunned silence followed as the three people stared at Kela's still form. They ignored the decapitated general's slide to the floor.

Ani sobbed as she touched her companion's head, *Kela?*

Why didn't you just tell me where you were headed? I could've helped.

She wiped away a tear. *I had to do this myself. I couldn't endanger you.*

But you were in danger and he would have killed you. You must live. You . . . must return home.

I am home.

Kela tried to laugh in her head. *Not yet, but soon. Leave, now.* He whined in pain.

"I won't leave you," she whispered as she bent to examine the wound across his spine.

I'll heal. It's just a flesh wound. He rolled onto his stomach. *The hair will grow back in time. Give me a few moments. Go. You're still in danger. If you remain here he will kill you.*

Dalkey kill me? He is . . . was . . . no threat. She glanced at the body, more curious about the lack of blood than anything else.

Not Dalkey, someone else. Kela wobbled to a standing position.

Who?

I don't know. He was behind me in the hall.

"The hall. He was in the hallway," Ani said aloud.

"Yes, Kela came from there," Taryn said. He looked confused at the sudden change of events.

"The laser came from the hall, Taryn," Renloret said as he headed to the doors. "I can hear one set of footfalls. We should follow."

"Wait!" Ani stroked Kela.

No, you must go. I'll follow shortly. He pushed against her legs.

Taking his head between her hands, she kissed him between the eyes before joining Taryn and Renloret at the doors. A brief glance down the hall showed it to be clear, and the trio left the cafeteria in pursuit of the unknown.

CHAPTER TWENTY-THREE

Her chosen route quickly became a machine-bored tunnel with widely spaced light fixtures that brightened as she approached and dimmed after she passed. In one long stretch, she noticed the light dimming ahead of her. She was catching up.

The tunnel dumped her into a natural cavern. Puzzled at the sudden change in her surroundings, she turned to look at the artificially smoothed surface of the tunnel. Why hadn't she noticed this before? When had it been constructed? Was it an escape route? Had it been in use before or after the attack on the research center?

A shuffling sound interrupted her thoughts. Cursing, she turned, bringing up her blade. Too late. Jerking her head away from the flash of a blade saved her throat from being cut but her cheek stung as the edge nicked through the skin. She dropped to the ground and rolled toward the center of the cavern.

A shadow flitted between stalagmites. She looked ahead of the movement, saw that another tunnel offered escape, and ran toward it, hoping to cut off the assailant's flight. A curse from her left brought a thin smile to her lips. Now she had a chance to get some answers before she finished this.

"Why hide? You won't get past me, and the sheriff will be here shortly. Come out where I can see you."

Dressed in a full black bodysuit that included a mask revealing only his eyes and mouth, the man stepped out to face her. A sword was in his right hand and a waist holster held at least two hand blades of some variety. Ani studied his movements. His rapid breathing betrayed him as not physically fit and the slight tremor in his blade hand indicated he was scared. He was not a professional, though he seemed to have some blade knowledge.

"Who are you and what did you have against Dalkey?" If she got a name perhaps she could reason with him.

"You don't remember me? I worked with your uncle and mother at the research center until about ten years ago. My name is Isul Treyder and it was *I* who invented most of the machines and technology that came out of this valley, *not* your dear Uncle Reslo. I had hoped to share my latest invention with Reslo since your mother was rude enough to die before I could show it to her. So like him to run crying to Southern when his ideas were frowned upon. I just wanted to prove my genius to him. But obviously, Reslo Chenak still has no stomach for real science." His teeth showed an eerie smile surrounded by the mask. "And now that I think of it, you might make a more impressive test subject."

The assailant continued his babbling as he advanced toward her. "As for Stubin Dalkey, I have no feeling toward him one way or the other. He was the perfect diversion to bring your uncle within my reach. I thought Reslo would come back to help you, but I guess he hasn't the courage to face a deluded man either."

A slight shake of her head helped clear the buzz of his ramblings. Why was it difficult to focus on the man in front of her? He had brought Dalkey back just to prove his superior scientific intellect to Uncle Reslo? None of it made sense, and being a test subject of any kind didn't sound healthy at all.

Treyder waved the sword again. She could see the blood smear on the blade edge where he had nicked her cheek. At the thought, she realized her cheek no longer stung. She rubbed at it with the back of her hand. The cheek was numb. Good. She could ignore it.

"So, Isul Treyder, is this wonderful invention of yours the weapon you used to kill Dalkey?"

Maybe if she distracted him with Dalkey, she'd discover why he was prepared to do her remaining family harm. Her uncle would most definitely have been interested in a killing light beam, though she didn't think it was a fair way to fight when compared with blades. You didn't have to look your enemy in the eye or take responsibility for their deaths or injuries with a killing light beam. Killing someone at such a distance required no courage, strength, or intelligence. To her thinking, the closeness necessitated by blade use made war less likely.

She jabbed at Treyder, allowing room for escape but keeping him engaged. Though she had prepared herself for killing Dalkey, she found she was not inclined to kill this new opponent before she gleaned as much information as possible. He obliged her by continuing to talk around the fits of awkward blade work.

He said the killing light was one of his discoveries and that he had intended to offer it as a diversion tool on the battlefield. He didn't realize it would kill, but now that it had been proven an actual weapon, he was rethinking its use. If the right people heard about it, he envisioned making a profit. Treyder laughed about his luck in killing Dalkey, whom he saw as a fool. He had been more concerned that Dalkey would injure or kill *her*.

That really confused her. Didn't he know she had won the continental championships against professional blade ring combatants, that she trained military recruits in blade basics? How could he think Dalkey would damage *her*?

A shiver traced down her back. This was not what she expected, and it probably was not going to end well or to her advantage. She remembered her mother's warning when she began training recruits as she continued to assess Treyder. "Beware the beginner and the fanatic because they are less predictable and more dangerous than any of the professionals you have ever faced. Beginners don't know the rules and fanatics don't care, so be very aware and learn from them." This Isul Treyder was sounding more like a fanatic, and he appeared to have had at least some training with a blade. Truly a double edge.

Between the give and take of blades, Treyder expounded on his delight at hearing that a Southern aerial observation craft had crashed in Star Valley. The incident had played right into his plan. And he had used Dalkey's alien obsession as the perfect cover. Somehow he had convinced a higher up to let Dalkey loose. Pride in his plan was evident when Treyder described his assumption that her uncle would rush back to the valley to investigate a real crash. But her uncle had not come and now, it seemed, Treyder was planning to use the invention on her to prove something to her uncle.

They grappled, pushed away, and reengaged. Treyder tripped and Ani whipped her blade downward. He cried out as it left a thin line along his sword arm. She knew it wasn't bad enough to prevent him from using it, although his weapon clattered away as he caught the fall. He scuttled out of her range and she backed off, curious about his statement.

"You planned to use the invention on *me*?"

"Yes, you, because you're available and alive. My invention only works on the living." He glanced at his sword and started to crawl. "By the way, Miss Chenak, how's the cut on your cheek?"

"You were lucky." She cocked her head. "What is this invention?" Ani continued to follow the blade ring code of honor, allowing her opponent to retrieve his weapon. It allowed time to get answers. None of what he was saying made any sense. She glanced across the cavern. Where were Taryn and Renloret? Was Kela really all right? His presence was still in her mind, though it was flickering oddly.

Snatching up his blade, the man scrambled to his feet. Now that he was armed once more, Ani attacked. She couldn't wait any longer for Taryn to arrive; she'd have to end this now and ask questions later.

Throughout the exchange he prattled on about the disrespect he received from her uncle about his inventions, especially when he talked about making them so small you could inject them into a person's bloodstream. These microscopic machines would hunt out and kill tumors and germs and even repair broken parts of the body—anything doctors wanted them to do. He said he'd even hoped that he could invent one that would bring his wife out of an eleven year coma. It hadn't, and she had eventually died. Somehow, he seemed to be making a point by using Ani as a pawn.

The cavern air vibrated as they slashed and stabbed. Treyder seemed more intent on running away from her than fighting her, as if he were waiting for something. Then she stumbled, barely able to wrench herself out of the slashing arch of her opponent's blade.

"Finally." Smiling, Treyder reset his position.

"Finally what?" Ani asked, bringing her blade into position, ready.

"The drug on the blade is taking affect. That little cut on your cheek was enough. Soon you'll be unable to—"

Lips tucked between her teeth and eyes narrow and fierce, Ani moved swiftly, pushing the man backward. He parried frantically. The man cursed as he slipped again and was knocked to his knees. Ani hesitated, her vision blurry. The sword seemed to have gained weight.

"Unable to what?" she asked. Her words slurred as she staggered and her sword tip dropped.

He laughed as he swung his sword up and lunged forward catching her too slow block on the hilt. Using his weight and momentum he slammed her against the cavern wall. Dropping his sword so he could pin her wrists out of the way, he brought one of his waist knives to her throat. "Oh, I won't kill you. I need you to be alive for this," he hissed.

Ani was stunned. Muscles would not obey her commands. She couldn't focus. What in all the hells of Teramar was happening? She sent a call to Kela. He was coming, but not fast enough.

"Now you'll know the power of a true scientist," Treyder said, almost growling. He shifted the blade from her throat to shove it upward into her chest. "Here's my finest achievement."

Ani felt the pressure of the blade as it was pushed through the fabric of her shirt and passed through her skin to grind between her ribs. There was no pain at first, only surprise. How could she have let him slip under her guard, and with such a small blade?

Anyala whispered through gritted teeth, "Hells, I should have worn a vest." She flinched as he twisted the narrow blade. She heard a small click before he laughed again.

"There. Don't be too upset, I just needed to nick your skin. The poison I used on the blade was the one way to get this close so I could deliver my invention." He leaned closer, lips brushing across her ear. "It'll travel to your brain and essentially put you to sleep. It's smaller than anyone else can see so it will be most difficult to remove without my assistance. And I don't plan on being available for a while—about eleven years should do it. I want to see how this turns out. So, until then, enjoy your sleep."

His voice blurred to soft static. Ani tried to shake her head to clear both her vision and her hearing. *Poison, Kela! Help me!* Would this poison shut her off from everyone? Would she die? Numbness seeped out from somewhere in her body smothering the pain of the wound but not the pain of her mistakes. *Poison . . . can't . . .*

"No!"

Ani wasn't sure if she smiled or not, but she heard Renloret and Taryn yell in unison. They had arrived. A blade rocketed passed the assailant's torso and clattered off the cavern wall. A Lrakiran curse echoed.

"Ani!"

Was that Taryn?

"Taryn! Renloret . . ." It wheezed out as a whisper.

His breath felt hot on her neck as he leaned close. "Gotta go. See you in eleven years." Treyder released her hands and Ani slid into a heap.

She thought her body trembled at his whispered words but she couldn't feel any of her extremities. He moved out of her blurring vision toward the back of the cavern. He was getting away. She could hear boots grinding the gravel and dust on the cavern floor near her. Surely that was Taryn. Hadn't she heard his voice?

"You can't die, Anyala. Our people need you. You are my heart."

Renloret. It was Renloret. She had to tell him. Could she still speak? Struggling to inhale she pushed the words out.

"Poison allowed him . . ." She coughed. A bloody tang sparked saliva, slurring the words. "Something . . . inside head . . . sleep." She fought to pronounce each word. "Poison." She was losing her battle to communicate aloud. *Kela? Love* . . . Air whispered through her lips. He was there and then he wasn't. Her eyes closed as she lost contact.

"What kind of poison?" Taryn asked. His breathing was rapid but controlled.

"She didn't tell me," Renloret said while continuing his exam of her. There was a nasty cut on her cheek and a small handled blade protruded from below her rib cage. Precious blood seeped out. He put his hand around the handle to pull it out.

"Stop!" Taryn put his hand over Renloret's. "She may bleed out if you do."

He released the handle.

"For all the hells, you're from another world, you travel between stars! Can't you do something, now?" Taryn screamed.

"A Stone Singer could, I think. But I'm just the pilot. I'm not a Stone Singer."

"But you *are* a singer, Renloret," Taryn said.

"You don't understand. Only a Stone Singer can help." He stopped as he remembered that S'Hendale's gift of the blade to Ani meant she might be blood bonded to the Stone's blade. That connection might save her. He swept the cavern with his eyes. "Where's the blade, Taryn?"

"The crystal blade?" Taryn asked.

"Yes, where is it?"

"In the cafeteria, I assume."

"If she's who I believe she is, it's imperative that we have the blade!" Renloret shouted. "That blade can save her. I can't lose her. My . . . I . . . Lrakira needs her." His voice broke. "It might work, but I need the blade."

Taryn tore off back down the tunnel.

"There's not much time." The word turned Renloret's stomach. "Hurry."

CHAPTER TWENTY-FOUR

Renloret shook his head. Was there enough time? If Taryn found the blade and returned with it, could he remember the words from the dusty old books he'd found in the library? Could he remember the ludicrously simple instructions from the ancient medical book? What was the tune? He knew it had not been in the book. Would any tune be sufficient?

He hugged Anyala to his chest. "You're a Stone Singer, Ani. The blade will know you. I will sing *for* you and the blade will heal you because you are its Singer."

Would the healing song work with a non-Singer holding the blade and singing? Would the blade really know Ani? It was his only hope—Lrakira's only hope.

He heard a muffled bark as Kela ran into the cavern followed by Taryn carrying the blade box. Relief flooded through Renloret.

"Now what?" Taryn asked as he offered the box.

Kela nuzzled Ani's limp body, whining.

"Open it," Renloret said.

Taryn obliged and presented it to the pilot.

The blade nestled in a shaped depression on the finest silteene fabric Lrakira produced. The fabric was blood red to complement the green of the crystal. Renloret hesitated at the beauty of the Anyala Stone's blade. Only Singers touched the crystal blades. He cursed under his breath. Did he dare touch it? Would it burn his hands, too?

A sharp slap on his shoulder snapped his attention back to the girl before him. Reverently, he picked up the blade. It did not burn and he did not question why. Perhaps the blade knew it was needed. He poised the weapon above the bloody wound, expecting the words to come. They did not. Tears did.

"Renloret? How is this helping her?" Taryn demanded.

The pilot hung his head. Indeed, how could he help her? He was not a Singer. He was a simple pilot who liked to read about the history of the Stones. And now, when he needed the ancient words, he could not remember them.

"I can't remember the words."

"What words?" Taryn asked, his eyes still on Ani.

"The words to an ancient healing song. Long ago, the Singers healed wounds in a ceremony of some sort. They used their blades and sang. But now we have *modern* medicine and so many other things that my people have forgotten the old ways to heal. I think the majority of people have forgotten the Stones themselves." He paused. "And those same people will vanish and be forgotten if she dies. All because *they* no longer believe and *I* cannot remember the words." Tears fell unheeded.

Kela whined mournfully.

"Please, Renloret," Taryn said, his eyes now on the grieving man. "You're her one hope. I have no concept of how a song and a blade will heal her. You know how to fix it, to bring her back to us. You've got to believe—to hope."

Renloret focused on the word "hope." The Anyala Stone said he was its hope, the one who would bring the cure home. The "cure" lay in front of him, dying, waiting to be brought back to life so she could save what to her was an alien world. He gathered air deep into his lungs and slowly let it out, focusing his energy and thoughts as if he were in the blade ring.

He pulled the sliver blade out and quickly pressed the crystal one over the wound hoping the mere presence of the Lrakiran blade would stop the flow. Blood did not gush as he thought it might, but it continued to seep around the blade. He had to remember the song. Renloret knew the ancient words were somewhere deep in his memory. Years of secretive study would not be wasted. He closed his eyes and turned the pages in his memory, searching. Then he started to hum. A tune began as he hummed louder, but it faltered, and he began again. The crystal shimmered with internal light while a pale green mist appeared and blanketed her body.

A tear slipped from under Ani's eyelashes. Her lips moved. "Nahnah." Her body shivered as the mist wrapped her chest.

Renloret continued to hum and the tune finally settled into a pattern. The crystal's light intensified. The mist gathered, weaving between the blade and the wound.

Renloret interrupted his humming. "Sing with me, Taryn." He recited some unintelligible syllables.

Taryn shook his head. "I don't know those words."

"Sing with me." It was an order.

Taryn joined in and the mist danced to the rhythm, between the blade and singers. The words and melody echoed throughout the cavern and down the hallways.

Blood ceased its escape from Ani's body. Flesh appeared to bind itself, but she remained unresponsive.

Taryn harmonized. The crystal blade sparked and Renloret was startled by the sudden heat radiating from the blade. He stared at the glowing blade, unaware that it had found and struggled to eliminate the poison.

Ani's body jerked. It seemed to be responding to the rhythm and harmony of the ancient healing song. But she remained unresponsive. The blade's light faded. The song was hoarse in Renloret's throat and he could hear that it had lost its power in Taryn's throat as well. He stopped singing and Taryn followed.

"That's all one blade can do. I think only real Singers with their blades can bring her totally back—that is, if I can get her to Lrakira in time."

"There are other blades?" Taryn whispered, hoarse from the singing. He turned to Ani and his fingers found the steady beat at her throat. Then he looked up at Renloret and said, "Thank you."

Nodding, Renloret answered, "I thank you for believing—in so many things." He bent close, brushing his lips across Ani's forehead.

"How do you get her to Lrakira?"

Kela nosed between them to snuffle at Ani's neck.

"He knows." Renloret looked at Kela. There was still a mission to complete, even if he was twenty years late and the cure was comatose at the moment. At least she was alive.

The canine blinked.

"Knows what?" Taryn asked.

Renloret held Kela's eyes. "Kela, *is* there another ship?"

"What are you asking him for? He's just a canine," Taryn said.

Kela barked once, backing away from the trio toward the tunnel.

Renloret gathered Anyala and stood. "He's as intelligent as either of us, probably more. Bring the blade." He started back toward the research center through the tunnel.

Kela led the men back to the launch tube. The large circular room was empty and the control stations dark. Renloret placed Ani's limp body on a bench. He brushed long tendrils of hair off her face. Another necessity became apparent. Without shifting his eyes from Ani's face he asked, "Kela, are there any stasis bags here?"

Kela paced back toward the door, stretched up on his hind legs, and pointed at a symbol etched into the surface with his muzzle.

Taryn, who had remained at the door observing, shook his head in disbelief. "Renloret, I don't know how much more I can take."

"From what I have seen, you are far stronger than you think or I imagined. Can you open the compartment Kela pointed out?"

Taryn pressed the symbol and the wall slid away. Shelves were stuffed with packages of varying sizes. Renloret looked at the array of colors and guessed. "Unless things have changed in twenty years, I need one with three gray stripes. I will know for sure when I open it up."

After a quick search, Taryn pulled down the requested package, ran back, and shoved it into Renloret's hands.

Pulling a small black tab, Renloret said, "I need help getting her into it." He peeled the case off and unfolded a rectangular silver-colored bag.

"Into this?" Taryn was aghast. "If she wakes up and she's still in it, you'll have real problems on your hands. She's terribly claustrophobic."

"Do not worry. I can set the mechanism so that will not happen. Besides, she will need all three blades and Singers to heal her fully. Help me."

Together the two men lifted Ani from the bench to the center of the bag.

"What did you call this?" Taryn asked.

Renloret positioned her legs. "A stasis bag."

"What're they supposed to do?" Taryn asked as he pulled the long strands of Ani's hair into his hands and wove it back into a loose braid. He bound the end with a leather tie from one of his wrist sheaths.

"Depending on the type of bag, they can hold a body in suspension until a burial can be performed or a cure can be found for an illness or a wounded person can be transported to a medical facility. All of our teams carry them." He paused as he remembered Ani's comment about his dead crew members. She'd said that they were safe until she could notify their families. "I think Ani knew about them."

"Wouldn't surprise me, now that I know she's an alien. I think her mother kept a lot of information from her so she could live a proper life, but Shendahl would also have told her about certain advances the research center was working on. That would explain why no one else knew about these bags. There'd be a lot of people who would pay anything to stay alive until cures could be found, but stasis bags are just a bit beyond our current technology."

He paused and it seemed to Renloret that Taryn was studying his face.

"You really don't look anything like an alien."

Renloret shrugged and bent to seal the bag. "That's a mystery we'll have to solve later, Taryn. I didn't expect such a close resemblance so far from Lrakira." He nodded for the sheriff to complete the seal over her face. "It's just one of the questions I've got for my superiors." He turned to watch Kela cross the room from the control station to the opposite wall. "Where's that ship, Kela?"

Kela growled deep in his throat and glared at the men. He stopped in front of a section of wall and appeared to study its blankness.

"Guess he's having trouble with the controls or something," Renloret said as he clicked open a small box near the center of the stasis bag's seal. "His paws can't hit the controls correctly. Why don't you help him out while I set these?" He didn't even look up to see if Taryn would comply with his request.

Taryn joined the canine at the wall. "So, Kela, he says I'm supposed to help you."

Placing his paws as high as he could on the wall Kela mimed a pushing motion. Taryn nodded and began pushing the wall. Kela dropped off the wall and leaned on Taryn's legs, moving him several steps to the right.

"Ah, I felt something move."

Taryn aimed the push more to his right. A large section of wall sunk a palm's thickness away and slid minutely before grinding to a stop. Redoubling his effort, Taryn wedged a foot into the space and pushed again. Kela backed off, shaking his head vigorously at the horrendous screeching that filled the launch tube. The door's painful opening squeals moved higher in pitch as Taryn was joined by Renloret. They pushed and pulled until they heard a pop and sigh as the door edge settled flush with the right wall section. Kela returned to the control station and barked in warning.

Both men stepped back as the floor beneath them started to move. Renloret grinned in apparent anticipation while Taryn stood slack jawed as a sleek Lrakiran star runner rolled into the center of the room. The floor rotated a quarter. Symbols on the ship's fuselage brought a smile to Renloret's face. "Her name is Lansoret. It means far flyer."

"You fly this between stars?" Taryn asked, incredulous.

Renloret saw several emotions flash across the sheriff's face. He looked awestruck, confused, resigned, and amused, all in quick succession. No doubt he was struggling with the fact of the spaceship before him, confused about how to process the information, resigned to the fact that no one would believe him if he told them about it, and amused in the way that people are when they need to sit down and get a grip on the outrageousness of what was happening. Renloret knew how he must feel. He'd had similar feelings many times since the crash.

Renloret placed a hand on the sheriff's shoulder. "Are you okay, Taryn? The first time I was close to a ship like this I felt the same way."

"No, I don't think so," Taryn replied. "You grew up with the knowledge you could travel between stars and planets. You have to realize I've never seen such a ship. I'm just beginning to imagine the possibility." He sighed. "I probably shouldn't be here."

"You shouldn't even know that we've been here. That was the plan, anyway." Renloret moved to the underside of the ship, stroking the metal. "All of this was supposed to be gone, returned to Lrakira. I wonder what went wrong."

A growl from Kela brought their attention back to the control counter. Ears lay flat against his head as he stared at one of the screens. Renloret walked over to view the readings.

"We need to get out of here," he said.

"Why?" Taryn asked from the opposite side of the ship. He touched a panel and jumped aside as a horizontal line appeared and widened to reveal the interior of the ship as a ramp extended.

Renloret looked up at the whooshing hydraulic sound. "Good, you opened it. You're a natural, Taryn. Now help me with Ani."

They laid her in one of six alcoves that lined the passageway.

"Is there time for a tour?" Taryn asked, looking toward the front of the ship.

Sliding the alcove's door closed to seal the stasis bag and Ani's body within, Renloret shook his head. "My apologies, Taryn, as much as I would like to show you around, I must answer no. That security screen showed soldiers working their way back into the research center."

Kela joined the men inside the ship.

"I think I know how to stop them, but I have two questions," Taryn said.

"All right, what's the first?" Renloret asked.

"Do you need any assistance in launching this ship?"

"No, I can open the top from inside the ship. Now, how do you propose to stop them from finding us?"

"Second question first. What about Kela?"

"Why don't we ask him?" Renloret replied.

Taryn stifled a grin. "Sure." He turned to Kela. "Do you want to stay here with me or go with her?"

Kela sat up and offered a paw. Taryn grasped it as Kela gave him a quick lick on the cheek then he pulled his paw out and moved to sit next to the alcove where Ani lay.

"Okay, it's settled. You have two passengers, pilot. Fly well." Taryn stood and grasped forearms with Renloret. "Drop me a note if you ever get back to this part of the galaxy." He couldn't stop the grin that accompanied the statement.

"I will do that and I will try to bring her with me," Renloret said.

"If . . . if it doesn't work out on Lrakira, you're welcome here. You do fit right in, even if you are from Southern." With that, Taryn winked and grinned.

Renloret laughed and released his grip. "Again, I thank you for believing."

Taryn waved his arms at his surroundings. "It's kind of hard not to when it's all around me. Safe journey." He brushed away a tear as he touched the alcove door. He mustered a pat on Kela's head and a nod to Renloret before he turned to leave the ship.

"Taryn?" Renloret asked.

"Yeah?"

"You did not tell me how you were going to stop the soldiers."

"Let me worry about that. Just get her home and save your people. If you come back, I'll tell you all about it. I won't forget, even if it's another twenty years." He slapped the panel on the side of the ship and the ramp retracted.

Renloret and Kela moved to the cockpit of the star runner. They watched Taryn run to the launch tower exit.

"He is a good man, Kela. I almost wish I could bring him along." A few touches across the panel and varied colored lights danced and flickered. He toggled a switch. The mountain tower's launch window opened and the engines started up.

CHAPTER TWENTY-FIVE

When the star runner and its pilot's identity blipped onto the screen, the flight command room became silent. The swoosh of the doors brought all eyes to Noret, Lrakira's galactic flight controller, as she entered the multitiered amphitheater. At her tight smile and short nod the dawn bells shift manager stepped away from his console. All other flights were already in preplanned holding patterns, leaving the landing field almost empty. Two transports blinked orange on the screen. They could wait until this all important star runner had arrived.

Her voice carried without artificial enhancements. "Let's get this runner down. This is not a drill." She straightened her jacket and seated herself at the communications console.

"Star runner, Lansoret, you may approach. You have full clearance. You're a sun-time or two ahead of schedule. Welcome home, Renloret." She nodded in response to the acknowledgment from the pilot. "Of course I'm still the GFC, why wouldn't I be?" There was a short pause. "You've only been gone about one moon-cycle. Your return notification reached us eight sun-times ago. We planned on the trip taking nine, so, yes, you are early." Her light chuckle ceased. "Twenty? That's not possible." Her mouth made a small "O" and her eyes widened in surprise.

The bell shift manager approached and leaned over her shoulder. "Anything wrong?"

She nodded. "He'll explain as much as he can later. Right now he asks to have a medical team ready. A passenger is in a stasis bag."

The manager snapped his fingers and a junior officer dutifully touched her earpiece to make the request. "Does he need anything else?"

"He says Commanders Chenakainet and Trimag must be notified of his arrival immediately." She hesitated. "He also demands that the Stone Singers meet with them all at the medical center in a private conference room."

Eyebrows went up in surprise. No one ever made demands of the Stone Singers.

Commanders Chenakainet and Trimag were summoned. Both quickly dropped what they had been doing when told why they were needed.

Alone, at least for a few chimes while he waited for the physician's report, Renloret wondered if he could have managed his arrival better. He was most concerned about his demand to have the

Stone Singers at the first conference. Looking back, now, he knew that had been a mistake.

In the bedlam following his initial report, Renloret had been mesmerized by the lack of emotion from Selabec, the Anyala Stone's Singer and Ani's grandmother. She'd sat in the chair, a haunted shell in a golden robe, despair in her eyes. She had not acknowledged the fact her daughter, S'Hendale, had not survived and that it was her granddaughter who was being examined by the physicians. Though he had tried to explain multiple times, Selabec seemed unable or unwilling to actually hear what he had said.

At the other end of the spectrum, Commander Chenakainet had erupted with anger and disbelief. Spewing questions at Renloret without giving him a chance to answer, Chenakainet had paced and ranted at the undisciplined behavior of a pilot too young and inexperienced to identify people correctly. How could Renloret *not* have found a five sun-cycles old child? Chenakainet had only been gone for barely a moon-cycle. It was not possible his daughter was twenty-five and his wife was dead. How stupid did Renloret think he was? It had only been when Renloret had shouted him down by reciting the words from the gravestone that the commander had put his fist through a wall and crumbled into a chair. That had quieted almost everyone.

Selabec chose that moment to ask, yet again, when she'd be able to see S'Hendale, insisting there was much planning to be done for the Singer Transfer Ceremony. It was then that Renloret realized there was something deeply wrong with the Anyala Stone's Singer. The other Singers had shaken their heads at him, forestalling his statement that S'Hendale was dead. They had simply whispered in Selabec's ear and bracing her between them had shuttled out the door. What had happened to cause such a stunning change in the most revered Singer in Lrakiran history?

After the singers left, Trimag had moved to stand next to Chenakainet, placing one hand on the distraught man's shoulder. Renloret wanted to escape. He had not planned on being so abrupt, but he knew that the sooner the information was out the more quickly Chenakainet could deal with the results. It was supposed to be easier to handle extreme happenstance if you had all the facts. Renloret did not like being the one to pronounce those facts. Not one iota.

Though he had managed to complete his mission by bringing the savior home to Lrakira, Renloret honestly did not know how he should feel. What should he do? What more could he say? He had saved an entire species, yet he was filled with grief. Sobs from the commander only made it worse. He wished he could punch a hole through a wall. It wouldn't help, but perhaps he'd feel better afterward.

Trimag had quietly suggested that Chenakainet's hand should be examined for broken bones. The pair had left, but Trimag had promised they would return shortly. Renloret hoped the physician examining Anyala would have his report by then as well. Fighting tears he wished Kela had been there. He could use a friend.

When Commanders Trimag and Chenakainet returned, Renloret was surprised and relieved that there had been no broken bones, only bruising. The three men had waited impatiently for the physician to arrive. When he did, he remained standing, a deep frown creasing his face as he fidgeted with his tablet. Renloret held his breath. After all of this, had she died? Had he lost the race against time? Was he truly too late? Was Ani really the savior his people hoped for? Or was she just a young woman who would die like all the others? Renloret flopped into a seat, suppressing all of his questions, and looked at Chenakainet. The commander stared at the physician, hope glittering in his black eyes.

The physician carefully placed the reader on the table. He laced his fingers together and brought the folded hands to his lips, tapping several times while exhaling, as if undecided about something.

"Well?" Chenakainet asked.

"She won't wake up," the physician said, moving his hands behind his back and rocking back and forth on his heels.

Renloret leaned across the table trying to get closer to the physician. "What do you mean she won't wake up?"

Commander Chenakainet placed a restraining hand on the pilot's arm. "Let him finish."

Renloret glared at everyone in the conference room but nodded, sitting back in his chair and folding his arms tight across his chest. Had they thought about bringing in the Singers? Surely *they* could wake her. He paused his thoughts. Perhaps whatever was wrong with Selabec was preventing a full healing. Would they even know how to use the blades or the Stones to heal her? He waited.

The physician scrolled through the report, alternately nodding and shaking his head. He looked up and said, "Evidence of a blade healing was found and no toxin was present. We are testing her blood for the needed antibodies. Everything about her is fine . . . except she won't wake up." He stared at the defensive pilot. "I think we are missing some very small but vital piece of information. We need to know exactly what happened. What or how was this coma induced?"

The chair slid backward, colliding with the wall as Renloret jumped to his feet, "I've told you everything. It's all in the report I sent after leaving Teramar. The only other person who might know more is . . ." He stopped. Why hadn't he thought of this before? "Where's Kela?"

"The canine?" the physician asked. "As a foreign creature, it was placed in quarantine with all the other off world animals. We have no idea what pests or germs it might be carrying."

"Yes, the canine, her *telepathic* canine. He's as sentient as the governor of Slerdon," Renloret spit out, barely in control.

All eyes turned to Renloret. He could see the sudden understanding.

"That's not in your report," Commander Chenakainet said.

"She asked me not to tell anyone, and I didn't think it was going to be so important. She said Kela couldn't communicate telepathically with anyone else. But I do know he understands what is said, and he can respond to questions. I think he can even read, sir." The close confinement on the star runner had taught Renloret much about Kela.

"So, as long as we can frame questions for a positive or negative response, we should be able to get details we don't have? Is that right?" the physician asked.

"I believe so, sir," Renloret replied.

Commander Chenakainet went to the wall communicator and pressed a few buttons. "Cranvorg, I need you to get the port authorities to release the Teramaran canine from quarantine and bring him to the hospital. Now. I'll be at the entrance to guide him."

"Yes, sir."

Obviously Chenakainet didn't care about the six sun-times minimum quarantine for off world animals, especially with his daughter's life on the blade edge. Conveniently, he was able to order Cranvorg to deal with the vets. Chenakainet turned away from the communicator, nodded to those in the room, and exited.

Kela tilted his head and raised his eye brows at Renloret. *I'm not a puppy, but one word at a time is ridiculous. And his grammar is awful.*

"Sir, perhaps if you stated your questions as if you were talking to me, then I or the commander can translate in Northern and you won't have to look up the words. It would be faster," Renloret said.

"All right, I need a baseline for his communicative skills. In what age range would he put his vocabulary?" the physician asked.

Renloret translated offering three ranges he thought would be suitable. Kela barked twice.

"He says twenty to thirty."

The physician notated the range on the report board and then asked, "Is this a natural occurrence on Teramar?"

Instead of translating, Renloret explained what Anyala had told him about the connection between canine and girl.

"Is it artificially enhanced?" the physician asked.

Renloret translated. Kela barked three times.

"He doesn't know."

"Can he sense her now?" the physician asked.

Kela hung his head with a single soft bark. Renloret shook his head.

"When did he stop sensing her?"

After Renloret's translation, Kela began growling and whining as he tried to verbalize the answer.

The physician glared at Renloret. "What kind of an answer is that?"

Renloret chuckled. "I'm sorry. It wasn't worded as a positive or negative. He's honestly trying to tell us when." Kela was still making noises. "Let me try again." Renloret switched to Northern.

"Kela, do you have a good sense of time?"

Kela stammered to a halt. *What?*

"Can you tell me how long before you arrived in the cavern you lost the connection?"

Yes, yes, I can! Two barks.

They quickly refined a time line until Renloret held up his hand. He switched to Lrakiran. "Oh blades, that was just after—"

Until now, Commander Chenakainet had maintained silence

during the interview, observing the interactions of the canine and the two humans. "Just after what, pilot?"

"Her last words," Renloret whispered.

"And they were?" the commander urged.

Trying to mimic the desperation in her voice, the pilot spoke each unforgettable word. "Poison . . . allowed device . . . head . . . sleep . . . poison."

He exhaled slowly, tears tracing his cheek unnoticed. "And then I thought she had died. But she continued to breathe, too slow. Kela arrived shortly after that with the blade. We sang a healing song. I figured if she were connected to the blade, it wouldn't hurt me. I don't know how long we sang. It was a long time. The wound appeared to heal but she didn't revive. I thought the poison was too alien and that all three blades, their Singers, and perhaps even the Stones themselves would be needed for a complete healing. So we put her in a stasis bag and I brought her home."

He turned to Kela and switched languages again. "Did you feel her at all during the flight?"

Kela shook his head. He whined and put a paw on Renloret's knee. Renloret knelt in front of Kela. "I'm sorry. I didn't realize you couldn't hear her at all. I just assumed. All this time together and I never even asked and you couldn't tell me. I'm so sorry."

Kela ran his rough tongue across the pilot's cheek.

The physician cleared his throat. "Can we get back to the patient?"

"Of course," Renloret replied. Returning to his chair, Renloret kept one hand on the base of Kela's ears, rubbing his fingers through the fur. Kela sighed softly.

The physician was quick to recap his notes. "The patient sustained a minor wound on the cheek that introduced a fast acting toxin to her system. The toxin slowed her response time, allowing the assailant to insert another blade, which released a 'device' into her bloodstream. This device traveled to her brain. Within a short amount of time it effectively put the patient into an artificial coma, and in the process, somehow removed or interrupted the telepathic connection." He harrumphed and tapped the tablet. "All we have to do is find and excise it, then all should be well."

"You got all of that from a one-sided interview with a telepathic canine?" Commander Chenakainet asked.

"The simple answer is, yes." The physician closed his tablet and stood. "Now, excuse me. I need to get your daughter into surgery."

The conference room door whooshed open. He turned back at the threshold to look at Renloret. "After that, we need to discuss other aspects of this rescue mission, particularly the blade healing. And I've been told to pass on that the young woman is indeed the commander's daughter, so you did bring home the correct child. A sample of her blood passed the first round of testing for use as a vaccine against the plague. More tests will be necessary before we can manufacture enough doses, but the prognosis for our people is much improved. I'm not as sure about Anyala's, but at least I have something to look for."

The door swished closed leaving the pilot, commander, and canine staring after him.

Kela whined and pawed at Renloret's knee.

Commander Chenakainet called to Kela, who padded over to him. They took a few moments to study each other. A slight smile twitched at the corners of the commander's mouth.

In Northern the commander said, "I bet it was my brother's idea to enhance an animal's innate empathy to become a type of telepathy. What was his reasoning to do this?" He stared into Kela's eyes. "Do you really understand all of what we say if we speak Northern?"

Kela barked twice and held out a paw. Chenakainet grasped it. He smiled at the pilot still quiet in his chair, staring at the closed door.

"According to Trimag," Chenakainet said, "you are his best pilot and the Anyala Stone specified your assignment to fly the rescue ship. Your report does not mention a reason for your crash. Perhaps we can discuss the connection between the crash and a certain event here on Lrakira while we wait.

Renloret straightened in his seat. "A connection between the crash and what?"

"Time." Chenakainet chuckled. "Time seems to be involved with every aspect of this. Yes, due to timing, I don't believe the crash was your fault. I'd like to bring in Trimag and two of the Stone Singers to participate in this discussion."

"What do the Singers have to do with my crashing on Teramar? That makes no sense."

The commander motioned at the door as it slid aside, allowing entrance to Renloret's mentor, Trimag, and two golden-robed Singers. "I'm hoping it'll all make sense in the coming bell."

CHAPTER TWENTY-SIX

"So you're saying that an interrupted song triggered the crash? How did you come to this conclusion?" Renloret asked. He leaned across the table, studying each face. He couldn't believe that a simple song, even if sung by the Stones, could cause his ship to crash.

The two Stone Singers exchange worried looks. The younger one, Layson, spoke with downcast eyes and tightly clasped hands.

"The time of the attack, the time of your crash, the length of time you were on Teramar, and your subsequent arrival here provided us with most of the information. And since your arrival, we have regained communication with two of the Stones. After the interruption of their song, they had been silent. We believe they are focused on sustaining the Anyala Stone."

She paused for a moment to let this last bit of information sink in, then continued. "We were not in the chamber during their song and their attacker was . . . is . . . close to the Stones. No alarm was sounded until the crime was committed. Diani and I did not know precisely what occurred, and neither of us was able to communicate with them immediately afterward. And there was no word from the rescue team until eight sun-times ago."

Her eyes flicked from her hands to Renloret's face, as if beseeching him to understand.

"We weren't sure how the song was supposed to help." She managed a slow breath. "But when the communiqué arrived that you were successful and would arrive within the few sun-times, we went to the chamber and told the Stones you had retrieved the child." Her chin trembled with the stress.

"And?" Renloret asked, pressing but not sure if he wanted to know more. This was bad enough.

"I'll finish," Diani said, placing a hand on Layson's shoulder. "Their song had been interrupted at a critical moment, and even they did not know if anyone had survived. The Anyala Stone has been compromised beyond our understanding, though Pericha and Kita assure us it is still alive, barely. There have been flickers from its life light, but no communication."

Renloret shifted in his chair and swallowed hard. He had one question. "Outside of convenient timing, what does this interrupted song have to do with my crash?"

"My Stone said a 'time song' was needed to bring about the preferred scenario so The Blood and The Balance would be returned to Lrakira and we would be saved." Diani drew in a deep breath. "I don't understand it all. They admitted that the attack came after your ship had safely entered the time bubble the song had created around Teramar. The Stones said you should have had no problems due to this time bubble, but the attack caused them to lose control of events and the Stones were only able to tell us they thought the pilot had survived. Whether or not the mission would succeed was unknown, even to them. We have waited since then to hear from you.

"When the port received your first communication, they came to us. They never received your distress signal, so we had to tell them what had occurred. Layson and I were not sure how long we should wait before explaining and asking that a new rescue team be sent. The Stones and we are grateful you survived and were successful in your rescue. The Stones rejoice in their own way." She inclined her head toward Renloret as she touched her forehead with her left index finger.

Renloret sucked in a sharp breath at the acknowledgment. Only the Stones themselves were supposed to be given such an honor. He did not feel he had earned it. "Singer Layson, I'm—"

Layson interrupted with a wave of her hand, "The general populace does not know any details of this save that a cure has been discovered and vaccines are being prepared. The people are jubilant, of course. However, some uncertainties still exist. We do not know if your Anyala will awaken. By bringing her home, you have saved Lrakira, but according to legend, only she who is the Blood and the Balance can save the Anyala Stone. If she does not live, the Stone may perish."

Renloret stood. Comprehension lit his features. "I remember reading an old text." He snapped his fingers as he stepped to the display board on the wall and began writing. "Something about The Blood and The Balance."

Circle of Seven sing safe passage,
Divide by two and send in deep sleep,
The Blood and Balance shall each save one,
Awakening three to rejoice with time's message.
Time will soon come for reunion's leap,
Six will Sing joining three homes and suns.

"Do you recognize it?" He turned a hopeful look on the Singers as he finished.

They read in silence.

"Well?"

Diani shook her head. "It is incomplete, I think."

"This is the part that mentioned The Blood and The Balance. It's actually the last piece I was reading right before the meeting . . . uh . . . the one I was late to." He glanced at Trimag.

His mentor smiled. "You've never been more than a quarter of a bell late, until now." Trimag's expression turned serious. "Twenty years late." He shook his head in disbelief.

Renloret blushed and glared at his superior. "That was obviously the Stones' doing, not mine."

Tremag raised his palm. "It was an observation, pilot. The Anyala Stone chose you for the mission and I concurred. But as to why the three of them chose to accelerate time around Teramar . . ." He rubbed his chin, thinking. "Unless, after verifying the child had been born they needed to quickly age the child past puberty so she'd have the correct levels of hormones or enzymes or something."

The pilot, Stone Singers, and commander all stared at him.

Trimag cleared his throat. "Pardon. It was just a thought."

Layson reached across the table and placed a hand on his arm. "No, you are quite right. None of the prepubescent girls seem affected. Only those of child bearing age are vulnerable. It is the hormones during pregnancy that seem to be damaged. We've already looked into that, but the hormone therapy tried so far has not stopped the cellular disintegration."

Now it was the Singer's turn to be stared at. She blushed then whispered, "At least that was what we were told by our physician at my last appointment."

"Continue," encouraged Diani.

"He said that research had pointed them to seeking off planet solutions. Some thought that if a Lrakiran child was conceived on another planet under special conditions, which he did not specify, she might have the correct blood chemistry to provide a cure."

Diani said, "I sense a 'however' at this point."

Layson nodded. "They've spent the last three sun-cycles testing girls conceived and born on thirty-seven planets. A half dozen have remained on their birth planets past puberty and they have all tested negative. Also, there were some flaws in the research. The mothers had all left Lrakira well before the plague started, so that line of research is no longer a main study area."

"So the Stones decided to help us by creating a time bubble around Teramar to age Anyala so she would have the blood we need," Diani said, finishing the train of thought.

"Not just that, but Pericha said the child had to be the daughter of a Stone Singer."

The commander raised a hand. "But S'Hendale was not a Stone Singer, her mother is—or was. That would make Anyala the granddaughter."

Diani stood abruptly, her chin quivering. "No, S'Hendale was the Anyala Stone's Singer. She had the blade. The Stone itself anointed her and requested her service. That much we do know . . . now."

Shaking his head in denial, the commander said, "She did not have the blade. At least, I never saw it in all the six sun-cycles we were together. And she never mentioned it." He stood and turned away from the table, his hands clasped behind his back.

"I'm sorry, sir," Renloret said softly, "but, I did see the blade. I used it to heal Ani."

Kela whined.

Renloret realized that all the conversation had been in Lrakiran, leaving Kela uninformed. He changed languages, apologized to the canine, and summarized the discussion before continuing in Lrakiran for the Singers and his commanding officer.

"Taryn told me Ani had been gifted a ceremonial blade by her mother when she attained a continental championship ranking in the blade ring. That was a little over one sun-cycle before S'Hendale's death. Taryn assumed it was purely decorative because the blade was crystal. Taryn said Ani had frequently handled the blade without repercussion, so I assumed she'd somehow been chosen. After she was wounded, I thought the blade might be able to heal her if a Stone Singer was present."

"I'd like to know, pilot, how you even thought of a healing song. And I'd like to understand how you accomplished a healing without one of us there," Diani said.

"I couldn't let her die! I had to try something, and using the blade and an old healing song I'd read seemed to be my best option."

The others waited expectantly. Even the commander had turned from the window.

Renloret shrugged. "I guessed that with her in a critical situation the blade wouldn't hurt me, especially if she was the only Singer available. I didn't know if it would work without the actual Stone being present." He felt he was babbling but he continued. "It just seemed the correct thing to do. I wasn't thinking beyond how to keep her alive." He shrugged again, unable to continue.

The room was quiet for a moment.

"Excuse me," said Layson. "I'm a Stone Singer and *I* don't know any of the healing songs. How does a pilot?"

Her gaze touched Diani, who refused to look at her or to offer an answer.

A soft chuckle preceded the pilot's response. "Since childhood I've read all I could about the Stones, their blades, and their Singers. I think my mother was afraid I'd pinned my future on becoming a Stone Singer."

Everyone laughed, for they all knew only females held that role.

"But as I aged, the stars drew me more and more. Still, I couldn't leave the books alone."

"So you memorized the words from the ancient texts?" Diani asked.

"Not exactly. I just knew there was a healing song. I didn't know the tune but . . ." His thoughts drifted back to the cavern and Taryn's plea. "I don't think it would have worked without Taryn."

"How would he know?" Chenakainet asked. He returned to the table and sat down.

"He didn't. He demanded I do something. He said I had to believe—to hope. Then the melody began in my head; the words came later. I thought if he joined me, the song might be stronger. Together we sang, and the blade healed her as much as it could." He paused. "It was . . . unexplainable."

Again, silence permeated the room. A soft chime announced the return of the surgeon. He approached the table and placed a tiny object in the center, his smile broad.

"Once I had an idea of what to look for and where to look for it, it was simple to extract it. Anyala is in recovery and you can see her in a few bells. I've ordered several additional blood withdrawals to ensure an adequate supply for the vaccines. She should be back to her normal self by sunrise."

Renloret knelt on the floor, pulled Kela roughly into his arms, and whispered the news. His tears dampened Kela's fur.

The commander peered at the miniscule device on the table. "What exactly is it?"

"Don't know yet," the surgeon replied, "but I thought I'd show you before the lab techs abscond with it. If it was doing what I think it was, there are so many possible uses. I'm astounded at the complexity of this device. I did not think Teramar would be capable of such for many sun-cycles."

"I think the Stones' time song has something to do with that," the commander said.

The surgeon looked confused. "Time song?"

Chenakainet began to explain but was interrupted by Kela's sudden bark. The canine turned end for end, then bounced around the room, deafening their ears.

Just as quickly, he stopped and turned to look from the door to Renloret and back.

Before anyone could react, the door slid open again allowing a security guard to charge through. "We've got a problem. The patient has a hostage."

CHAPTER TWENTY-SEVEN

Ani remembered the sterile starkness of the hospital room, the coldness pushing her away from her mother's bedside. She had strained to hear the voice she loved, now shredded by pain and ineffective drugs.

"You must survive. You will save my world," her mother had said, her voice brittle and faint.

She had pleaded with her mother to not go, to not die. But her mother pressed on, as ill as she was. She'd said things that were inexplicable, things like, "He will come," and, "Remember, Anyala. You are The Blood."

It intruded on her consciousness now like a nightmare.

She opened her eyes to subdued lighting and quiet surroundings. This was not the hospital where her mother had died, nor was it the cavern. A lightweight but warm blanket covered her. Her body felt leaden, stiff as if she hadn't moved in days. She tentatively commanded her fingers to move, swallowing a whimper of pain as they tingled awake. Continuing to flex and fist her hands, she studied the ceiling. It was definitely not the cavern. Gentle twisting of both arms assured her of their cooperation, though the muscles complained as if she hadn't worked out in weeks. Keeping her breaths slow and even, she wriggled her toes. The onslaught of sensation jolted her control and released a single shocked gasp before she gritted her jaw closed. A scraping sound alerted her to another presence in the room. She closed her eyes, ceased all movement, concentrated on regaining control of her breathing, and listened.

Footsteps shuffled softly, then the blanket was moved. Warm hands moved along her torso. She tightened her grip on her jaw as the hands reached where she'd remembered the sliver-blade entering. She almost cried out in relief at the lack of pain. Her body seemed to wake as the hands moved its length. Awareness was now balanced with control.

Opening her eyes to mere slits, she watched the young man as he leaned closer to study the scars on her wrists, reverently running his fingers across her skin. He folded the blanket down and placed a disk against her chest in several places, then moved to place it on her neck. She decided.

His wrist broke easily and as he doubled over in pain, she struck again. Blood burst from his nose. He pushed away from the bed, overturning one of the carts as he stumbled toward the single door. She didn't remember leaving the bed. Bloody smudges identified several pads or buttons which he managed to touch before she stepped in front of him to cut off his escape. She allowed him credit for quickness. He sighed as she pointed to one of the furthest corners. Then he wiped his nose cautiously across his unbroken wrist and pinched the bridge of his nose as he shuffled into the corner. She waited for him to sit on the floor before turning to examine the door.

No handles or buttons were visible on the door itself. "Open," she said. It did not. She pressed her hand to a large pad on the wall, assuming it would open the door. It flashed red. A disembodied voice made some sort of announcement in a foreign language. She muttered a curse and struck the door with her fist, then kicked it. It remained closed. The man in the corner said something and she glared at him. The flat of his hand and a turned head offered no offense, so she turned once more to the door. She stepped up to the small window to ascertain what was on the other side, but her view was limited.

A man's head appeared, startling her. His mouth moved. She heard nothing. She shook her head and stepped back in a defensive stance, waiting for him to open the door. He continued to move his mouth. She glanced at the injured man in the corner and pulled open a drawer on the nearest cabinet to find several large blades in it. She shook them at the man in the window and pointed them at the injured one in the corner. Several slashing movements and a flourishing pantomimed drawing of the blade across his neck brought tears of fear to the injured man's eyes, though to his credit, he remained still. Turning back to the window, she launched herself at the door, turning and twisting until her feet thumped against it. Widened eyes registered her intent and the face in the window disappeared.

Rummaging through more drawers, Ani collected several more wicked blades, all surgical and, therefore, sharp enough to be used as needed. Frustrated, she again brandished them at the man in the corner. He turned away, good hand to his stomach trying to hold back vomit. Clearly, he was not the threat she'd assumed. Frowning, she located a stack of towels on a rolling table. She dampened several in one of the sinks along the wall and tossed them to him so he could clean up his face now that his nose had ceased bleeding.

Ani assessed her situation. Obviously the man in the corner had little knowledge of even rudimentary self-defense skills. She didn't feel threatened by him but kept him in her line of sight. A closer scrutiny of the room registered that it was more of a laboratory or medical facility than a military interrogation lockup.

She put the blades down and ran her fingers across her cheek before grabbing a metal tray to use as a mirror. No stitches; not even a ridge of a scar marred her skin. Had the nick on her cheek been her imagination? She put the tray on the counter to pull the flimsy gown above her ribcage. A button-sized indentation between the last two ribs marked the sliver-blade wound, now completely healed and pain free. She considered the length of time it would take for that type of wound to heal. How long had she been in this place? How had she gotten here?

Movement from the corner of the room was met with a glare. He resettled but continued to stare at her—not at her face, but lower. She dropped the gown's hem with a disgusted snort. "Grow up and get over it."

A slight coloring of his face let her know he understood her meaning without recognizing her exact words.

What had happened after the stabbing? She remembered not hearing Kela. She remembered a song, haunting in its beauty, and her mother wrapping her in a warm, green blanket. After that, darkness, silence, nothingness in her mind until a few moments ago. Tears stung her eyes. Had she died? She bit her hand to stop a sob. Had her assailant returned with the milits Dalkey had brought and managed to capture her? Had they brought her here, brought her back to life? For what purpose? So many scary, unreasonable questions chased chaotically after one another, tying her thoughts in knots. What had happened to Taryn and Renloret? Were they still alive? What about Kela? She couldn't feel him at all.

The man in the corner moved again. "Quiet," she hissed at him.

Another thought occurred. This could be a different form of torture: lock her in a room full of deadly weapons with an unarmed, inept watcher—she couldn't call him a guard—who didn't speak or understand her language and whose language she didn't understand. How did they know she wouldn't kill an unarmed, injured person?

The man spoke and pointed to the door. Ani shook her head. "I don't understand a word, but I'm sure as blades not going to fall to that trick and take my eyes off you. Besides, if there was someone at the door I would hear them." A wry smile curved her lips. "Perhaps no one is coming to rescue you."

He continued to stare at the door behind her.

Shifting her weight against the counter, she raised one of the surgical blades to study its edge. "Perhaps you are the unwitting bait to trap me into revealing my real identity. In spite of what they think they know, alien or not, I will never eat you." She pointed the blade at the man and smiled as his eyes rounded in some semblance of understanding. "You're not worth the challenge. Even the hooded man fought better than you." She rubbed her ribcage and silently called again for Kela. The complete absence of him in her mind terrified her. Was he dead?

The small window allowed Renloret limited viewing. An overturned instrument cart and empty bed were near the middle of the room and an injured attendant huddled in the furthest corner. Ani backed into partial view, the surgical gown swinging open as she turned and leaned against the central counter. He could see the surgical blade in one hand. This was going to be a problem. "Explain again why the door won't open and we can't communicate with those inside?"

The security guard repeated his earlier dissertation. "It's an isolation room, sir. We're not supposed to disturb the patient after surgery. There's always at least one attendant who can handle all medical emergencies."

"One attendant for emergencies?"

"Surgery patients rarely make a ruckus or take hostages, sir."

Renloret did not smile. "Why can't she open the door?"

"The door is keyed to staff personnel. Patients are usually incapable of even sitting on their own, let alone walking over to open the door.

Truly, we've never had a problem with this system before."

"Never?" Renloret asked.

"Never," the guard answered.

Renloret stepped away from the door, pulling Kela with him.

"All right, you're on the staff aren't you?"

The guard nodded.

Renloret raised his eyebrows. "So, open the door."

"I can't sir. Not even Physician Sholoret can, from this side."

Sholoret stepped forward. "It was deemed unnecessary for anyone, including the physician, to enter unannounced."

An exasperated whoosh of air punctuated Renloret's response. "And how does one get announced?"

"The intercom system. But we've tried that already. It must have been turned off in the scuffle. There's a switch pad near the door."

Kela jerked out of Renloret's grip and bounced against the door. His muttering growls sounded perfectly frustrated. Every so often, he would stop and cock his head to the side as if he were listening for something.

Renloret watched Kela's efforts. "Perhaps we don't need the intercom system."

"What do you mean?" the guard asked.

Renloret pointed at the canine.

"He's telepathic with her," Commander Chenakainet explained as he pushed his way between the guard and pilot to look in the window.

"Really? Like the Slerdonians?" the guard asked.

Renloret smiled. The young man was quicker to make the

connection than anyone else. "Similar, but not exactly. Kela's telepathic ability may not be natural. We think it was engineered, or at least enhanced."

Kela growled. He rose on his hind legs and began pushing and bouncing against the door, his frustration evident to everyone in the hallway.

"Kela!" Renloret yelled.

Ceasing his scratching and growling commentary, Kela sat and looked at the pilot expectantly.

"You can hear her, correct?" Renloret spoke in Northern.

Kela barked twice.

"Good. Now, can she hear you?"

Kela softly woofed once.

Without turning away from Kela, Renloret said, "He can hear her but she's evidently unable to hear him."

"As I suspected," the surgeon said, "the device suppressed all mental activity. My guess is that now it has been removed, it will become active again, though it is impossible to know when."

"That makes sense but how does that correlate to her regaining consciousness so soon after surgery?" Chenakainet asked.

Everyone turned to look at the surgeon, who shifted side to side under their scrutiny. "I didn't take into account the blade healing. You must understand that blade healing is difficult to study because it is quite rare in this era. I believe the residual effects may last for an extended amount of time."

"May?" Chenakainet raised his voice and eyebrows.

"How long?" Renloret asked, stepping closer to the surgeon.

The surgeon backed away. "I don't know. I can surmise from

medical history and ancient Singer notes. But in this case, after I removed the suppression device, those residual effects may have rid her system of the anesthesia, bringing on a hyper-rapid recovery. I might be able to guess at her behavior if the effects of the blade healing roused her fully healthy and conscious.

Kela whined and pawed at Renloret. Holding up a hand to forestall further conjecture by the physician, Renloret explained to Kela, with occasional interjections by Chenakainet to correct the pilot's word usage or grammar. At each interruption, Kela turned a baleful glance to the man claiming to be Ani's father as if to say he did not need exactness to understand.

When the pilot finished, he nodded to the surgeon to continue.

"What were the circumstances under which the device was implanted?" the surgeon asked.

"The implantation caused the wound, which caused the need for the blade healing. In addition, there was the poison to deal with."

Obviously excited, the physician rushed on. "That explains her behavior upon awakening. Don't you understand? The device probably suspended sound, thoughts, actions, and even memory at the moment it reached its implantation destination. So when she awoke, she started where she left off, defending herself."

Renloret groaned and translated for Kela, again. The canine growled and returned to scratching at the door.

Sholoret touched Renloret's shoulder. "But she'll be confused, too, because she's not actually there. She may be able to hear the canine once she's calm enough."

"Possibly," Renloret replied, "but she's not your normal patient. She's a weapon, and with the surgical tools available in that room, she could do a lot more damage to the attendant, especially if he tries to escape."

"But he only has to explain—"

"She doesn't speak Lrakiran and neither does *he*," Renloret said as he pointed to the still scratching Kela.

"How is it that your daughter does not speak Lrakiran?" the surgeon asked in an accusing tone, turning to Chenakainet.

The commander shrugged. "She was five when I left and we were under the strictest orders to blend in. The easy part was blending in physically. But we couldn't speak Lrakiran, even amongst ourselves, for fear of unconscious slips. We were never sure if we could pass off as true Southerners, so it was Northern or nothing. I think the valley residents assumed we were from Southern, so we let them believe that. Since no Southerners had ever been to Star Valley, no one knew their language. Even the Northern audio news media never had someone on from Southern. Continental politics assured us there was little chance we would be discovered as non-southerners. When we told them we were from Southern they accepted our foreign accent without question."

"Then I assume we'll just have to wait for her system to recover enough for the telepathic enhancement to become functional again, so she can hear the canine." The physician crossed his arms and leaned against the wall, evidently confident in his conclusion. "Patience will get us access to the patient."

CHAPTER TWENTY-EIGHT

Reviewing details of the attack built up an inner anger and self-recrimination. She'd been distracted by a fanatic with revenge as his focus. Most importantly to her, she'd failed to adhere to the most basic of lessons, and her current situation was entirely her fault. Beginners and fanatics *are* unpredictable. She'd learned from her own experience as a beginner that her mother's words about beginners were true. Now she also knew from personal experience that her mother's words about fanatics were also true. She remembered cutting her mother in her first blade lesson at the age of seven. Ani frowned. Had it been that long ago? Her heart ached at the memory. She'd been frightened by all the blood, but her mother had just praised her ingenuity. Then her mother had sung a song. Ani covered her mouth as the words and tune wound themselves through her memory. The song she'd only heard once at the age of seven was the one she remembered hearing sung in the cavern.

She pulled in a deep breath, holding it until the tune appeared in her head, then exhaled in a hum, feeling the buzz radiate from the back of her throat. Her mother's words came first in her memory, followed by male voices. A solo baritone, anguished and searching, was joined by Taryn's familiar tenor, tentative in the beginning, then intense and harmonizing. Those voices combined to create powerful music for a powerful need.

Though she did not know the words, she felt the meaning. She whispered, "A healing song for me." Ani hummed the tune, trying to remember the foreign words from so long ago and yet so recently. Her body relaxed, her headache eased. She hadn't realized how much it hurt until it lessened. She sang without a plan, enjoying the irony of her situation and wishing Kela would comment in her head. She breathed deep and using her diaphragm, she put power behind each note and syllable.

In the corner, the injured attendant stared, mesmerized by the song being sung—in Lrakiran.

Ani turned to face the door. She looked at the window and Kela's face peered in at her. The song ceased. Was this her imagination or had the song brought Kela? She shook her head. The window was still filled with Kela. He appeared to bark, but she heard nothing. Was the room soundproof? That would explain a few things. Ani ran to the window and slapped the flat of her hands against the glass. Again, no sound was heard; not even a vibration was felt. Then she ran her hands along the doorjamb for a toggle switch or depression to push. Nothing. She glanced back at the window. Kela was still barking. She struck every panel and pad within an arm's reach of the door. When it still did not open, she cursed.

The attendant in the corner said something. Ani turned away from the door to point at him. Using a few of what she thought were curse words or phrases she'd heard from Renloret, she pulled her hand across her neck and pointed at him again. He sank back into the corner, but he smiled as he raised a palm toward her. Hoping she'd gotten her point across, she returned to study the window. Kela was gone.

"No! Come back!" Her hands hit the glass repeatedly. "Why won't it break, why won't the blade-damned door open? I can't hear you! I can't feel you, but I know you're there. In all the hells of Teramar, someone open the door! Kela!" She pounded at the unrelenting barrier.

Someone must have lifted Kela up so he could see into the room. Did that mean Taryn was here? Renloret? Nothing mattered now that they were here to get her out. She paused her useless pounding. Her hands throbbed. The bruises would show themselves in the coming hours. Where was Kela's sarcasm in her mind?

Stretching up on her toes, she looked out the window, trying to see where Kela had gone. She didn't even blink when a face filled her view. Not Kela, but Renloret. She stopped shouting and drank in the concern and frustration from his gaze, thirsty for much more. Her soul sobbed in relief. Fiercely, she grabbed at the window frame. A fingernail tore but she ignored the momentary pain. Renloret was here. Kela and Renloret had found her.

The touch on her shoulder shocked her. She jerked her elbow backwards catching the attendant on the chin. He collapsed to the stone floor. Ani cursed at her own inattention and left the window to kneel beside him. She was embarrassed by her reaction. He had not deserved it. Her tingling hands had difficulty finding a pulse, but there was one. His chest rose and fell. She glanced at the window. Kela's black-masked face had replaced Renloret's. She could see that he barked, but she heard nothing. She sat on the floor and stared at the window, concentrating on opening herself to her four-legged companion, and decided to hum the healing song again. It had helped with the headache a few moments earlier, so perhaps it would help restore Kela to her.

Ani inhaled, exhaled, hummed. She felt the release at the base of her neck, as if a cramped muscle had finally relaxed, and reached up to rub at the spot. Her eyes widened as she realized the headache was completely gone.

Idiots if you ask me. And then he has the fangs to say I'm fat!

Her smile was radiant as she sent her response. *Who says you're fat?* The black emptiness of her fractured soul refilled with his boundless joy. He did not need words; he sent his heart to her. They reveled in rediscovery.

"Is he all right?" Chenakainet asked as Renloret placed the canine on the floor.

Renloret studied the trembling canine. "I don't know." He glanced through the window. "She's just sitting there with the most beautiful look on her face. Her eyes are closed."

Chenakainet pushed the pilot to one side to have his own look.

"I think she hears him."

"That was my thought." Renloret crouched to Kela's ear level and whispered, "Sorry to bother you, friend, but can you tell her we need help in getting her out?"

Kela opened one eye to glare at the pilot then turned his attention back to Ani. After a few moments, he turned back to Renloret with an expression that suggested he'd done what he'd been asked to do. Then he turned back to the window, tail wagging gently.

Renloret put a hand in the middle of Chenakainet's chest, restraining him from being the first through the door. "Remember, she's twenty-five, not five, and she doesn't know you."

The door slid open. Kela leapt across the threshold, knocking Anyala back a few steps, her laughter joyous.

Renloret entered and knelt next to the attendant. A quick check at his neck confirmed a pulse. Without turning he said, "Commander, please see that he is attended to." Oblivious to the fact that he'd just ordered his superior to do something below his rank, Renloret heard the quiet response while he moved to embrace the savior of his people.

Her arms clutched him. Then she sagged as the adrenaline ebbed away and new emotions rushed in. Clinging to him, her tears came with sudden gulping sobs. He couldn't hold her tight enough, long enough. He kissed the top of her head and stroked her back. He had no sense of how many chimes had passed before he felt Kela's paw scraping down his leg. One more lingering kiss on her forehead, then he turned to look at the commander, whose black eyes glared a warning.

Renloret pulled her closer and wondered how to proceed. He could just blurt out that she was on another planet, that she carried the immunities needed to save an entire race of "aliens," of which she was a member. A wry grin slid across his face as he contemplated what Anyala's reaction would be if he just laid out the facts. He didn't really want to know.

Ani looked at Renloret, her eyes showing a bit of concern. "Kela says I should apologize for my behavior and actions even though they weren't my fault." She extracted herself from his grasp and retreated a few steps toward the center of the room as a gurney arrived and several medics lifted the attendant from the floor and whisked him out. "He didn't deserve that, but he surprised me." She returned the stare from the uniformed officer who seemed to be in charge of the medics. She thrust her chin at the man and asked, "What's his problem?"

Renloret looked back at the commander, shaking his head to warn him not to speak. "That will take some explaining, but not right now. Besides, he won't hurt you."

The commander backed up to stand against the wall just inside the door with his arms crossed. His eyes did not leave her.

Ani glanced at Renloret. "So can we get out of here?"

"Not yet. You apparently recovered from the surgery much faster than expected. More tests are needed to ensure your response is not a complication or reaction to the anesthesia." He thought that might be close enough to the truth to be believed.

"I'm not being held prisoner?" she asked, her voice soft and shaking.

"No."

"What kind of surgery did I have?"

Sighing, Renloret answered. "That's also complicated. You had brain surgery . . . after they repaired your wounds and flushed poison from your system."

Her exclamation was an octave higher than normal speech. "Brain surgery?" Her hand went to her head, fingertips feeling her scalp for any outward signs. Her hair had not been cut. "But the headaches went away when I sang the song."

Commander Chenakainet unfolded his arms and spoke in Lrakiran. "Renloret, we should do this in the conference room with everyone clothed appropriately."

Renloret nodded.

"What did he say?" Ani's eyes took on a steely sheen.

"That this discussion should be held in another location, under less revealing circumstances." His smile widened as he noticed that the surgical gown had slipped off her shoulder, nearly baring one breast.

Kela dodged away, tongue laughing across his canines as Ani advanced unexpectedly toward the pilot. Her fist struck Renloret's upper arm hard enough to tingle his fingertips and rock him off balance.

"Ow!" He rubbed the offended muscles.

"That's for whatever you're thinking."

The pilot's sidewise catch-step brought a quick grin of approval from the commander.

Ani snatched the top of the flimsy gown back over her shoulder and gave a sharp nod, "Lead the way, student." Glaring at the commander, she said, "You next, officer. I don't want anyone but Kela behind me."

Kela made an audible sound resembling a snort. Whatever he said, Ani swiped at him but missed as they filed out of the room.

The yellow-green of the pullover was definitely not in her usual color range but it was the smallest of the available tops the medics could find on short notice. It was probably from the "the patient won't need this anymore pile," but at least it was clean. Ani arranged the neckline again as she looked in the mirror. "Isn't there some type of belt I can use?" she called out to the men waiting in the hallway.

"Do you need one?" Renloret replied.

She frowned at her reflection. "When can I have some real clothes? Or am I still being held prisoner and this is a weird form of torture?"

"We can order an entire wardrobe later. And no prison or torture is involved, I promise."

He hasn't seen you in that color. Kela perused the image in the mirror. *The surgical gown was better.*

"Thanks, Kela." She spoke aloud as she turned the hem of the drawstring pants one more time. "At least this prevents prying eyes."

Ani could hear muttering on the other side of the door and while she couldn't understand a single word of the Southern dialect, the tone was clear. She glanced at Kela. "I think they want me to hurry." She gathered her hair by twisting it tight around itself until she could tuck the end. One last look at the mirror and she opened the door.

Renloret turned away from the commander. A frown creased his brow as Ani stepped out of the changing room. "I suppose we can't argue color choices with the giver." He shrugged then mumbled, "The medic gown was better."

Ani laughed in unison with Kela's barked agreement. "That's what Kela said."

She glanced at the officer leaning against the opposite wall. He seemed to note every move she made, but his eyes were laced with sadness. Why was he so sad? Her thoughts flitted from topic to topic, question to question. Were they really on Southern? She hadn't seen any signs of military action. No milits rushing around containing insurgents or taking prisoners. Was she truly free from whatever confinement she'd been in? Who had held her? Had she even been a prisoner? How serious had her wounds been? How long had she been in that room?

Struggling to stop her mental ramblings, she stepped in front of the pilot and wrapped him in an embrace. "How many people at this meeting will understand Northern?" she whispered.

"A few, perhaps," he whispered in return.

Ani shut her eyes for a second, relieved. She would be able to talk to Renloret without anyone else understanding if she was careful and spoke softly. Snuggling closer, the feel of his body against hers brought a different onslaught of thoughts. There was intensity in the way he held her and she reveled in it for a fleeting moment. Why did his embrace remind her of the dance? Her heart was racing. In this unbelievable circumstance, how could she behave this way? He didn't seem to mind. She smiled at that.

When she opened her eyes again, she could see that the eyes of the commander in the corner were still on her. He was frowning. Why did his scrutiny make her feel like a five-year-old caught doing something terribly wrong? Did Southerners disapprove of such physical contact? Would her behavior bring trouble to Renloret? Perhaps she should back off, let go.

She released her arms and stepped away from Renloret. In a show of defiance she slid her hand down his arm to nestle inside his palm, a silent request to continue the contact. He laced his fingers between hers. Evidently, holding hands was more acceptable.

With a long look, Ani dared the commander to separate the grip. He opened his mouth to say something but closed it again without speaking. There was a shine to his eyes and his chin trembled. What was she doing that was upsetting the man so? Renloret pulled her down the hall. She followed but kept her eyes on the commander, who had slipped behind them. Ani heard several of Renloret's Southern expletives within his muttering.

A mental chuckle from Kela caused Ani to look down at him with upraised eyebrows, an unspoken question on the air between them.

Later. His tongue lopped over his teeth as he sidled next to Ani.

Upon entering the conference room, Ani's survey showed that two sides of the room were covered with display screens. A third wall was actually a large bank of windows that overlooked a small park surrounded by glass fronted buildings, and a centrally placed table echoed the blue of the sky beyond.

She loosed her grip on Renloret's hand and walked along the wall of screens facing the windows. There were maps on the screens with dozens of flashing markers within areas shaded different colors. It appeared more military in nature than she expected to find in a medical facility. A ripple of unease settled within her. Had Renloret been truthful about where they were? With the exception of the officer who couldn't keep his eyes off her, everything she'd seen since waking had led her to believe she was in a medical facility. Was this actually a military facility or perhaps a military facility that also housed a hospital?

Ani chose a seat near a corner with her back to the windows. That allowed her to face the door they had entered. She could not discern a secondary exit and her unease grew.

Kela seated himself close enough to rest his muzzle on her thigh, his tail curled around his front feet. He bumped her hand with his muzzle.

Her fingers immediately found their way to the base of his ears. She smiled at the contented sigh it elicited. It was comforting to feel him in her mind. He was not concerned. The others began arranging themselves around the table. Renloret settled next to her, scooting the chair close enough to take her free hand, which he held protectively.

The door swished open and a man who appeared to be a physician bustled in. Once seated, he placed a tiny metallic device in the center of the table and fixed a broad self-satisfied smile on Ani. Both Renloret and the officer edged away from the table.

"What's that?" Ani asked.

"The device that held you unconscious until one bell ago," Renloret said as his shoulders shivered.

"Really?" She leaned toward the table to study it more closely.

The door slid open again and another uniformed officer strode in. Renloret jumped from his seat and stood at attention. The door whooshed closed. Striking his right fist to his shoulder in salute, the officer's smile was warm and directed at Renloret. Renloret responded with a similar salute, adding a deep nod of his head before relaxing his stance.

"Ani, this is Commander Trimag," Renloret said. Then he moved back into what she assumed was Southern for everyone else's benefit. She glanced at the officer in the back corner also standing at attention. The two officers shared short nods but no salutes. Perhaps they were equals. Commander Trimag pulled out a chair while the other retreated to the wall, his arms folded and eyes back on Ani.

Ani nudged Renloret to get his attention and lifted her chin toward the officer in the back. "Is there something wrong with me, Renloret," she whispered, leaning in close. "He hasn't stopped staring at me since he followed you into the recovery room."

"He has a good reason, I assure you. We'll get to that topic, among other things, later. I was told more important things need discussion first."

"Such as?"

Renloret ignored her question.

The physician opened one of his readers and started talking excitedly. At one point, he nudged the tiny object in the center of the table. Renloret and the others joined in what Ani could only assess to be an animated discussion. The only thing she understood was her name, uttered by Commander Trimag as part of a response to something another said. The doctor, who seemed to be leading the discussion, finally sat back in his chair and stared triumphantly at her.

The officer behind her stepped to the table, pointed to the device, and queried the doctor. But he kept glancing at her as he did. There was something very familiar about him, though she could not quite place him. Had he worked with her parents?

She reached out to pick up the device in the middle of the table.

Renloret sucked in a breath and restrained her hand. "Please don't touch it."

She chuckled. "It's not alive, you know." She pried his fingers from her wrist.

"It held you unconscious for more than two of your weeks. Not just unconscious, but completely isolated. Even Kela couldn't hear you." His eyes held her in their grip. "Without Kela, we might never have found it. Thank you for telling me about your connection with him."

"Can you answer why this was placed inside me?" she asked.

Renloret shook his head. Ani noticed a reciprocal shake of the officer's head. He opened his mouth to say something, but once again stopped himself and continued in Southern.

Renloret translated. "He wants to know if you recognized your attacker."

Ani studied the officer, a vague familiarity still nagging. "No, but he said something about my mother letting his wife die and that this was some type of repayment for his loss." She watched the officer's ebony face twist slightly. How had he known her mother?

Again, the officer opened his mouth and hesitated. This time when he spoke his tone was angry. His gestures included everyone in the room except Ani and Kela. The physician interrupted only to be shouted down by the dark skinned officer. Commander Trimag added his comments to the verbal fray, his tone conciliatory. The physician and officer ignored him.

A bemused smile crossed her face. They were behaving no better than toddlers. She had to know who the dark skinned officer was and how this Southerner knew Northern's language, seemingly better than Renloret.

Ani jumped from her seat and slapped the table with the flat of her hand. "Quiet, children!" She waited as the startled occupants shut up and looked at her. No need for translating that, she thought. "That's better. Now, sit." She pointed at the physician and officer both still leaning across the table, almost nose to nose. She pointed at the chairs. "Sit down and listen." She spared a glance at the pilot. "Renloret, you have been remiss in your duties."

"I've what?" His eyes were wide in surprise.

"You have not properly introduced me to either of these gentlemen." Her eyebrows arched and she tipped her head toward the pair she'd reprimanded as they took seats. Only the officer reacted with a weak smile. "Arguments will not be tolerated as long as I am unsure of who is on whose team or who can answer my questions. Understood?"

Renloret answered, "Yes, Master."

The officer's raised eyebrows gave her confidence that he fully understood Northern.

"May I introduce Surgeon Sholoret?" Renloret said with formality. "He's the finest on Lra . . . the continent. And after a detailed discussion with Kela and me, he was able to locate and remove the device, which we now know was the reason for your continued unresponsive state."

"Renloret, how do you Southerners say thank you?"

There was a slight hesitation before he said, "Traseevat."

Ani nodded to the surgeon and carefully pronounced, "Traseevat, Sholoret."

Sholoret responded, "Chidore, Anyala."

He leaned across the table and picked up the device. Then he launched off into a barrage of information, as if speaking one word in Southern qualified her as being fluent. He didn't even give Renloret a chance to translate—let alone give him a chance to introduce the others in the room.

She decided to take this opportunity to test the officer's knowledge of Northern. Waving her hand in front of Sholoret to get him to stop talking, she said, "Renloret, translate, now."

She didn't wait for an acknowledgment, just sallied forth as quickly as she could, keeping the officer in her peripheral vision. She was sure Renloret was not familiar enough with the Northern language to keep up. Perhaps the commander was.

"I know you want all sorts of information I do not have. I don't believe mere coincidence is responsible for Dalkey's arrival and the attack on me. Larger blades need melting down. Before

Dalkey was murdered, he said that someone higher up had gotten him released from the hospital and sent him to Star Valley on a mission to find alien spaceships on my property. If you believe that, we should also discuss some other myths, such as talking rocks. But let's leave that for another time."

She heard Renloret stumble over words. The officer offered assistance. They were playing into her plan.

Ani continued. "I believe that this 'higher up' knew the kind of commotion Dalkey's presence would cause, thus distracting us from their true purpose, which I have yet to figure out. I just didn't expect a Southern pilot to take the opportunity to actually crash on my property, thus providing even more fodder for Dalkey's obsession. But Dalkey provided ample opportunity for the attacker to get to me."

She stopped and observed the officer, who had taken over the translation entirely. Renloret was just staring at her, a smirk on his lips as he nodded.

Again there was silence in the room.

"How long did you live on Northern?" she asked. Why hadn't he just been introduced as another translator? What about him were they all hiding?

The officer straightened his jacket and answered, "About six of your years."

"So you are here at this meeting to verify Renloret's translations?"

"One of the reasons," he said, his voice trembling as if he were about to cry. Opening and closing his mouth several times, he seemed unsure of something. After a deep breath, he appeared to translate for the others. Then his expression turned serious as he nodded to Renloret. "Introduce me."

The pilot stood at his side and with a sharp Northern salute to Ani said, "To you, Anyala it is my honor to introduce Commander Yenne Chenakainet. Your father."

Commander Yenne Chenakainet offered a Northern blade salute. His black eyes glistened with unshed tears and he bit his lower lip.

The smile left her face.

Kela whined in warning as Ani shut him out.

She rose from her chair and walked around the table. Her eyes never left this Yenne Chenakainet, measuring every inch as if she were his commanding officer. Then she planted herself in front of him. Her face was stone, her eyes a chilling green. A tear tripped over and traced a track on his night sky dark skin. Her hand caressed it away.

Kela sidled over to lean on Renloret's leg, trying to warn him.

"What is your age?" she asked without taking her eyes off his face.

"Thirty-six, miss," he answered as a recruit to a commanding officer.

A smile crept across her lips but did not soften her eyes.

Kela whined again in warning.

The crack of her hand across the commander's cheek echoed in the room. Everyone flinched. Though he was rocked off his feet, he recovered enough to stand again in front of her and lick a bit of blood from the corner of his mouth

"First, you are not old enough to be my father. Second, my father would have returned to get us after the attack when I was five. My father would have been at my first blade competition. My father would have overseen my crowning as a continental champion. My father would have been at Mother's side when she died." She bit her lower lip to keep it from trembling. "My father would have kept her body safe. My father would have been with me when I woke up. He would have hugged the fear away, he would have . . ." A ragged breath escaped. She had caught the slight wince on his face with each accusation, but had kept going in shear anger.

"I was waiting for the right moment to explain, a time when we might be alone," he said.

The tremble in his words seemed real to her, but she shook her head. "There is no right moment. This is unexplainable." She shivered. "This is impossible. You're an . . . an . . . imposter." She had hesitated for a moment as new threads wove about her thoughts. "This is a crazy kind of torture."

As fast as the blade champion she was, she stepped behind Renloret and wrenched his arm between his shoulder blades. "Of what use am I to Southern? My own military didn't trust me with any but the newest recruits. I'm not worth any ransom. Northern will not pay for a female who intimidated every male trainer on Northern and yet delivered soldiers who could actually defend themselves so they could fight. I'm sure they are more than happy that I'm no longer on Northern to remind them of their weaknesses. What would Southern gain by kidnapping me?" She hissed into Renloret's ear, "Why would you do this to me, Renloret? Were you in on this from the beginning?"

She pulled him around the table and made her way towards the door. "Was the dance a lie?"

Everyone heard her heart start to break, though her voice did not.

Renloret shook his head. "Never a lie," he whispered through clinched teeth as she tightened the twist.

She stopped for a moment and Commander Chenakainet stepped closer. "Please, Anyala, it is not his fault. Let him go."

"You are *not* my father. You have no sway with me. What do you want from me? Is it information about Northern's military strategies? Even that idiot Dalkey would have been a better choice."

Commander Chenakainet shook his head. "What we want has nothing to do with military strategy."

"No, for some reason, you just need my blood. Why didn't you take it all while I was unconscious? By not removing that device, you could have kept me alive interminably, taking blood any time you wanted. Why am I so all hells important?"

The surgeon approached. He spoke calmly, though his tone had a pleading edge to it. Ani shook her head. She didn't understand a single word. She looked at the imposter of her father for a translation.

"Sholoret says that because this disease attacks only females of child bearing age, our people will die out within one generation. Yes, we need your blood, but just enough to create the vaccine. We only ask two things of you, Anyala. First, that you stay and assist us in the creation of that vaccine and second, that you save—"

Trimag interrupted the translation. Southern words flew between everyone around Ani. She felt Renloret stiffen his attention on the argument.

She whispered in Renloret's ear, "I have three questions: What are they arguing about now? What else am I'm supposed to be able to save? How in all the hells of Teramar did I get chosen for this honor?" She eased the pressure she'd put on the pilot's hand.

"This has nothing to do with the military. It has always been medical. We've spent over a decade searching for a cure. Apparently, you are in sole possession of the right combination of factors that will save our people." He hesitated, obviously choosing his words carefully. "Can you stop imagining all the wrong reasons we want you, even need you, and listen to the full story before passing judgment on us?"

She hesitated but did not relax her grip enough to allow him to extricate himself.

"So I'm still not a prisoner?" she asked.

"No. You are our salvation."

"No pressure there."

She sighed and lowered the shield against Kela. *What do you think, Kela?*

Can we leave them to argue and go outside? I need some fresh air after all this. His tongue hung over white canines.

Ani bit her lip, deciding. "Can we leave the building?"

Renloret nodded.

"Okay, let's go." She released his arm and pulling on his shirt to keep him with her, she backed the few extra steps to the door. It opened without a sound. Kela brushed passed them. The door closed again as soon as they were in the hall.

Are they still at it?

Kela snickered in her mind. *Yes, they're still arguing. They haven't even noticed we're gone yet. Follow me.*

Ani switched her grasp to hold Renloret's uninjured hand, and the trio ran down the hall to a large lobby. Ani did not notice the crowd of staring people as they left the building and entered the paling light of the late afternoon sun.

They ducked into and out of several streets and alleys. Ani relished the teasing breeze as it brushed her cheeks. It was good to be outside. She slowed her gate to a walk and looked at her surroundings. The tang of autumn was in the air. Renloret walked beside her, his good hand still folded around hers.

She signaled a pause at the edge of a small plaza so she could examine the pilot's injured hand. "Sorry." A hiss of air intake made her aware of the pain the mere touching of the now swelling fingers caused.

"Want me to pop them back in?" she asked.

He nodded.

Without giving him a chance to brace himself, she jerked the fingers, snapping them back into place. Renloret sagged against her as he muttered curses into her shoulder. She patted his back.

Straightening from her shoulder, Renloret said, "Our physicians usually give us something for pain before they do that."

"Where would be the fun in that? Besides, you said yes when I asked."

He grimaced and wiggled all the fingers.

With Renloret's attention on his fingers, Ani took the moment to appreciate the courtyard. Potted blooms in brilliant purples and reds complemented the iridescent golds of the three trees surrounding a central fountain where water splashed out of the mouth of some antlered herbivore. At least she thought it was a plant eater. A quadruple set of pointed tusks split the water flow so it fell into four distinct streams, each aimed at the open pool-like mouths of other equally unusual animals. The water continued its path over the edges of the beasts' mouths, dribbling into the larger basin that surrounded the sculpture.

Ani walked closer to admire the fountain. She did not recognize either species of animal and reasoned that Northern education may not have included all species found on Teramar. Perhaps these were found in isolated areas on Southern, but a shiver sent a worrisome note across her back. A shell-shaped leaf fell from one of the trees distracting her from this musing as it seesawed through the air to settle on the water's surface.

Another leaf began its journey, but Ani snatched it before it could decorate the pool with its gold. Though it looked delicate, the veining was strong and supportive of the cuplike curve. Ani broke the stem and sniffed at the golden bittersweet fluid that erupted from it. She glanced at Renloret, who was now watching her intently.

How long was I unconscious? She asked Kela while continuing to smile at Renloret.

About two weeks. Why? Ani?

Pointing at the fountain she asked, "Are these native beasts?"

"Of course," Renloret said. He pointed at the antlered herbivore. "That is a wapitan from the western highlands and the others are found in the swamps of Digosan. The only time I have seen them together is in this sculpture." He stopped, a quizzical look on his face.

Ani took a step back and waved her hands toward the sun. "It feels different."

"Of course, you are on Southern." He forced a laugh.

"Surely?" She tipped her head, a puzzled expression wrinkled between her brows.

He nodded vigorously as if trying to convince her.

"Come, let me show you," he said, holding out his uninjured hand.

"Kela?" Ani wanted to know his opinion. She was having difficulty reading his reactions to the surroundings. They seemed partially disguised. Perhaps the suppression device was still effecting their telepathic connection.

Let's wander with him. Perhaps we could find a way to contact your uncle?

She felt the hint of falseness in that last comment but could not fathom why.

Falseness. There was a topic more important than how her surroundings felt: the man claiming to be her father. It could not possibly be true. Now was a good time to clarify that ridiculousness, before Renloret could distract her again.

"Before we go anywhere, I need the real scoop about what's-his-problem."

Renloret frowned.

"Don't pretend to be stupid. You know as well as I do that he is *not* my father. Were you forced to introduce him so your people could get some sort of weird reaction out of me?"

Turning his back to her, he stared at the fountain, hands on his hips and chin at his chest. Obviously, the topic disturbed him. Ani stepped up to him and grabbed his elbow.

"You *were* forced, weren't you?"

Shaking his head he finally faced her.

"There is no logical reason that you would understand, but he *is* your father," Renloret said softly.

"Damn right it's not logical," she shouted. "Kela, what do you think of this?"

Ears flat to his skull, Kela turned away. *I don't believe I can answer any better than Renloret.*

Exhaling sharply between her teeth, Ani stalked toward the narrow path between buildings. "This is not over by a long blade. If I am truly not a prisoner and this is not torture, that imposter and those who put him up to this will answer to my blades!"

Renloret caught up to her. "You cannot confront him. He is in shock."

"*He's* in shock?" she asked, incredulous. How could he be in shock when she was the one who'd just been introduced to *her father*, who had been dead for twenty years? If it was true then, where had he been the last twenty years? Why hadn't he come home? Had he been a prisoner in Southern all this time or had Northern's military been the culprit. That made more sense. She scrubbed at her temples trying to come up with something logical.

Renloret pulled on her sleeve. "Yes, in shock and grieving. He was informed only a few bells ago that his wife is dead and his daughter is all grown up. He doesn't understand why twenty years have passed any better than you or I do. If you were in his boots, you would be in shock too."

Ani turned, her eyes wide, to stare at him. "And I'm not?" Could this situation be any worse?

Holding her by both shoulders, Renloret's eyes seemed to plead for understanding. In a voice soft as new grass he said, "I am not discounting your feelings, Ani. I am trying to explain his reaction to the circumstances."

He tugged at her, heading between the buildings once more. She placed a resigned smile on her lips and followed. Kela seemed content to follow as well. He had been relatively silent during the entire exchange.

They wandered the streets for a short time, pausing to purchase three meat rolls from a street vendor. She licked the savory sauce that leaked through the flat bread wrapping onto her hand while Renloret talked about his Southern capital. His circuitous route seemed to be leading somewhere, and she realized she was right when they finally came to a vantage point where the spires of a cathedral jutted into the skyline like the coniferous trees of Northern's Tashim Mountain Range. More of the cup-leaf trees, as she now called them, towered above a multitude of rooftops below and the magnificent religious building. The sun's fading rays flicked and fluttered through the cathedral's crystal dome, holding her attention until unease settled back over her. She couldn't shake the feeling that something was amiss. Even the air felt wrong.

She shrugged and tried to decipher the unease, ignoring Renloret's details. A shiver slithered down her spine. She wondered what else they should be discussing. Some necessary details were missing. A reluctant tone undercut Renloret's voice indicating he wasn't speaking the whole truth. She gave a perfunctory nod as Renloret rambled on about how much better the older stone buildings in the valley below were when compared to the newer metallic and glass architecture of the city's business section, which apparently could be seen on the other side of the hill and which he seemed reluctant to show her.

"Where's Taryn?" That's what was missing. No one had mentioned Taryn's name, even in the conference room.

Uh, oh, Kela said. He lay down facing away from her.

She peered at Kela from the corner of her vision. *Yes?* She drew it out in her mind. She felt his internal barrier slide into place.

Renloret stopped in mid word and lowered the arm he'd been using as a baton to direct her attention. A drawn out sigh escaped from his lips as he picked at the turf between them.

The rhythm of her heartbeat increased. Her attempt to slow it was unsuccessful. "He's alive, right?" she asked, alarmed.

"The last time I saw him, yes."

"How long ago was that and where?"

"Near where you were injured. He assisted me in getting you

to safety and then left to tend to his sheriff's duties."

"That was a couple of weeks ago?" she asked. She was trying not to panic. What had happened to Taryn?

Renloret nodded but refused to look at her.

"You haven't talked to him since?"

He shook his head.

"He doesn't even know if we made it to Southern?"

Another shake. Renloret was frowning now.

"Of all the stupid . . ." She was furious and confused, all at once. She realized that her breath had become more and more labored as they had climbed to the vantage point, and even in her anger, she knew the air was heavier here, not like at home. Disgusted, she turned away from Renloret and headed to the crest of the hill.

The vista below stretched her imagination even as it stuffed her breath back into her lungs. The metallic and glass city spilled away from the hill with geometric precision. Straight avenues were lined with mirrored towers, reflecting the last vestiges of orange-red from the setting sun. Occasional dark blocks broke up the gridded pattern, suggesting more tree-filled parks. Ani put her hand to her throat, gasping for air to clear her mind. It didn't. She stabbed her hand at the city.

"Where in all the hells are we?" Her blood seemed to coagulate as her heart beat ever faster trying to move the sluggish fluid into her lungs and on to her brain.

Southern? Kela's soft suggestion snuck into her consciousness.

"Uncle Reslo sent me photos of Teramar from Southern's satellite. Southern does not have a city this large and neither does

Northern." Her arms were spread horizon to horizon trying to corral the city in her vision. "This is just not possible, Renloret. Not possible."

CHAPTER THIRTY

This was not the way Renloret would have revealed the truth of who and what she was. He knew her true identity could no longer be disguised or ignored, and he certainly could not deny what was before her eyes. What could he say?

A distant rumble announced the launch of some cargo shuttle from the spaceport. Its hot flame drew a bright line across the darkening skyline. Renloret watched as Ani traced the ship's flight, her arms still outstretched. Other lights blinking yellow and green appeared above the horizon signaling the whisper glides of the evening work shuttles from the docking station halfway between Lrakira and her largest moon, Erid.

At that thought, he glanced at the horizon and groaned as he saw the twin glows of the late autumnal double moonrise of Erid and Cranite. He knew the third and smallest moon, Denert, would follow in just a few hours. All of these sights unequivocally placed Anyala on another planet. She had not moved. Renloret was cautious as he moved to her side, waiting for her reaction.

Not a word or sound passed Ani's lips for the entire quarter of a bell it took for the moons to float clear and reflect the light from Shashoon, Lrakira's sun. Autumn was Renloret's favorite time of year because of the closeness of the moons and because the seasonal paired rising made it look as if Erid and Cranite were almost connected, though they were actually tens of thousands of piases apart. The spectacular unveiling in the cloudless sky sent a pleasant chill down his spine and he smiled.

"Oh, blades be damned to all the hells." The whispered curse was followed by her retching the meat roll. She fell to her knees and continued until there was nothing left. Sobs shook her slim form.

"I'm so sorry, so very sorry. Please forgive us, but we are desperate. You are the only one who can save us."

"You lied!"

The fist struck his chin. The fact he'd been behind her saved him from being knocked out. The ground was hard on his backside and his head buzzed. He threw up a blocking arm as a whirlwind of jabs pelted him. Obscenities dirtied her ragged voice with every blow. He started to roll, but a resounding kick to his chest slapped him to his back, knocking the breath out of his lungs. Kela barked and Ani eased off on the attack just enough for Renloret to twist onto his hands and knees and crawl several body lengths. High pitched whining echoed in his head and he couldn't seem to get his limbs to follow instructions, but he finally turned to sit until the blurry scene refocused.

Ani was in an animated one-sided argument with Kela. Her arm movements were angular and sharp, as was her tone of voice.

Gradually, his hearing cleared up enough for him to appreciate her frequent use of choice phrases from Lrakiran. He hadn't realized how quick she was with languages, and while some of the phrases meant nothing close to what she assumed they did, the words did not matter nearly as much as her tone. And her accent was delightful. Renloret almost enjoyed the tableau. When she appeared to run out of things to swear at or argue about, her arms dropped to her sides. She turned away from Kela and advanced toward Renloret, who wobbled to his feet.

"Take . . . me . . . home!"

Her hands and arms flailed across his meager defenses between each word. She finally stopped with a lung-draining sob.

Renloret was suddenly grateful she'd been weaponless. He straightened and wrapped her in an embrace. She buried her face and continued to sob. The bell towers chimed. Her sobs slowed to hiccoughs.

"Renloret?"

"Ani."

His jaw hurt, but he was reasonably confident that she was spent, so he loosened his grip just a bit to stroke her head. He could not imagine what she was thinking or feeling. He'd grown up knowing about other worlds and beings, and he'd been intrigued by the stars. He could not imagine *not* knowing these things and being thrust into that expanded reality without warning. He kissed the top of her head and patted her back. She shifted her weight, turning her head to peer at the moons.

Kela pawed at the pair, whining.

"What does he say?" Renloret asked.

"That we should sit and talk before I do you more harm."

"Are you all right with that?"

"The sit and talk or the doing harm?"

He thought he heard a smile.

Another full bell had passed, signaled by the cathedral's carillon joining other bell towers across the city to serenade night's arrival. The trio on the hill had moved to sit under one of the cup-leaf trees.

"I did not lie, Ani."

"What about you being from Southern?" she asked, her tone accusing him.

"You assumed I was from there and I had to let you believe that because of pre-contact oaths. Really, I am just a rescue mission pilot. Many research teams were sent to a variety of star systems in search of a cure. Your parents, uncle, and several others were sent to Teramar. The disease was spreading slowly enough that the expected years of research were not of great concern. And depending on what each team found, our people hoped to have a cure in five to ten sun-cycles. We thought we had enough time."

"Why did they need to get rescued?" Hiccoughs still interrupted her breathing. She shivered every time she looked at the moons.

"Your father was quite certain you were the answer, a living cure for our people. I do not know all the details, but the research lab on Teramar was attacked before your father could send us the news. His ship sustained a certain amount of damage during that attack to its communication system, so we did not know he was coming or that a cure had been found until he arrived." Renloret smiled at her.

She hiccoughed again but did not smile.

"It took two of your weeks for him to arrive. Another couple of your weeks passed before the rescue team was put together." At her puzzled looked he added, "It took some in the medical field that long to analyze the pieces of research he had managed to bring with him to agree that you were, indeed, The Blood. We really were looking for a woman and her young daughter. You were about five when he left Teramar. The plan was to land and locate you, your mother, your uncle, and the others and return to Lrakira without ever interfering with the Teramaran peoples.

"I do not know what went wrong, but something altered time and perhaps caused the crash, allowing you to rescue the rescuer." He smiled again.

The corners of her mouth twitched.

He skipped over the events on Teramar. "Since returning to Lrakira, some of the discussions have centered on the Stones themselves as the cause of the time shift. Something about a time song, but there has not been an opportunity to talk to the Stone or the Singers. You woke up at that point in the discussion."

"Why not go talk to them now?" she asked.

"Because the Singers are reluctant to let just anyone close to the Stones, I was planning to get support from Commanders Trimag and Chenakainet. You know, your father engineered my audience with the Anyala Stone before I left on the mission. But even then I had to ask several times."

"So, don't ask," Ani said.

"Don't ask?" He had never even considered that.

She leaned forward, her nose almost touching his. "Sometimes, if you need a straight answer, it's best to sidestep the middles and go to the source. We say 'talk to the top.'" A tentative smile finally curved her lips. "It often saves time."

He laughed. "All right, come on. Anyway, that's probably the last place they'd expect to find us."

"Won't they be searching the city for us?" she asked.

"Oh, I am sure when they finished arguing about whatever it was and they realized we were gone, they got organized and started a search. But I know other routes to get there." He started back down the hill to the old sections of the vast city. "Besides, the Stones are not where most people think they are."

CHAPTER THIRTY-ONE

"Pericha said, 'The Blood and The Balance shall save us all.' I don't understand how everything can be corrected with a simple vaccine? Casset and I aren't exactly dying to have a family, but dare I believe her blood will allow us the opportunity?"

"We must believe she is the one, that she will save us all—even the Stone." The response was barely audible.

A rustling of robes, a door closing, and then hurried footsteps fading away allowed Renloret to peek once more around the corner. The Stone Singers had left the corridor without looking back. He flashed a grin at Ani. Though her answering smile was wane, her expression was lit with unvoiced questions. He held up his palm, forestalling them. She sighed and tipped her head toward the now empty hall. He led the way to the intricately carved door. Her hand caressed the detailed mosaic patterns, and he nodded at her upraised eyebrows.

"Yes, similar to yours." He pushed the door open.

Anyala pulled him back from the opening. "Tell me again why

no one's supposed to know we're doing this?"

"Because," he said with a sigh, "because if you are not a Singer, you must ask permission for an audience, and that takes time. Time is one thing we do not have. Historically, the Singers protected the Stones from unwanted contact, but I am sure the Anyala Stone will not mind. It spoke to me before I left. I think it will be pleased to speak to you. It said I would bring you home and you would save our people. And you are named after it."

Ani rolled her bottom lip between her teeth, apparently nervous and worried. "This is more than a little over whelming. I mean, real talking rocks?"

He took her hand and pulled her into the room. "It's more like singing than talking. You'll understand in a moment. Come on."

They crossed the room to another door on the opposite wall. Renloret watched as her fingers traced the faded tattoos that decorated the ancient handprints near the middle of the double doors. She gasped. Pulling up her sleeve she pointed to a particular scar pattern, then traced the exact design on the carved hand. Then she offered her arm for Renloret's reaction as he, too, compared the tattoos.

"By the Stone's Blade, you *are* Anyala." His voice quavered with reverence.

"What does that mean?" she asked.

Kela whined, reminding both of his presence. Ani stroked his head as she waited for Renloret to continue.

"This tattoo is ancient Lrakiran script for Anyala. Your mother must have known the likelihood of her not being alive by the time we arrived, so at the Marking Ceremony after your championship she tattooed the Stone's name in the ancient language as a sign of your identity. She was positive we'd come, even after twenty years, and she was faithful to her promise to the Stone." He shook his head. "But I'm not sure anyone else on the rescue team would have recognized it because only the Singers and a scattering of scholars are even familiar with the first script of Lrakira."

"I thought you were just the pilot?"

"I am, but I have too much curiosity for my own good." He paused, understanding finally showing in his face. "That was why the Anyala Stone chose me. Somehow it knew I would recognize the markings. But how did the Stone know what would happen more than twenty years in the future?" He pulled her wrist closer to read the tattoos. He cursed under his breath. "If I'd taken the time to notice these markings, I would have known who you were. Ani, your story is right here on your skin! I could have gotten you to come back with me without the intrusion of Stubin Dalkey, without the poison assailant, and without the coma. Why didn't I see?" He was twisting her arm as if it wasn't attached to her body.

"You can let go, now," she said, prying his fingers from her wrist.

Her whisper brought him out of his shocked musings. "Yes, the Singers might return any time." He pushed open the doors and pulled her through the opening.

The lush wall hangings were as he remembered, but instead of a solitary pedestal, there was a trio, each cradling a large crystal. The inner life light of two glowed softly, illuminating a stunning view of an amber crystal blade buried hilt deep in the dark green lump on the center pedestal.

"What?" Renloret couldn't get another sound out. Unbidden tears stung his eyes and traced hot trails down his cheeks. He couldn't move to wipe them away. He couldn't take his eyes off the trio of Stones. Was the Anyala Stone still alive? Could the Stones be killed? Why hadn't the Singers told him this had happened? He understood their reluctance, but if they had been forthcoming with just how serious the situation was, he would have waited to bring Ani to the Stones. Now he could only watch as Ani drifted toward the pedestals, drawn to her namesake. Kela followed, hackles raised in alarm. Even the canine seemed to sense the crime. Amber and blue life lights began to pulse in rhythm. Ani turned around to stare at Renloret. "They're singing, to me." Her eyes were wide in surprise and delight. "Here. They're here." She pointed to her temple.

He nodded his understanding; he also heard their greetings.

Kela rose on his hind legs to sniff at the dull green lump that sat on the pedestal at the apex of the triangle. He whined and ran a tongue across the Anyala Stone, then sat at the base of the pedestal and lifted his muzzle. A mournful song began deep in his chest and rose and fell in minor harmonics.

Renloret shivered. It was a fitting tribute to what he saw.

Ani stepped up next to Kela and placed her hands on the dark crystal. A pale glow emanated to the left of the blade. From the expression on her face Renloret knew the Stone sang to both of them. To him its song sounded tired and sad.

Singer S'Hendale was true to her promise. I shall miss her soul. The whispered hum faded as the pale glow weakened within the Anyala Stone.

Ani turned to Renloret. "Are they truly living beings?"

"Yes." As he walked toward the trio of Stones he could feel the energy from two of them ripple across his mind. "My apologies, Ani." He pointed at the dull green stone. "If I had known about this, I would have waited. The Singers only said that one of the Stones had been injured, but it was still alive. I could not have imagined this and I cannot explain it." He shrugged in defeat and sorrow.

The pulsing life light within two of the Stones shimmered, but the green light barely flickered.

Pericha sang in warm amber tones. *We greet The Blood and give honor to the pilot for transporting her home. We are to explain as we are able. As it was foretold, many generations ago, The Blood shall return to a home she did not know to save our people. The Balance shall remove the blade and we shall unite what has been divided.*

It was clear to Renloret that Ani was trying to reconcile what she saw and heard with what she had known until a few bells ago.

She looked at Renloret with eyebrows raised. "So, why hasn't that blade been removed?"

He shrugged. "I have no idea."

Ani fit her hand around the grip of the blade and pulled. It did not move. She tried again. "Renloret, come help me."

He joined her at the dais. They braced each other against the Stone and pulled. Their combined efforts did nothing.

Kela barked to get their attention.

Renloret saw a flash of understanding cross Ani's face and asked what Kela had said.

"He suggests that this Balance might be a specific person other than me; perhaps another Singer."

Renloret considered the possibility and with a shrug turned to the Stones and asked them if it was true.

A tired tune hummed from the pale life light deep within the Anyala Stone, which seemed to be addressing the answer to Ani though he could hear it.

It is your twin who can remove the blade and thus restore balance to our existence.

"Twin?" Ani gasped aloud.

Renloret gaped in return. "Twin? What twin?"

The marbled door swung open. Two golden-robed women and a host of others paraded into the audience room.

"What's this about a twin?" the older of the Singers asked.

Ani pointed an accusing finger at the green crystal. "It says only that The Blood's twin can remove the blade and bring balance to the Stones. But I don't have a twin." Ani turned to look at Chenakainet, who was among those who had entered the room. "Not that I know of, anyway."

All eyes turned toward Commander Chenakainet.

"I have one child. I would have known if there had been a twin."

The Singer Diani approached him. "Are you sure?" she asked.

"S'Hendale gave birth prematurely, while I was away. Perhaps the twin died and she never told me." He slumped down on the step of the dais, his head cradled by his hands.

Kela again barked for attention.

Ani repeated his question aloud. "Wouldn't these Stones know if the child still lived?" They all looked at each other.

Ani turned to the dimly glowing green crystal and placed a hand on its surface. "Is the twin still alive?" She nodded in understanding then turned to the others. "The Stone says that The Balance lives."

"How can we be sure it's her twin who is The Balance," the commander asked. Perhaps there's a twin here on Lrakira who is The Balance. You could test every twin on the planet."

All three crystals pulsed, though the green Anyala Stone's hue was pale. Ani, Diani, and Layson shared looks.

Singer Layson spoke. "We have tested every child, Commander. The Stones say The Blood and The Balance are twins and we know Anyala is The Blood."

There was a painful silence as all considered this information. Ani frowned and let out a sigh. "Are you positive that the vaccine will work and more of my blood is no longer needed?"

At their nods she seemed to make a decision.

"If you are certain that I am not needed here and I obviously cannot accomplish this task." She pointed at the blade sticking out from the Stone. "Then, alien or not, in order to save the Stone, I have to go back to Teramar and find her."

ABOUT THE AUTHOR

Allynn Riggs began telling stories before she could write them down. Though she has worked in numerous capacities including as a parochial school English teacher, youth soccer coach and referee, dance instructor, and assistant office manager at a CPA firm, by August of 2012, Allynn decided to focus on more intriguing areas of her life. She surrendered to the driving need to fulfill a decades-old promise to publish the stories of some very demanding characters who lovingly reside in her imagination and dreams. When not writing, Allynn is an avid square dancer who, up to six nights a week by her husband's side, actively participates in and teaches others the joy of the dance. She is also a big game hunter who manages to keep the freezer full of meat. The mother of three grown daughters, Allynn lives in Centennial, Colorado with her husband, Bob.